I WANNA BE YOUR LAGER

GIA STEVENS

I Wanna Be Your Lager: A Brother's Best Friend Romantic Comedy by Gia Stevens

www.authorgiastevens.com

Published by: Gia Stevens

Copyright: I Wanna Be Your Lager: A Brother's Best Friend Romantic Comedy by Gia Stevens © 2025 Gia Stevens

Editor: My Notes in the Margins, Davenport Edits

Proofreader: The Final Touch

Publisher: Wild Clover Publishing, LLC

Cover Art: @aksi.art

Print ISBN: 978-1-958286-21-0

V011026

All rights reserved. No portion of this book may be reproduced in any form without permission from the publisher, except as permitted by U.S. copyright law.

This is a work of fiction. Names, characters, places, and incidents either are the products of the author's imagination or are used fictitiously. Any resemblance to actual persons, living or dead, business, companies, events, or locales is entirely coincidental.

Find your person who will take you to the bookstore and whispers these four words to you:
"Get whatever you want."

While this story is a romantic comedy there may be situations that are triggering to some. For a list of those content notes please visit my website and scroll to the bottom of the page.

Chapter 1

OUTHOUSE GETS TOSSED INTO THE WINDMILL

Eve

Goosebumps spring over my naked body as I rise to my feet. The comforter falling away. I lift my pastel pink dress off the light wood floor and slide my arms into the sleeves. Once in place, I tug the zipper along my side until it's securely fastened. The light cotton is soft against my skin. Using the oblong mirror on the wall next to me, I finger comb one side of my disheveled hair. The moonlight shimmering in through the sheer curtain gives me just enough light to see what I'm doing. "The wedding was really beautiful, wasn't it? Her dress was gorgeous. The way the tulle floated in the breeze made for some amazing pictures." I glance at Pax from the mirror. His hand emerges from under the blanket with the used condom pinched between two fingers. He tosses it onto the nightstand and picks up his phone. My nose scrunches. If he thinks I'm cleaning up his mess, he's delusional. I run my fingers through the other side of my hair and continue talking to myself. "When I get married, I think I want a beach wedding, but a mountain lodge would be pretty too." Once I'm satisfied my sex hair is tamed, I spin to search for my shoes. "Want to go to the bar for drinks?" Bending over, I snatch one sideways heel off the floor and slide my foot in, buckling the strap around my ankle.

Pax, my boss, drops his phone to the mattress and leans against the headboard. The white comforter falls to his lap, exposing a dark smattering of chest hair. "I hate to say this, but I need you to leave."

My body goes rigid. Did he just ask me to leave? No. He *told* me to leave. Slowly, I rise and twist to face him. His shaggy, dark hair flops over his forehead, and his chest rhythmically rises and falls. A smile tugs at my lips. "Oh. You need some alone time to reflect on the amazing sex we just had." It was mediocre at best, but some things you keep hush-hush. We have plenty of time to fix it.

He shakes his head. "No."

I lift an eyebrow. "Is this so you can wax your chest again? If you aren't aware, I've already heard you scream like a twelve-year-old girl." I hobble toward the bed on my tippy toes to match the height of my one three-inch heel. "If it changes your mind, I actually like the chest hair." As I reach the side of the bed, I bend over and rest my palms on the mattress, so my face is inches from his.

His gaze drifts away. "No, I have company coming."

"Like a client? I would love to sit in on that meeting to get an understanding of what their needs are."

"My wife is coming for a visit." He shifts away to rub the back of his neck.

An anchor drops in the pit of my stomach. Blinking rapidly, I process his words. Is there a possibility *wife* could mean something besides the person you're married to? I rise to my full height and prop a hand on my hip. "Back this infidelity train up. You're married?" My gaze drops to his left hand in case I blocked out a wedding band. Nope. Nothing.

"Yeah." His eyebrows knit together as if I'm speaking Latin.

"And she's coming here?"

"Yes."

My vision floods red. "Don't you think this is something you should have told me, say… before we started fucking?" I clench my fists because if I don't, my hands might accidentally wrap around his throat. He's married. And I've been sleeping with him for six months. Sure, there was mutual flirting, but he pursued me. He kissed me first. But I didn't know he was married.

"Why are you yelling? You saw the pictures in my office."

I rear my head back. His invisible handprint evident across my cheek. "When I asked about those pictures, you told me she was your sister. I would remember if you told me she was your wife. Sister and wife aren't remotely close enough to be misunderstood."

His lips purse together, and his face scrunches as if he's trying to take a giant shit. And maybe he is. All over my life. "I'm pretty sure I told you she's my wife."

"Um. I'd remember if you said wife. Again, it's kind of hard to mix up wife with sister." I'm drowning in a sea of red.

"Anyway, you can get your own room. Or you can catch an earlier flight back to Knoxville, and I'll see you when I get back."

My heart pounds in my ears as adrenaline races through my body. "Hold on. Your wife is coming for a few days, and you expect us to pick up right where we left off afterward? I want to make sure I'm understanding you correctly." Is he delusional right now? What kind of woman does he think I am? He assumes I'm okay with this when I. Thought. We. Were. In. A. Relationship.

"Yeah." He shrugs. "We have fun together."

Son of a bitch. I'm seconds away from reaching across the bed and smothering him with the hotel pillow. Right when I thought I had my life together, the outhouse gets tossed into the windmill. Shit everywhere. Very similar to an automatic robotic vacuum running over a pile of shit and smearing it into the living room rug.

Sometimes in life, you have no longer than the bat of an eyelash to make a decision. Right now, my choices are to pack my shit, quit my job, and never see this lying, cheating bastard again or unplug the lamp and strangle him with the cord. As appealing as the second option is, I think it's best if I go with the first. Frantically, I scan the room before hobbling around, picking up everything that belongs to me, and cramming it into my suitcase. I slam it closed and yank on the zipper. I'm surprised it doesn't snap off. My other heel falls from my grasp and hits the floor with a thud. I shove my foot through the straps and secure it at my ankle.

"Thanks for being so understanding." He rolls out of bed, still naked.

Quickly, I divert my gaze. For someone I once found attractive, he now makes bile rise in my throat. He's living in a fantasy world if he thinks this is a "to be continued."

I snap to my full height and square my shoulders. "Understand this, I'm leaving and never coming back. And if that isn't clear, I also quit." I yank the suitcase handle until it clicks into place.

"What do you mean?" He tugs on a pair of sweatpants, but his foot gets caught, causing him to hop around to maintain his balance. The urge to push him over is strong.

"We have that big Holland/Pryor wedding to shoot next weekend."

"You should've thought about that before you started sleeping with me! While. You. Are. Married." I stomp toward the door, my suitcase trailing behind me. I throw open the door, and halfway across the threshold, I spin around. "I was lying! It wasn't amazing. In fact, I used every agonizing second to make a mental note of my grocery list. And those orgasms you thought you gave me? Fake! Every! Single! One!" Before he says anything, I slam the door behind me. What an asshole! My hands tremble as I lug my suitcase down the hall. I can't believe he would do this. Not only to me, but to his wife. My head throbs in rhythm with every footfall. When I reach the elevator, I stab the down button. Immediately, the doors open, and I'm thankful I don't have to wait. I need to get far away from here. From him.

At the rental car in the parking lot, I toss my suitcase in the trunk and climb into the driver's seat. I shove the key into the ignition and turn it over. The car purrs to life, and I grip the steering wheel. Just when everything in my life was falling into place, it burns to ashes in seconds. My life was blue skies and sunshine. I had a good job that was going to put my life back on track—no more derailments. I had what I thought was a good relationship. Then, it all went up in a plume of smoke. Hello, old friend, rock bottom. We meet again.

What am I going to do? Where am I going to stay? My flight back to Tennessee doesn't leave until tomorrow. Sleep at the airport? Anger, anxiety, frustration, and hurt all flood my body at the same time. It's overwhelming. I inhale a deep breath and let it all out in a blood-curdling scream as I beat my fist against the steering wheel. Once I've emptied my lungs, I drop my hands to my lap.

Movement to my left draws my attention. A terrified young man in a blue plaid polo and khakis stares back at me. I jab my fingers on the button to roll down the window. "Nothing to be alarmed about. I'm okay. Just working out some frustration."

Without saying a word, he nods before scurrying away.

Glad I can now cross off terrifying young adults from my list of things to do today. I press the button, and the window rolls up. Screw Pax. He doesn't get to control how I feel. I shouldn't be the one hurt and frustrated while he doesn't have a care in the world. My plan was never to go back home. Failure wasn't an option. Or at least it wasn't supposed to be. But here I am with a giant *F* stamped on my forehead.

I pull out my phone and send a text message.

EVE

I'm coming for a visit. I'll see you soon!

Chapter 2

WHAT AM I DOING?

Eve

After changing my flight—thanks Pax for paying for my ticket. I won't see you in Knoxville—I stick to my original plan—a drink. Turning off the ignition, I push the car door open. My heels click against the smooth pavement as I hoof it across the parking lot and toward the resort. As I pass by the pool the moonlight ricochets over the rippling water, almost blinding me. What was I thinking sleeping with my boss? My life isn't a romance book. There is no happy ending. I blow out a deep breath. The clattering of my heels against the hard cement echoes between the buildings.

"Eve! Wait up!"

Pax's voice grates on my nerves. I glance over my shoulder, and he's rounding the edge of the far building, jogging toward me. If he thinks I'm stopping, he's a bigger idiot than I thought. I quicken my pace. Now is a good time to test out my ability to run in heels. Several feet ahead of me, I spot the main bar. Vacationers crowd the entire bar, occupying all the seats. I slip past a few people. Since Pax has spotted me, there's no way I'm stopping here. I'll lose him in the crowd. I sidestep through the jungle of people and emerge on the other side. Without looking back, I race down the sidewalk and zigzag between buildings until a smaller bar comes into view. Edison lights swoop over a wood deck as a woman in a white dress twirls around on the dance floor. Crashing a wedding wasn't on my BINGO card, but I guess I'm stamping a red dot on that tonight.

"Eve!"

My name rolls over the crowd, smacking me upside the head. Peering over my shoulder, I spot Pax hot on my heels. Do I have to drown myself in the Gulf to lose him? I'm seconds away from hurdling the railing and sprinting across the sand. It might be the easiest way to ditch him. I pause, eyeing the railing before my gaze drifts down to my three-inch pumps. Heels and sand don't mix. I huff. After dodging a few wedding guests and ducking past a few more, I find a stool at the dark end of the bar. I pray the guy in black slacks and a white button-down with the sleeves rolled up, exposing colorful ink, will shield me. Glancing past the random stranger, I catch sight of Pax. He scans the dance floor and I hold my breath as he spins toward me. I dart my gaze to the left and come to an immediate stop on my bar mate. Dark irises stare back at me in bewilderment as if I were a Pomeranian, wearing a tutu, riding a unicycle.

"Can I buy you a drink?"

His deep voice snaps me back to reality. I drop my gaze to his left hand resting on the bar. There's not a ring on his finger, and he's asking to buy me a drink. He must be single. But maybe my judgment isn't always the best, considering my last situation.

"Eve!" Pax's voice carries through the crowd.

I need Pax to fall in a hole and for the tide to bury him. I'm done with him and his sleazy ways. My hands slide up the smooth fabric covering the stranger's thighs. "You're not married, are you?"

His brows pinch together. "Um. No."

Relief washes over me. In the softest, smoothest, sexiest voice I can muster, I whisper, "Good. In that case, I'd rather have some of yours."

The corner of his lips twitch into a smile, and I give him one of my own. This guy has barely said two words to me, yet I find him oddly charming. At this point, I'd find a rat lugging around a slice of pizza charming compared to the dumbass in the crowd who doesn't get the hint.

"Eve!"

I'll have to double my efforts to make him jealous. Engulfing the stranger in a hug around his neck, my fingers play with the short hairs on the back of his head, and I fuse my mouth to his. Shifting my weight to the side, I peer around the stranger's head, and sure enough, Pax's beady glare is aimed at us. His jaw clenches. Nostrils flare. Fuck you, Pax. A guy who appears to be a security guard steps in front of Pax. Before I know what happens next, a hand on my lower back draws my attention to the man, tugging me closer to him. His bulge presses against the apex of my thighs—and holy shit. Forget one tube sock. He must be using the entire ten-pack in his slacks. I moan into his mouth, and he takes that as his opportunity to swipe his tongue across the seam of my lips. What's-his-nuts is quickly forgotten, my attention fully on the hot guy with his tongue in my mouth. Our tongues caress each other, soft and erotic. With every stroke, I inch closer to him, needing to feel more of him because it's unlike anything I've ever felt. It's warm and inviting and turns me on more than it should. My nipples pebble against the fabric of my dress. I break our kiss. My lashes flutter open and I'm met with deep sapphire eyes with shimmers of gray swirling in his irises. I'm drunk on them alone.

"Do you want to get out of here?" My words come out soft and breathy.

"Should we exchange names or something first?"

I lift a brow. I've heard my name enough thanks to the douche canoe. "Are names necessary?"

He shrugs. "How will you know what to moan later?"

A soft giggle escapes me. Oddly, I'm intrigued by his cocky charm. "How about this?" I drag the tip of my finger down his chest. "I'll be Kat," when I reach the waistband of his slacks, I nibble on my bottom lip, slowly releasing it, "and you can be Patrick." It's one of my all-time favorite movies. Plus, he's giving me Patrick vibes that would make my panties instantly wet—if I was wearing any.

He clears his throat. "Now that's established, where are we going?"

I sink my teeth into my bottom lip. My plan wasn't to come down here and hook up, but Patrick has my vagina in a chokehold. Plus, I could use the distraction. "Where's your room?"

He pushes his stool away and rises to his feet. Even at five feet eight inches on top of three-inch heels, I'm still a couple of inches shorter than him. With a hand on my lower back, he escorts me through the crowd of people. His thumb softly brushes back and forth, shooting tingles through my body. A simple touch shouldn't cause my nipples to pebble. As we move through the sea of people, I scan all the faces as inconspicuously as I can. I exhale in relief when I don't find Pax. Security must have done their job.

Once we're away from the crowd, the music and chatter slowly blend into the sound of the waves crashing onto the shore. I spin out of his grasp and move in front of him. While walking backward, I drag my hand down his hard chest. As seconds pass, I get more adventurous and inch my fingers farther south until I graze the side of his cock. Holy shit! He's huge, and there is no way he's fully erect. But I want to find out. I throw my arms around his neck. His footing falters, but he quickly recovers and wraps an arm around me to help regain his balance. While I kiss his neck, inhaling the crisp sandalwood of his cologne, his hand roams down my waist until his fingertips graze the curve of my ass. The touch sends goosebumps springing up over my entire body.

When we finally reach his hotel room door, I'm no longer thinking about how shitty the last sixty minutes of my life have been but instead how much I want this hot guy in front of me. I slide my lips along his jaw while I hook my fingers under the waistband of his slacks. My body is on the verge of spontaneously combusting. While I've always been a sexual person, it's never felt like this before. It's like someone has a voodoo doll of me, and instead of sticking me with pins, they're rubbing me in all the right places.

My irritation increases as he fumbles with his keycard. I almost rip it from his hands and do it myself, but it finally flashes green. He pushes it open and once inside, he spins us around. My back hits the door with a soft thud. Without missing a beat, his lips are on mine in a searing hot kiss. Tingles catapult through my entire body. I moan into his mouth as he slides his hand down my leg until he reaches my knee. His fingers mark my skin as he lifts, hiking my leg over his hip. Another greedy moan escapes me as he thrusts his hard erection against me. If he's trying to turn me on, he's already there. Foreplay isn't necessary. The fore is already well played. I grip his wrist, pulling his hand off my leg. He breaks our kiss. His brows pinch together, unsure if I want him to stop. The answer is no. I need him to speed things up. My lips tip up into a smile as I slide his hand under my dress. I suck in a sharp breath when his fingers graze my bare pussy. His lips crash to mine. Hot and demanding. The pad of his finger slides through my wetness, and I moan into his mouth. I gyrate against his hand, needing anything and everything he'll give me. It's the sexy voodoo doll again.

My head falls back against the door. "Oh! Yes! Patrick! Use your fingers. Fuck me."

His strokes falter, but he quickly recovers and fills me with two fingers.

"Ahhh! Yes! More!"

He continues to thrust into me, harder and harder with each pump. The palm of his hand rubs against my clit. I'm seconds away from exploding around him. Like a professional finger banger, he spears and scissors his fingers inside me. A finger bang should not feel better than sex, but somehow, he's doing it. He presses his lips to my neck, nipping and sucking.

A shiver jolts up my spine. Stars burst behind my eyelids, and my orgasm rips through me. "Oh. Oh. Yes!" My mouth falls open on a gasp. Slowly, my eyes flutter open, and I'm met with lust-filled eyes staring back at me.

He removes his hand from under my dress, and my leg drops to the floor. Lifting his hand to his mouth, he spreads my orgasm over his bottom lip before sticking his fingers in his mouth. I'm mesmerized by the way his tongue swirls around his fingers as he enjoys the taste of me. He releases his fingers with a pop.

"Fucking delicious."

My gaze drops to his cock, tenting his slacks, and I back up. "Do you have a condom?"

"No. But I can get one."

"I suggest, if you want to keep the party going, you do that."

His hands grip my hips, pulling me away from the door. I can't help the giggle that escapes me. He slams his mouth to mine in a fervent kiss before he opens the door and closes it behind him. The taste of myself lingers on his lips. It's erotic.

I press my fingers to my lips and blow out a deep breath. Strolling to the other side of the room, I sit on the edge of the bed. I'm going to have sex with this sexy stranger… right after my boyfriend told me he's married. What am I doing? Hot sex—or what I'm assuming would be hot sex based on the earlier orgasm—with a stranger will not fix anything. It'll be fleeting. In the end, it's only a band-aid on an amputated limb. And I certainly don't have enough band-aids to stop the bleeding. Ugh! I just need to leave and figure out my life… again. I jump to my feet and walk to the other side of the room. With my hand on the door handle, I glance over my shoulder. "Goodbye, Patrick. It was fun while it lasted." I lower the handle and poke my head through the crack. Once I confirm the hallway is empty, I slink out the door, down the corridor, and disappear into the stairwell.

Chapter 3

THANKS FOR CELEBRATING
MY BLUE BALLS

Lach

Twenty minutes. That's all I'm giving myself to sit here and be a piece of shit, pining over a woman I met an hour ago. This isn't what I do, and I'm not starting today. But damn, tonight would have been fun—scream-my-name type of fun. I prop my elbows on my knees and scrub my hands down my face. Something about her spoke to my soul. The gleam in her eyes, her soft hands on me, the way her lips would part when her gaze met mine like I took her breath away. She certainly stole mine. Then she disappeared without a word. Maybe we were moving too fast? But she could have stopped things. I was perfectly content with my fingers tangled in her hair, kissing her. Maybe she got an emergency phone call and didn't have time to tell me. Fuck. I've been hanging out with Rylee and Dessa too much. I rise to my feet. Twenty minutes is over.

Back at the bar at Dessa and Garrett's wedding reception, I spot Trey and Rylee as they wait for their drinks from the bartender. As I sulk toward them, Trey notices me first and does a double take.

"Weren't you just making out with someone?" He glances at his watch. "And you're already finished? My guess is you left her completely unsatisfied. Poor girl. Probably sworn off men forever now." He presses his lips together and shakes his head in disappointment. Rylee glares at him. At least someone is on my side. The bartender passes them their drinks, and I order one for myself.

"I'll have you know it's actually the other way around."

"Wait. She left you unsatisfied?" Trey asks.

"She got hers and I didn't." I lift a shoulder and let it drop.

"Damn. Too bad she bailed. I'd love to buy her a drink for taking what she wanted." Trey raises his glass of whiskey.

"Thanks for celebrating my blue balls." The bartender slides a lowball in my direction. I raise the glass in a toast before taking a sip. The whiskey burns as it flows down my throat. "Honestly, I don't even know what happened. I was following her lead. Then she asked if I had a condom. I didn't, so I went to find one, and when I came back, she was gone."

"Oh, the old looking-for-a-condom trick. Happens to everyone." Trey pauses. "No. Actually, it only happens to you." He clasps my shoulder, a smug smile on his face.

"Thanks." I swallow another gulp of whiskey. "It's my sign to not hook up at destination weddings. Been there, done that, and have the blue balls to prove it." Rylee opens her mouth, but before she can say anything, I spit out, "Don't tell me I'll find my *one* because if I was looking for my *one*, I'd find her, and I'm not looking."

She pinches her lips shut. "Well then, I guess I don't

need to say anything more. We'll let you enjoy your whiskey. Trey." She spins to face him, resting her palms on his chest. She whispers, and unfortunately not quietly enough, "Let's finish our drinks, go back to our room, and you can sour cream my burrito."

I gag, the whiskey burning my nostrils. "Something tells me you're not talking about an actual burrito."

Trey shakes his head, a giant smirk taking over his face. "Nope."

"Yep. That's what I thought." I frown and point at my mouth. "I just threw up a little."

"The night's still young." He waves his hand over the crowd. "You can find someone's burrito to sour cream."

"I'm never eating a burrito again."

"Suit yourself." Trey raises his glass, swallowing the last gulp of his whiskey. I wave them both off as they stroll across the dance floor and toward the courtyard of their hotel block. Twisting on my stool, I face the bar. Sitting here isn't going to make the night better. I throw back the rest of my drink. I might as well do the same, minus the burrito. And sour cream.

Chapter 4

OH. SHIT.

Lach

The whiskey didn't do its job last night. Instead of passing out, I spent the night tossing and turning while visions of Kat invaded my dreams. Her soft hands brushing over my cheek. Her warm body pressed against mine. Her soft whimpers as she rode my hand. All of it played on repeat throughout the night. I've never been this affected by a girl, especially one who got hers and disappeared. Call me a glutton for punishment, but I want more. Maybe it's because I can't have more. Either way, I'm ready to get out of Florida and back to Harbor Highlands. More importantly, I'm ready to forget about Kat.

I shuffle down the cramped airplane aisle, careful not to bump into any passengers, but it's kind of hard when they make these aisles so damn small. Even an inch or two would be fine, but no. They cram us in here like the floor at a rock concert. I glance down, checking my seat number on my phone—18 A. When I'm a few rows away from my seat, a familiar face with blonde hair cascading down her shoulders catches my attention. A hot pink travel pillow encircles her neck, and her eyes are glued to the paperback in her hands.

"Kat?" She doesn't move. So I call her name again. This time, she glances up. Her bright hazel eyes grow wide as all the color drains from her cheeks. Apparently, she's just as surprised to see me. "Fancy seeing you here. What happened to you last night?" I tilt my head and flash her a smirk. My gaze drops to the man seated in the aisle seat, then back to Kat. Without a second thought, I tap the guy on the shoulder. "Excuse me, sir. It seems my girlfriend and I got separated from each other. Would you mind switching seats with me? I'm only a few rows back. It's a window seat."

Before he can respond, Kat rests her hand on his arm to get his attention. His gaze flits from me to her. "Ex-boyfriend. Right now, he's being a little stalkerish." She peers up at me, flashing me the same smirk I gave her.

"Hey man," a guy says behind me, "let's keep the line moving. You can chitchat later."

"Don't keep the line waiting, Patrick." She smiles before lifting the book entirely too close to her face to read.

I huff out a laugh and make my way to my seat a few rows behind Kat before plopping down. Never in a million years did I expect to see her again, let alone on my flight. I was content not knowing why she left, but now that she's here, I want answers.

After all the passengers are seated, the ground crew pushes us back from the gate to taxi to the runway. The entire time, I can't tear my gaze away from Kat. Twice, she turns around to sneak a glance my way, and I catch her both times. Perhaps she's having the same thoughts as me, but instead of ditching me, she's daydreaming of what the night could have been. Fuck. Now that's what I'm thinking about.

Once we reach cruising altitude, the captain turns off the Fasten Seatbelt sign. I contemplate if I should get out of my seat and demand she explain why she up and left or if I should let it go. Normally, this wouldn't bother me, but I've also never had someone ghost me like she did. Not going to lie. It bruised my ego—not that I'd tell anyone else that. She missed out. The first orgasm I gave her would have been a minor tremor compared to what I had in store for her next. She'd still be walking on wobbly legs. The head of the guy next to her falls forward. If he's going to sleep like that, he's going to wake up with a sore neck. I roll my head back and forth, imagining his looming stiff neck. My gaze drifts back to Kat when suddenly his body convulses. "Oh, shit," I mutter. Kat twists her head to the left. She jumps from her seat, her head inches from smacking against the overhead bin. Her eyes widen as she plasters herself against the window. All the color drains from her face as panic spreads over her features.

"Help! Help! Someone help!" Her gaze flits from the back of the plane to the front, desperate for help. I'm seconds away from hurdling the person seated next to me, even though I don't have the slightest idea what to do. A mixture of murmurs and gasps floats through the cabin. A flight attendant from the rear galley rushes past me and down the aisle to Kat.

A woman two rows in front of her jumps up from her seat. "I'm a nurse." Passengers move out of the way to give the nurse and flight attendant as much room as possible. Another flight attendant from the front galley of the plane races down the aisle. Time slows to a halt as they assist the passenger with the medical emergency.

My attention drifts to Kat. Her hands cover her mouth;

the whites of her eyes are the only thing visible as she stares at the guy who's now lying in the aisle. I want to wrap her in my arms and shield her from what's happening next to her. The fear, terror, and concern on her face are unbearable to witness.

"Attention, passengers," the captain's voice sounds over the intercom. "We'll be making an emergency landing in Huntsville, Alabama. Please take your seats. We'll be on the ground in about thirty minutes. Flight crew, prepare for landing."

Kat disappears as she lowers herself to her seat. I grip the armrest and rise in my seat, wanting to go to Kat, wrap my arms around her, and tell her everything will be okay.

"Please take your seat and fasten your seatbelt," the flight attendant says as she walks by. Without taking my eyes off Kat, I lower myself to the seat. Even after the wheels touch down, I never tear my gaze away from her.

Chapter 5

MORE WORSE.
THE WORSTEST.

Eve

Worst flying experience ever. I'll take all the crying babies. All the toddlers kicking my seat. The person in front of me who insists on reclining their seat all the way back. I'll even take the person who forgot to apply deodorant and sprinted across the airport as my neighbor over having to witness someone almost dying in the seat next to me. It was like a bad car accident. I knew I shouldn't have stared, but then again, it happened two feet away from me. As soon as we touched down, the paramedics rushed on board and carted my neighbor away. There was a slight twitch to his fingers, so I take that as a sign of life, and I'll pretend he makes it to the hospital alive and will continue living a full and happy life because I don't want to think about the other option. I thought I was having a bad day, but he's the winner. But is that really winning? Maybe the winner of the shittiest day. But that doesn't sound like anything worth winning.

The captain comes over the intercom to announce the cancelation of our Chicago flight and it's rescheduled for tomorrow morning. We need to see the ticketing agent to arrange hotel accommodations. My night just went from worse to worser. More worse. The worstest. Either way, zero stars. Do not recommend.

Passengers shuffle down the aisle, collecting their carry-on luggage as they go. When it's my turn, I rise. Twisting to peer over my shoulder, I spare a glance back at Patrick, and I'm met with soft blue eyes.

"Are you going to go?" a guy behind me asks.

I shake my head. With everything that happened, he's the last person I need to think about. "Yeah. Sorry," I mutter before grabbing my tote bag from the overhead bin and shuffling down the aisle to exit the plane.

While waiting in line to collect the hotel arrangements and rebook the flight for tomorrow, I never saw Patrick. He got buried in the chaos. It's better this way. I'm sure he'll again ask why I ditched him in the hotel room, and I'd hate for my answer to be, "My boyfriend is married, and his wife was stopping by, and I wanted to make him jealous." He just happened to be in the right place at the right time. Or the wrong place, depending on how you look at it. I exhale a deep yawn. Sleeping in my car didn't offer me a quality night's sleep like a bed would have. After collecting my checked bag from the baggage carousel, I exit the small airport. A warm, light breeze floats by, flinging hair across my face. I brush it away on a huff. I scan the long line waiting for the bus and then the size of the bus. Math isn't my forte, but when I put the two together, the math isn't mathing. There is no way all these people will fit on the bus. Call me selfish, but I'm tired as fuck, and don't want to wait. I shimmy past a group of people, weave between another group, and squeeze past a few more.

"Kat!"

My fake name pierces through the air. I guess I found Patrick. Or he found me. Either way, there's no time for chitchat. The bus is filling up and fast. He calls my name again, but I ignore him. I squeeze into the line, pass my suitcase off to a worker to shove in the storage compartment, and board the bus before the doors close. I sink down in the last window seat, more than ready for this day to end. Patrick's crammed in the middle of a group of people like a herd of cattle, having to wait for the next bus.

After the longest fifteen-minute ride ever, the bus slows to a stop in front of the modest three-story hotel. Everyone races off and through the sliding door to the lobby, including me. People from all directions swarm the small, one-person front desk, wanting to claim a room. I yawn and rub the tiredness from my eyes as I stand in line. It's been a long weekend and an even longer twenty-four hours. All I want to do is snuggle under the blankets—in a bed, curse my ex for his shittiness—and drift off to a peaceful sleep. But all that soon dies a quick death as a familiar sandalwood scent wafts through the air. Peering around the broad shoulder of the guy in front of me, I spot him. Patrick. My heart rate spikes from anxiety or excitement. At this point, I'm not even sure anymore. More importantly, how in the hell did he beat me here? As the line inches closer to the reception desk, I refrain from making any noise or sudden movements. I don't need to draw attention to myself and have him turn around and berate me with questions. Sleep. That's all I want.

"Good evening, sir," the receptionist's soft voice floats across the desk like she's trying to compensate for our shitty situation. He replies with a greeting of his own. "You are in luck. You get our last room."

My ears perk up from her last two words. I step out from behind Patrick. "Excuse me? What do you mean 'last room'? What about the rest of us?" Patrick's gaze snaps to mine. Brows furrowed together.

"We'll have to take you to our sister hotel twenty minutes away."

Everyone's attention, including mine, drifts to the other receptionist as he announces that all remaining guests will have to wait to be transported to another hotel in another bus. A collective groan echoes through the lobby.

Oh hell no! I'm exhausted and just want to sleep. There is no way I'm waiting for another twenty-minute bus ride. "I'll share a room with him. He's my boyfriend," I blurt. Twenty-four hours ago, I was going to sleep with him. Might as well share a room with him now.

A deep rumble sounds from Patrick's chest. Bending down, he whispers, "An hour ago, you wouldn't talk to me, and now I'm your boyfriend?"

A fake laugh bubbles out of me, and I hook my arm through his. "Don't be silly." I pat my hand against his chest. The cotton of his zip-up hoodie does nothing to mask the hard muscle underneath. I turn to the receptionist. "He's just being funny. Always the jokester in the relationship. We got into a teeny, tiny argument about a little problem of his." I nod at the crotch of his jeans, then hold out a limp pointer finger. "It's a sensitive topic."

He leans down. His breath warm against my ear as he says, "If you want to stay in my room, fine, but you're also telling me why you bailed."

I glare at him from the corner of my eye. "I didn't realize this was a negotiation."

"It is now." He lifts a brow.

"Is your ego bruised that bad?"

"Call me curious."

"Curiosity killed the cat."

"Good thing I'm not a cat then."

I huff out a deep breath. He's infuriating. Yet, I'm intrigued just as much, if not more, than when we met last night. "Fine. I'll tell you. But not right now."

"If you think I'm going to let this go, you're delusional." He pulls his phone from his pocket and types on the screen with one hand.

"What are you doing?"

"Making myself a note to ask about this later."

I roll my eyes. "You're ridiculous."

When he's finished typing, he shoves his phone back into his pocket. He unlinks his arm from mine and wraps it around my shoulders, tugging me to the crook of his arm. His cologne invades my senses just like last night, when I was close to him like this, along with the taste of the smooth whiskey that lingered on his lips when they pressed to mine.

"She'll be staying in my room." The receptionist's gaze drifts from me to Patrick and back to me. I flash her a bright smile, and she nods before passing us two key cards.

"Your room is on the third floor. The elevators are on the left."

"Thank you," Patrick says.

It's going to be an even longer night unless I quickly fall asleep, or at least pretend, so I'm not subjected to a night of interrogation.

Chapter 6

TASTEFULLY FAKE AN ORGASM

Lach

The elevator ride is silent except for the whirring sounds as we travel up to the third floor. Her bright pink suitcase is the only thing separating us. I hike my backpack higher on my shoulder before stealing glances at her from the corner of my eye. She looks different from last night. More casual, but just as beautiful. She presses her pink lips together, and I'm instantly reminded of how those lips felt on mine. Plump and soft. It's hard to say where her head is, though. Not acknowledging me on the plane, avoiding me at the airport, and I'm sure she'd be sleeping in her own room if the hotel wasn't fully booked right now, all point to she's not interested. Why do I care? Tomorrow, we'll go our separate ways, just like last night.

The elevator jolts to a stop. Before the doors fully open, Kat slips through the crack and is down the hallway, suitcase in tow. My gaze drops from the back of her head to her hips as they sway back and forth. Fuck. I adjust myself in my jeans. She bailed on me once, and I'm sure she wouldn't hesitate to do it again. At the door, she slides the keycard into the reader and lets herself in. Not bothering to hold it open, she lets it click shut before I arrive. My lips twitch into a smile, and I shake my head. I'll give her a few minutes now, but she's not getting out of telling me what happened yesterday.

When I enter the room, a sliver of light shines through the bottom of a closed door, which I suspect is the bathroom. As I scan the rest of the room, the one king-size bed jumps out at me. This will be fun. I toss my backpack on the chair in the corner and throw myself onto the bed. Linking my fingers behind my head and crossing my feet at my ankles, I wait for the aftermath. Several minutes later, the door opens, and Kat strolls out with her suitcase, wearing cotton shorts and a hoodie.

No one should look as hot as she does right now, and I'm sharing a hotel room with her with only one bed. The temptation to pick her up and toss her onto the comforter while I crawl up her body is strong. Real fucking strong. Based on my read of the room, she'd probably grab the nearest object to clock me upside the head if I tried to touch her. It's in my best interest to stay exactly where I am.

She releases the handle, and her head drifts up. Her eyes connect with mine for a split second before darting around the room. "Where's the other bed?"

"This is it." I smirk. "And you best believe I'm sleeping like a starfish." I slide down the mattress and spread my arms and legs to each corner of the bed.

"There has to be a pull-out couch or something." She twists around, searching the room again in case a spare bed magically appears. Her hand slides down the wall, searching for a Murphy bed. Her frown confirms her answer.

"You can keep searching, but you'll have better luck with the other hotel. That is, if you want to wait even longer. Actually, I bet they're already sold out too." I lift my head and catch her glaring at me. "Or there's plenty of space here." I pat the spot between my shoulder and leg.

She eyes the comforter before blowing out a deep breath. "You'd think hotel rooms would have a pull-out couch nowadays."

"I'm sorry this isn't up to your standards, but I'll make sure you're cozy." I pat the bed again. "Just so you know, I only bite if you bite first."

She rolls her eyes but walks toward the bed. The edge of the bed dips as she sits. "Luckily, I am very comfortable sleeping in a ball." She pulls her hair from her ponytail, and the blonde tresses cascade down her shoulders. I'm mesmerized as she combs her fingers through the strands.

"So, how's it going?"

A small chuckle escapes her. "Is that really what you want to ask?"

"Not really, but I thought we'd ease in first. But we can dive right into the good stuff." I move up the bed and adjust the pillow against the headboard. "What happened? Why did you leave?"

She rotates on the bed and crosses her legs in a pretzel, getting more comfortable. "Would you believe your overpowering masculinity intimidated me?"

Fuck. She's sassy. All the girls I've been with always follow my lead. Afraid to have opinions of their own. "No. You don't seem like the type of person to fear anything."

"Thanks." She picks at a thread on the blanket. "But looks can be deceiving." She's silent for a moment before she says, "Would you believe I wanted to make someone jealous?"

"That sounds more believable. Did it work?"

Her face is soft as her hazel eyes meet mine. "I never stuck around to find out. I kind of got caught up in the moment and went back to a stranger's hotel room." A small smile graces her lips. "And I wanted to forget everything that happened earlier."

"Now we're getting to the good stuff. Keep going." I roll my hand between us, encouraging her to continue.

"You're genuinely interested in all my drama?"

"I never said *all*," she tilts her head and narrows her eyes at me, and I laugh, "just the stuff that leads up to you kissing me."

She taps her finger against her lips, drawing my attention to her mouth. Flashbacks of her lips on mine flit through my mind. Soft and perfect. *Don't be an asshole and reach across the bed and haul her to you just so you can kiss her again.* I doubt that's what she wants right now.

"The lighting of the fuse started when I found out my boyfriend for the past six months is actually married. After that, it was just a countdown until everything exploded."

"The explosion happened when you met me?"

"More like when I kissed you. And, not saying the kiss was explosive, but that was the moment things changed. It was no longer about making him jealous but making me forget."

I know a thing or two about wanting to forget. I've been doing it for over half my life. But this isn't about me. "So what did you expect to happen when you kissed me?"

"I don't know. I was being impulsive. Act first. Think later. At the moment, I wanted to make Pax jealous. Give him a tiny sliver of the hurt he gave me." She lifts a shoulder and lets it fall. "And I knew he was watching. Kissing you would achieve that."

"His name is Pax? He already sounds like a douche."

A laugh escapes her. It's soft and infectious. I'd spend the rest of the night listening to her if I got more of that sporadic laugh from her.

"He had to live up to his name."

"So, back to this kiss. You were using me?"

She shakes her head back and forth. "I mean, technically, yes. But I also enjoyed it. A lot. And kind of wanted more."

"It was a good kiss."

She bites her lips together. "It was an excellent kiss." She uncrosses her legs, stretches them out toward the top of the bed, and leans back on her hands. "I wanted to feel something besides hurt and betrayal."

My gaze drifts down to her sparkly pink polish on her toes. When did feet become sexy? "And sleeping with me would do that?"

"I was hoping it would give me five minutes to get out of my head."

I flinch. "Ouch."

She sits up. Concern etches her features. "What? What's wrong?"

"I'm hurt by you thinking I'd only last five minutes."

She grabs a pillow by her feet and throws it at me. It cartwheels through the air before I catch it, stopping it from smacking me in the face.

"I'll have you know I would have given you the best ten minutes of your life." I tuck the pillow behind me.

She giggles. It's the sound angels make. "A whole ten minutes." She gasps sarcastically and clutches her chest. "What would I do with all those minutes?"

"It's more than the five minutes you gave me credit for.

Based on your moans and whimpers, you would have enjoyed those ten minutes."

She raises a brow. "How do you know I wasn't faking it?"

"I doubt you were faking. No one is that good at acting."

She straightens her shoulders. "Want to bet? Oh! Uh. Yes." She tips her head back as her lips spread. "Oh. Oh. Yes. Right there. Patrick. Yes. Yes. Mmm, yes." She blows out a sigh before tilting her head forward. A smile tugs at her lips.

I shift on the bed, trying as discreetly as possible to adjust myself. I raise my hands and give her a slow clap.

She crosses her arm over her stomach and bows. "Thank you."

"I take my words back. With that performance, you could be an actress."

"You think so?" She rests a hand on her waist and lifts her chin, posing for the pretend cameras. Then a giggle escapes her, and she drops her hand to the comforter. "I never had dreams to be on the big screen. Plus, I think faking orgasms falls more in line with porn star than Hollywood actress."

"Or you could do that."

"But that's a lot of sex."

"And a lot of dicks."

"While I like both," she presses her lips together, "I feel like that would be overconsumption."

"You've put a lot of thought into this."

"Well, you put the thought in my head, and this is just what came out."

I rub my chin. "I don't think you can tastefully fake an orgasm."

"Meg Ryan did it."

"This is true."

"I could be the next Meg Ryan."

"You could."

"Your turn." She sits up straighter. "Since you think I was faking it. Let's see your best fake orgasm."

I laugh. "I don't think so."

"So you've never faked an orgasm?"

"No, I have. Mostly because I was tired and wanted to go to sleep, but this is different."

Now it's her turn to laugh. "Why is it different? I just did it."

"Because I'm not," I roll my hand between us, "going through the motions."

"If you need to dry hump the bed, by all means, have at it." She motions her hand over the comforter. "I won't mind the show."

"You would like that, wouldn't you?"

She nods enthusiastically. "Yes. Yes, I would." She scoots back to the edge of the bed. "The stage is yours."

I shake my head, but a smile twitches on my lips. What the hell did I get myself into? Performing fake orgasms in a hotel room with a woman I met yesterday when I don't even know her real name. I sit up but forgo the dry humping. Closing my eyelids, because this will most definitely be easier if I'm not looking at her, I open my mouth. "Uh. Oh. Uh. Mmm. Ooo." I follow that with a few grunts and groans. Slowly, I lift my lids to find Kat staring back at me. A few seconds of silence pass between us before a laugh bursts out of her.

"Oh. My. God." She tips over onto the bed, her entire body shaking with laughter. "I dodged a bullet if that's what's expected in bed."

I can't help the laugh that escapes me. "Hey! You put me on the spot."

She holds up her hand as if she's waving a flag. "Marked safe from Patrick's orgasm."

She continues to laugh, and I can't help but join her. I wouldn't want to have sex with me either if that's what I really sound like.

"I promise you, my fake orgasm is nothing like my real one. Enough about me and my terrible fake orgasm. You still haven't answered my question. Did you fake it the other night in the hotel room?"

She pushes herself off the bed and sits up. "A girl doesn't fake and tell."

I shift on the bed and lean toward her, invading her space. "I call bullshit on it being fake."

Her gaze casts downward and fixates on my lips before drifting back up to meet my eyes. She inches closer to me. "What are you going to do? Prove it?"

I lift my chin, mainly to test the waters. She doesn't back down, so I inch even closer. Her lips part a fraction. Her sweet coconut scent swirls around me, making it hard to concentrate. She intrigues me. I can't grasp what it is, but I want to explore the electricity between us. My lips brush against hers. "Is that what you want?" I whisper.

Her teeth sink into her bottom lip. Slowly, she nods. Mid nod, I crash my lips to hers.

Chapter 7

SUNFLOWER

Eve

I've missed this. As much as someone can miss kissing someone they not only just met but also kissed for the first time twenty-four hours ago. Never in my wildest dreams did I expect to see him again, but also locking lips with him? Again? His warm palms clasp both my cheeks, and I inch closer, resting my hands on his chest. My fingers curl around the fabric of his hoodie, holding on as his tongue sweeps along the seam of my lips. This kiss is hotter than the last. I want more. I need more. Parting my lips, I slide my tongue against his. A deep rumble sounds from his throat.

Reluctantly, I break away, but my lips are still a hairsbreadth from his. "Did you ever find a condom?"

"I did." A small smile forms on his lips.

"Impressive."

"An insanely hot and sexy woman wanted to have sex with me. I wasn't coming back empty-handed."

I chuckle. "Do you still have it?"

"I do."

"We should put it to use. Since you went through all the effort to find one."

He pulls away to meet my eyes. "Is this you being impulsive? Act now. Think later."

"Probably. But if it's memorable, I'll definitely be thinking about it later."

"Memorable is a guarantee."

"Prove it."

He grips the back of my neck, and I gasp. His fingers press into my skin, and he hauls me to him for another bruising kiss. It's rough and demanding and so scorching hot. He's on a mission to prove it, and I'm going to enjoy the ride.

Without breaking the kiss, I rise to my knees. His hands fall away and rest on my hips. I straddle his waist, pressing my chest against his. His fingers slide under the hem of my hoodie and with a feather-like touch, they brush my bare skin. Goosebumps prickle my arms as his hands continue traveling up and up. They drift over my rib cage and brush along the underside of my breast. I break the kiss on a gasp.

"Touch me," I whisper against his lips. His thumb grazes over one nipple, and I rock against him, his erection pressing between my legs. He lifts my hoodie but stops after a few inches. His gaze meets mine, silently asking for permission. I reach down and grab the fabric, yanking it over my head and discarding it on the bed next to us. The cool air hits my heated skin, and instantly, my nipples go hard. Patrick's attention leaves my lips and drifts down to my fully exposed chest. He cups both breasts and swirls his tongue around one nipple before wrapping his lips around it. I press closer to him while my fingers comb through his soft chestnut hair. I continue to gyrate over his hard cock. On every thrust, my clit rubs against him in the perfect spot. The thin fabric of my shorts is now soaked, and there's a good chance it's transferred to his jeans.

"Mmm. Your mouth feels so good on me. I can't believe I missed out on this before."

A laugh bubbles out of him. He pulls away. The spot where his warm mouth was is replaced with the chilly air. "Now you regret it."

"So much." I shimmy down his thighs. Sure enough, there is a tiny circle of dark fabric. The corners of my lips tip up into a smile.

He glances down and notices the spot. "Looks like you're using me for your own pleasure again."

"You're taking your sweet time, so I had to take matters into my own hands."

"Is that so?" Before I can answer, his fingers press into my ass, and he flips us over so he's on top.

His breath skates over my cheek as he says, "Since we're redoing our first night together, I'm taking a keepsake."

"What do you want, my bra or something?"

"Nope." His hand drifts over my rib cage and to my waist. He digs a finger under the waistband of my sleep shorts. I lift my hips, and he slides them down my legs.

"My shorts?"

"These." His hooded eyes meet mine. With both hands, he delicately slides my lace panties down my legs and over my heels. He holds up the fabric.

I laugh. "You're taking my underwear?"

"Yep."

"Are you going to sniff them?" The words are barely out of my mouth before I throw my head back in laughter.

"Not while you're watching." He smirks. He balls my

underwear into his hand and shoves them into the back pocket of his jeans.

"Wooow. I never pinned you as a trophy collector."

"Only when I win first place." Bending down, his lips press against my neck, alternating between soft kisses and gentle sucks. "And this is most definitely first place."

The short stubble on his face tickles my sensitive skin. A giggle escapes me as I squirm underneath him. I reach up and brush my thumb over his cheek before tugging on the collar of his hoodie. "This needs to go."

He sits up. With one hand, he reaches behind him and tugs it over his head. The bottom of his shirt rides up, and I catch sight of his taut stomach and a strip of hair that disappears under the waistband. Heat floods my entire body. I want to see him. All of him. He tosses his hoodie onto the floor and peers down at me.

"This too." I grip the hem of his white shirt, and with his help, I pull it off. My gaze rakes over his ink-covered chest and down his arms. I run a finger over his bicep, tracing the swirls of colors. Tattoos have never turned me on, but on Patrick, it's like a canvas of art. Beautiful and mesmerizing. I want to spend the rest of the night studying them, but my throbbing vagina has other plans. Especially when I see how his cock strains against the denim. "Since we're on a roll, might as well remove these as well." I dip my fingers into the waistband of his jeans and pop the button.

"Someone's eager." He winks while his lips curve into a smile. Hovering above me, he pulls the zipper down and slides his jeans and boxer briefs over his hips, freeing his cock. It bobs up and down. Long and thick. Holy fuck. Regret that I never got to enjoy this last night washes over me. Best I make use of my time now. Resting an elbow on the mattress to balance his weight, he continues to slide his jeans down his legs until he's able to kick them off. They hit the floor with a thud. Reaching down, I wrap my fingers around his girth. He groans from the contact. Slowly, I slide my hand up until I reach the crown, then I push down.

His eyes pinch shut. "Ah fuuuck," he draws out. "That feels so good."

His words spur me on. I alternate the tightness of my grip as I continue to stroke him.

A deep groan sounds from his throat. "If you keep that up, I'm going to come all over your stomach."

I giggle and release my grip on him. "We can't have that. Get the condom."

He bends down and presses his lips to my cheek, down my jaw, and to my neck.

"You're being too sweet."

He freezes, his lips still pressed to my skin. "What's wrong with sweet?"

"It solidifies everything I can't have." My body stiffens. Why can't I keep my mouth shut? He doesn't need to know all my issues. "Are you going to get the condom, or do I have to dig through your things myself?"

"You're bossy. It's hot." He rolls off the bed.

I can't help but stare at his tight, muscular ass as he digs through his backpack on a chair in the corner of the room next to the bed. When I'm finished drooling over his ass, my gaze drifts up to his back. Running along his spine is an intricate tattoo of gears. I want to run my fingers over the inked skin to see if they'll move.

He spins around and holds up the foil packet before tossing it onto the bed. Reaching over, I pluck it off the comforter. The ripping of the foil, along with the thumping of my heart, are the only sounds in the room. The mattress dips as Patrick crawls on the bed, coming to a halt a foot away from me. I sit up and pull the condom from the wrapper. His thick cock juts out toward me. With trembling fingers, I slowly slide the condom down his length. I've had sex before, but with Patrick it feels like the first time. When the condom is in place, he reaches down and pinches the tip before lowering himself over me. With his knee, he nudges my leg wider.

"How wet are you for me?" His warm breath skates over my cheek, sending tingles racing through my entire body.

"So w—ah!" I suck in a sharp breath when he shoves two thick fingers inside me and begins to thrust in and out.

"So fucking wet." He adds a third finger, stretching me even more.

I buck my hips, meeting his thrusts. "Oh! Yes! More! I need more."

The mattress dips. I whimper at the loss of his fingers, but seconds later, they're replaced with something much larger.

"Oh. My. God." My eyes roll back and my back arches. "Ah! Fuck!"

He slides out and slams back in. My fingers claw at the comforter. Stars burst behind my eyelids. His fingers grip under my knee, pressing my leg as he drives deeper and harder. My moans grow shallower with every thrust of his hips.

"Yes. Right there. Don't stop." I lift my lids, and his piercing blue eyes are staring back at me. A small smile flits over my lips. He gives me a smile of his own before he drives deeper into me as if that's even possible. The sound of our skin slapping fills the room. I lift my hips, meeting him on every thrust. "Oh god. I'm going to come!"

He grunts as he continues to pound into me like a

jackhammer. Fast. Hard. Rough. Primal. It's everything I need right now.

"You feel too good, Sunflower. I won't last much longer."

My heart stammers in my chest. No one's ever given me a nickname like that. The most Pax ever gave me was "babe," and it always made me think of the pig, which doesn't make the name very attractive. But Sunflower... yes. It's perfect.

My toes curl as a burst of tingles erupts in my belly. He rolls his hips, hitting my G-spot. My body jolts as my breath gets caught in my throat. "Oh, oh god! Harder!" He pushes my leg higher, driving deeper. His thrusts become more erratic, along with his own grunts and moans. Seconds later, he roars out his orgasm. He rocks his hips a few more times before eventually slowing to a stop. He lowers my leg to the bed. My chest heaves. If I tried to stand right now, I'd resemble a newborn fawn.

He slides out but doesn't move from on top of me. He reaches up, his finger lightly grazing my forehead and brushes a strand of hair to the side.

"Again, with the sweetness."

"I wanted to see all of you."

My breath hitches at his words. Why couldn't this man be Pax? Instead, he's a two-night stand. After tonight, we'll go our separate ways and never see each other again. It's better that way. With my luck, he's a serial killer, leaving a trail of bodies around North America. That's more than I want to deal with right now.

Chapter 8

YOUR CASANOVA SKILLS ARE SEVERELY LACKING

Lach

An annoyingly incessant beeping stirs me awake from the most amazing dream. I crossed paths with Kat again, and we spent all night exchanging orgasms. I crack an eyelid and groan. Reaching over, I blindly slap the nightstand until I find my phone. The easiest way to stop the noise is the snooze button. I twist my head on the pillow, and I'm greeted with a mop of blonde hair. Last night wasn't a dream. Rising on my elbow, I peer over Kat's shoulder. Her eyelashes fan over her cheeks, lips slightly parted as she softly snores. I glance over her body and around the bed. My shoulders shake from laughter. So much for sleeping in a ball. Instead, Kat is the one starfished across three-quarters of the bed.

My finger grazes her soft skin, brushing a strand of hair off her neck. Leaning down, I press a kiss to my favorite spot—the sunflower tattoo below her ear.

"Mmm." She stirs awake. "Are we doing this again?"

She stretches before rolling over to face me. I pull her into my arms and nuzzle the crook of her neck. "My legs are still sore from last night. I need to add more stretching to my daily routine."

"If I'd planned this better, I could have helped you with a few stretches, but it's that or me inside you. The choice is yours."

"Why do you ask such dumb questions so early in the morning?" She presses her lips to mine. "I'll take the stretches."

"Is that so?" I roll us over so I'm on top. Her laughter fills the room as I blow raspberries on her neck. She flails her limbs beneath me as I tickle her ribs. Then realization hits me, and I freeze.

She notices and turns to face me. "What's wrong?"

"I don't have a condom."

"Oh. Well, you can go find one again." She winks.

"And have you disappear on me again?" I quickly press my lips to hers, and she gasps in surprise. "Not a chance. I'll have to get creative." I lift the edge of the comforter.

"Using a hotel trash bag isn't creative."

With the blanket still in the air, I freeze, tilting my head to make sure I heard her correctly. "This is from experience?"

"No. It just seemed like the most logical idea since we're in a hotel room."

I smile. "No trash bags, but equally enjoyable." I flash her a wink before diving under the blankets and nestling between her legs. Since we didn't bother putting our clothes back on last night, her pussy is ready and waiting for me. With my thumbs, I spread her open and run the flat of my tongue up her center. Her body jolts from the contact.

"Oh. Yeah. This is definitely better than the garbage bag."

The last twenty-four hours have been... hell, there are no words to describe it. But it's been interesting, to say the least. And certainly not what I was expecting. But it was one of the best nights and mornings of my entire life. So much so, we almost missed the shuttle back to the airport. We agreed to go our separate ways. She took her seat, and I took mine. After landing in Chicago, I went in one direction, and she went in another. I'm kind of sad it was one and done. But it's better this way. No strings. Nothing messy. I can carry on with the rest of my life.

I hike my backpack over my shoulder as I push through the door of Porter's for the night shift. It would have been in my best interest to sleep as much as I could this morning, but Kat was in my bed. I wasn't going to waste a single second with her, so I'll have to power through the night. I can sleep later.

There are a few customers scattered around the bar, but it's a relatively quiet afternoon. I've been a bartender at Porter's for the past eight years. My life had been hell, and the owner, Jake, took me in. He told me someone was there when he needed help, so it's only fair for him to return the favor. I had nothing, so I wasn't going to say no. Since then, we've become best friends. There's no one else I'd rather have in my corner. In fact, everyone at Porter's is tight. It's our Porter's family. We have each other's back no matter what, and that's all I need.

When I'm halfway across the bar, Nora, the most recent bartender to the Porter's family, pops up from behind the bar. A wide, knowing grin spreads across her face.

Fuck. I know how my entire shift is going to go now. I give her a nod and quicken my steps to get to the back room.

"Oh no, you don't." Nora races toward me and grabs my bicep, twisting me around. "You're telling me everything first."

I feign innocence. "Tell you what?"

"Cut the shit." She pops her hip, hand resting on her waist. "Tell me about the hot blonde you were sucking face with at Dessa and Garrett's wedding reception."

"What the hell?" I throw my hands up in the air. "That was like thirty-six hours ago. How do you know about that already?"

"Rylee texted me the night it happened." She shrugs.

I shake my head. Nothing stays quiet around here. But it's stupid for me to assume that. Rylee was outed with her tryst with Trey, and Dessa got busted with her rendezvous with Garrett. I guess it's now my time. "Of course she did."

"She also said Trey wanted me to mention that you were barely even gone for five minutes." She presses her lips together. Her gaze drifts down my chest and stops at my crotch before it slingshots back up. "And that your Casanova skills are severely lacking."

"I can't say he's one to talk after getting Rylee pregnant in the back seat of his SUV in the Porter's parking lot. That's not very Casanova of him."

"Stop trying to divert the question. Who is she? Tell me all about her. Tell me everything. Every little detail." She rests her elbow on the bar.

I rub the back of my neck. "There's not much to tell."

"I'll take 'that's a lie' for five hundred. You can't wipe that grin off your face."

She's right. It is a lie. The memory of Kat will live rent-free in my head for eternity. But that's all it will be. A memory. Because I don't even know her real name. "Yeah, we had our fun and went our separate ways."

Disappointment etches her face. "So that's it? No late-night phone calls or text messages, making plans to meet up in the future? No a long-distance love affair?"

"Nope."

She frowns. "That's not very romantic of you.

"I never claimed to be romantic."

"That's the problem with guys nowadays." She waves a finger at me. "They only want flings and one-night stands. It's like they're allergic to relationships."

I shrug. "Why have a relationship when you can have flings and one-night stands?"

"It's annoying."

I wrap my arm around her shoulder and pull her to my chest. "Aww, is someone wanting a relationship? Is my little Nora finally growing up?" I am more than happy to divert this conversation away from me.

She shrugs. "A second phone call would be nice."

I pat the top of her head. "Your prince charming is waiting for you to sweep him off his feet."

"At this rate, I'm willing to settle for a semi-charming knight who can keep up with me."

"Good luck with that. Is my interrogation over?"

"No. But I'll let you put your stuff away." She steps out of my grasp.

It's been less than twenty-four hours since I saw Kat, and she's still at the forefront of my mind. Maybe I should have said "fuck it" and sat next to her on the plane. My skin tingles from where her soft hands roamed over my body. Visions of her even softer lips pressed against mine play in my head. Her moans and whimpers. There was only one tiny difference between her fake orgasm, which sounded just as good as her real one. Her nose would crinkle as if she was about to sneeze before she detonated around me. Initially, I overlooked it, but now it consumes my thoughts. I adjust myself in my jeans. The last thing I need is to be walking around work with a half-hard dick. I shove all thoughts of Kat to the back of my mind under lock and key. It was one and done. I don't even know where she's at right now. It was only a quick vacation fling. No more, no less. But fuck, a part of me wishes she was in Harbor Highlands. I toss my backpack into a locker. The metal door rattles as I slam it shut.

When I return to the bar, Jake's sitting on a stool, still wearing a jacket, shuffling through a stack of mail. He glances up. "Hey. How was the wedding?"

"It was great. Dessa and Garrett are obnoxiously cute together."

Jake nods along. "Good."

Nora strolls down the bar and rests her elbow on the worn wood bar top. "Did you know Lach hooked up with someone?"

I press my lips together as Jake swings his gaze toward me. I was hoping I was done with this conversation, but Nora wants to keep poking the hornet's nest.

"Congratulations," Jake says nonchalantly.

"Thanks, man."

Nora's arm drops to her side. "Wait, you don't want all the dirty details?"

"Not really." Jake shakes his head. We're not the type of friends who analyze each other's sex lives.

"Seriously?" She peers at Jake, then at me. "You two

are best friends. What the heck do you talk about if you're not talking about your random hookups?"

Jake lifts his gaze and meets mine, brows drawn together. "Sports. Beer. Video games."

"Jake helped me fix the brakes on my truck," I add.

"Lach helped me with my upstairs bathroom remodel," Jake says.

Nora closes her eyes and drops her head back, fake snoring. "Oh my god. You guys are so boooring."

"Alright, while you two discuss Lach's sex life, I have to go pick up my sister in The Cities." The barstool scrapes across the linoleum floor as he pushes away from the bar. "I guess her plane got delayed or something. A guy had a seizure, and they had to make an emergency landing."

Nora's eyes go wide. "That's so crazy."

"There was a guy on my flight that had a medical emergency. We had to make an emergency landing as well," I say. "What are the chances?"

"That's definitely out of the ordinary. Don't burn the place down." Jake's gaze flits between me and Nora.

Nora gives him a two-finger salute.

Jake rolls his eyes and strolls out the door, stack of mail in hand.

When the door closes, Nora turns her attention to me, a wide grin on her face. "Well, lucky for you, I'm not Jake, and I want all the dirty details."

I give Nora the briefest of rundowns of my hookup—just enough to satisfy her appetite. Luckily, a customer approaches the bar to distract her and, hopefully, she forgets all about me.

While Nora's serving the customer at the other end of the bar, I flip over a cardboard coaster and grab a pen from my back pocket. The black ink slides across the cardboard, leaving a small indent in its wake. With one long stroke, I loop around, connecting one end to the other. I continue all the way around the coaster until the loops connect to themselves. With small, soft strokes, I fill the center of the loops, forming a circle.

Nora peers over my shoulder. "Is that a sunflower?

"Yep."

"I didn't know you were into drawing floral arrangements."

"It's just a sunflower." Without taking my eyes off the coaster, I continue drawing.

She rests her elbows on the bar, watching me, not the pen. "But why a sunflower?

"Something that just came to my mind." Not because it's the tattoo on Kat's neck, right below her ear. I continue shading under the petals.

Nora pushes to her full height. "I call bullshit."

My pen falls to the bar top, and I turn to face her. "Why?"

"Because you're not a flower type of guy."

"Guys can like flowers."

"Yeah, but not you. I've watched you doodle tons of drawings, and you've never once drawn a flower." Her eyes flicker to life as if she discovered the holy grail. "Is that her name?"

"Sunflower?" I scoff. "Who has the name Sunflower?"

"The woman you hooked up with." She quirks a blonde eyebrow at me. When I say nothing, she continues. "Spill now, or I'll keep hounding you for the rest of our shift. And basically for eternity until you tell me."

"That's what I'm afraid of." She's like an annoying little sister. At times, you want to ignore her, but you'll also be the first person to have her back if she's in trouble. I exhale a deep breath. "She had a tattoo of a sunflower."

"Tell me more about her." With her elbow resting on the bar, she props her chin on her hand.

All my favorite things about Kat jump to the front of my mind. "She has the sweetest laugh. It's infectious. And the softest blonde hair and prettiest hazel eyes that are easy to get lost in."

She smiles brightly. "See, that wasn't so hard, now, was it? And you're in love with this Sunflower?" Her brows raise in question.

I swipe the coaster off the bar and shove it in my back pocket. "See, this is why I didn't want to tell you," I say over my shoulder as I stalk to the other end of the bar.

"Okay. I'm sorry." Her footfalls chase me from behind. "I didn't realize it was such a sensitive topic. Clearly, she made an impression on you. What's her name?"

Silently, a customer gets my attention for a refill. I grab a pint glass and fill it with beer from the tap before sliding it across the bar. "Kat. But that's not her real name. At least I don't think so. She gave us fake names. I'm Patrick. She's Kat."

Nora presses her fingers to her lips for a second before she spits out, "Ten things I hate about you."

My eyebrows raise. I guess the truth finally comes out. I thought we were good friends. Clearly, I was wrong. "What the hell? I can imagine maybe one thing you hate about me, but ten, really?"

She rolls her eyes and sighs. "No, the movie. *10 Things I Hate About You*. The main male character is Patrick. The main female character is Kat. There's a fake dating thing."

My heart jump-starts back to life. "But that doesn't make any sense. We're not fake dating. We didn't even know each other."

"Maybe it's your bad-boy vibe with a heart of gold. It's very Patrick Verona of you. And perhaps the mystery woman is feisty like Kat." Nora playfully swats my arm. "It makes perfect sense."

I shake my head, still confused. Kat was pretty feisty. It was one thing that held my attention. Not many girls would kiss a stranger at a bar, go back to their hotel room, ditch them, only to reunite with them at the airport and share a hotel room together. She left an impression, but it's over, and I need Kat out of my head.

Customers remain steady for the rest of the night, so I don't have time to stew about Kat. After Nora and I close the bar, she sets the alarm and locks the door. Streetlamps light our way as we stroll across the empty parking lot. Once she's in her car, I round the back of my truck and pull out my phone. With my thumb, I scroll through my contact list until I find the number I'm looking for. The call rings several times.

"Hey, Lach."

"Hey, Emiliee. I know it's late, but I wanted to see what you're doing."

I fish the keys out of my pocket and unlock my truck.

"I'm at home. Lying in bed. It would be more fun if you were here next to me." Her voice purrs through the speaker.

"I was thinking—" I pull open the door and lift my leg to get in. My brows knit together as something stiff in my back pocket stops me. Reaching behind me, I pull out the cardboard coaster I was drawing on earlier. The black ink sketch of a sunflower stares back at me. Fuck. Emiliee's not Kat. "Sorry, Emiliee. Something came up. I'll talk to you later."

"But Lach—"

I end the call.

How in the hell can a girl I've known for two days

throw my entire world off its axis? Better question: How the hell am I going to get her off my mind?

Chapter 9

SO MUCH BEIGE

Eve

After Jake picked me up from the Minneapolis airport, the two-hour car ride back to Harbor Highlands is fairly quiet. Luckily, Jake's not a big talker, and I certainly wasn't going to offer up any more information than I had to. How do I tell my brother, who I've always looked up to, that I quit my job with no backup plan? A job I was so excited to tell him about when I started seven months ago.

He sacrificed a lot of his own childhood to take care of me since our parents were terrible at it. He's always been my lifeline—minus the couple of years he went to a dark place, but he bounced back. I hope I can too. I don't want to tell him that my entire life is now a flaming pile of shit, all because of one disastrous decision. Like sleeping with my married boss and then quitting my job when I found out he was married. Keeping it vague is the best option until I figure out my life. I don't want to disappoint my brother.

Not only did I air out my dirty laundry to Patrick, I gave him the whole damn closet. It felt nice to have someone to vent to. He didn't know me or what was happening in my life. He made me feel seen, which oddly hasn't happened in a long time. A part of me regrets using fake names and not exchanging numbers. I could really use someone to talk to right now with zero judgment. It's not that Jake would judge me, but he would give me the "I'm just disappointed" look, which is worse. I'd love to have Patrick here with me right now, even if it's to make me laugh because laughing with him was everything.

"So you came home for a visit?" Jake's voice yanks me from my thoughts.

I rack my brain for an excuse I could tell him that makes sense without making it obvious that I'm running away. "It's been years since I've seen you, so I thought a visit was in order. Is there something wrong with wanting to see my big brother?" I spit out.

Slowly, he turns to face me. "No. It's good to see you, Eve."

I swear the corner of his lip twitches as if he were on the edge of cracking a smile, but as fast as it appears, it vanishes.

"How long will you be staying?" Jake asks.

I want to say indefinitely because that's where the road is taking me, both literally and figuratively. I certainly don't want to go back to Knoxville, but if I tell that to Jake, he'll have a lot of questions I don't want to answer. I opt to keep it more neutral. Not a full lie, just not the complete truth either. "Maybe a week or two. I have a lot of time off. Perhaps I'll stay for Thanksgiving. I don't remember the last time we spent Thanksgiving together." I twist to face him, eyebrows drawn together. "What do you do for Thanksgiving?"

"Work at the bar."

My mouth opens and then snaps shut. I purse my lips together. "You work on Thanksgiving?" This shouldn't surprise me. When I left Harbor Highlands, the bar was his life. I'd bet a hundred dollars there's a cot in his office so he doesn't need to go home.

He glances at me from the corner of his eyes. "Yeah. Sometimes people need a place to go—"

"And you're the other place." I nod.

"Nora, one of the bartenders, has named it Beersgiving. Everyone brings food, and all the bartenders have made an event out of it."

I'm happy to know my brother isn't alone. Also, I'm a shit sister for not keeping better tabs on him. "That sounds fun. I can't cook anything, but if there's a local bakery I can support, I'll happily buy a pie or two."

A small smile plays on his lips, but he doesn't say any more about Thanksgiving. Instead, he turns the conversation back to me. That was short-lived.

"Things are going well for you?"

I give him a tight-lipped smile. "Yep. Great. Fantastic. Couldn't be better." Lies. Lies. Lies.

"You still working as an assistant to that photographer?"

"Sure am." I wring my hands together in my lap. "But I'm contemplating a change. Maybe find someone else to work for or perhaps start my own business again."

Jake turns his head to face me. "Make sure you have a backup plan or a business plan before you make any rash decisions and quit."

A humorless laugh bubbles out of me. "Right. Who would do something like that? That's not responsible." Me. That's exactly what I'd do. That's exactly what I did. I can't tell him now, especially being trapped in the confines of his truck. His "I'm disappointed" glare would push me right out of the moving truck and onto the freeway.

"Either way, it's good to see you, Eve."

"It's good to see you too, Jake." I give him a warm smile. I've missed my brother. Sometimes, it's hard growing up with a sibling who's older than you are, and in my case, ten years older, but he's always been there for me. Even helped me during a few sticky situations I got myself into, like the time I got caught toilet papering my ex-boyfriend Joey Jamison's house because he's an asshole for dumping me after cheating on me with Susie Moore. I had to clean up the mess, but Jake stayed with me the entire time. Granted, he didn't help me and instead glowered at me every time I spared a glance in his direction. But knowing he was with me instead of out with his friends says a lot about his character.

"So enough about me. What about you? I'm assuming the bar is doing well, so I'll dive right in. Are you dating anyone?" I wiggle my brows at him.

His grip tightens on the steering wheel, but he doesn't spare me a glance. "Nope."

My shoulders sag. "Come on, Jake. Are you just going to live the rest of your life as a single man?"

"I don't see a problem with that."

"You don't miss the companionship of someone else?"

"I can find companionship if I need it."

I groan. "I'm not talking about sex. Anyone can find sex. Don't you want something deeper? It's been a long time."

"No, and I'm not talking about it."

I turn in my seat to face him. "You should really talk to someone. You're still harboring a lot of hurt and anger."

His knuckles turn white on the steering wheel. He's about five seconds away from crushing it into a pile of metal, foam, and leather. "Look, I don't need a therapy session from you."

"I'm just saying."

"And I'm just saying I'm done talking about this."

"Alright, fine." I raise my hands in defense before crossing them over my chest. Twisting in my seat, I stare out the window. A mixture of pine tree forests and rolling fields pass by. I guess the silent treatment is better than him hounding me about my life. It's only a matter of time before he kicks that door open.

It's dark outside when we arrive at Jake's house in Harbor Highlands. It's a modest ranch-style house, but it's his. Unlike me, who has more debt than actual assets.

"Lucky for you, I cleaned out the spare bedroom, so you don't need to sleep among stacks of boxes." Jake sets my suitcase in the corner of the room.

Beige. So much beige everywhere. On the walls. The comforter on the bed. The curtains. There's not even a variation of beige. It's all the same shade. I never expected Jake to be an interior decorator, but a little splash of color goes a long way. An accent wall. Pillows. Art. Anything to make it less institutional and more cozy.

"Thanks. And thanks for picking me up." I wrap my arms around his neck in a hug. His body tenses before resting a hand on my back. My brother's never been a big hugger.

"I'll let you get settled. I'm going to head back to the bar." He spins out of my grasp and turns toward the door.

"Wait. You're leaving?"

"Yeah. But I'll see you in the morning. Help yourself to anything."

"Oh. Alright." Jake's heavy footfalls grow quieter until I hear the door shut. I glance at my suitcase, not wanting to unpack. Instead, I flop down on the bed with my phone in hand. I wish I had Patrick's phone number. He's the one person I wouldn't mind talking to right now. But nope. Instead, my inbox is spilling over with messages from the married asshole wondering where I am. Apparently, it would take a brick to the face for him to realize I'm done with him. I should have done that. I toss my phone to the other side of the bed. Crawling under the covers, I curl into a ball and drift off to a restless sleep.

Chapter 10

FEELS LESS DEAD IN HERE

Eve

One thing I didn't take into consideration when I detoured to Harbor Highlands was clothes. November in Florida consists of sun and warm temps. November in Minnesota, not so much. I rummage through my suitcase, trying to find anything that would resemble warmish clothing. Tucked away in a corner, I find a pair of fuzzy lined leggings and a cardigan that will have to do for now. I guess I'm going shopping. After I'm changed, I step out of the bedroom and spot Jake sitting at the kitchen table.

I prop a shoulder against the doorway, evaluating his mood. His permanent scowl doesn't help me. "Who still reads the newspaper, anyway?"

Without looking up, he says, "I do."

"You can find everything online."

"I much prefer the peace and quiet while sitting here and flipping through the pages instead of being distracted by a pop-up of the next celebrity scandal."

I cross my arms and bite my lips together. "Sometimes I wonder if you're an eighty-year-old in a thirty-seven-year-old's body."

He folds the paper and sets it down. Finally, he glances up, a blank expression on his face. "What do you need?"

"Who said I needed anything?" I shrug.

"I know you. You're standing in the doorway, arms folded, bursting at the seams to ask me something."

My arms drop to my sides. "Fine. Can I borrow your truck for a couple of hours today?" On the counter, I spot a pot of coffee and a mug in the strainer next to the sink. As if I was on autopilot, my feet carry me to the opposite side of the kitchen. After I fill the mug, I rest my butt against the counter. With both hands wrapped around the mug, I take a sip of the hot coffee and frown. I now know what tar tastes like.

"For what?"

"I need to…" I can't say buy clothes because that will give it away that my trip was unplanned. Desperately, I try to think of something else to tell him. "I forgot to bring extra feminine products." That's something Jake won't have. I rest a hand on my stomach. "Being that time of the month—"

"Yeah. Drop me off at Porter's. Then you can take my truck. Plus, I can introduce you to everyone."

"Sounds great." My voice is extra chipper.

Jake continues to read the newspaper while I sip my coffee. Pulling my phone out of my cardigan pocket, I unlock it and scroll through the headlines of the latest celebrity scandals.

Jake pulls into the parking lot of Porter's. This place looks different from when I saw it ten years ago. It's no longer a rundown hole-in-the-wall bar but a well-established business—not something you'd find in a drug cartel movie to launder money through. My heart blooms with pride for my brother. Despite what he endured, he has done well for himself. I was eighteen when I left Harbor Highlands, expecting to find something bigger and better. For a while, I did. As they say, all good things must come to an end. Here's my end. I'm back here single, jobless, and sleeping in my brother's spare bedroom, contemplating what to do with my life because, as of now, nothing has gone to plan.

Jake strolls through the back door, and I'm only a few steps behind him. He gives me a mini tour, and in true Jake fashion, he uses as few words as possible. He points out the employee room, the storage room, and his office. I follow him down a hallway that opens up to the bar. Exposed wood beams and ductwork flow across the ceiling to create a modern industrial ambiance. It gives Porter's so much personality, which contradicts Jake's house. Clearly, it shows which one he cares about more. Behind the bar are two women, one with dark brown hair pulled into a ponytail and the other with her blonde hair twisted into a braid that dangles over her shoulder. Both are serving drinks to customers.

"Rylee, what are you doing here?" Jake asks.

The brunette's head snaps up. "I asked Lach to switch shifts with me. Trey needs me to go with him to some work event this evening."

"Okay. I want to introduce you to my sister Everly." He nods in my direction. "This is Rylee," then he points to the blonde, "and that's Nora."

"No one calls me Everly." I shoot Jake the death glare.

Tucking a strand of hair behind my ear, I turn to the two women and hold out my hand. "You can call me Eve."

Nora's face goes stoic for a second before her eyes widen.

Rylee holds out her hand. "Nice to meet you. Are you going to be in town long?"

"Maybe a week or two. I'm just taking a little vacation."

A warm smile forms on her face. "A vacation with this guy?" She hikes her thumb at Jake. "That sounds more like an episode from *My Trip from Hell.*"

We all laugh except Jake. His face doesn't even twitch from his normal glower.

"It's so nice to meet you. If you need anything, let me know," Rylee says.

"Thank you." I reciprocate with a smile of my own.

"I like your tattoo. Is that a sunflower?" Nora points to her neck, to the same place I have mine.

"It is. It's my favorite flower."

Her smile widens. "I really love it. So we can expect to see you around for a few more days. You need to meet everyone. Dessa and her stupidly hot baseball player husband should be back from their honeymoon soon. And, of course, Lach, who's equally hot." She nudges Rylee.

My gaze dances between the two of them. It's like they're sharing a secret no one else is in on. "Okay. A bar full of hot guys." I nod. "I'm on board." The last thing I need is anything resembling a relationship. Unless they want to come for a ride on my hot-mess express. Toot. Toot. "I'm looking forward to meeting everyone."

"I'm going to get some paperwork done," Jake interrupts. He holds out the keys to his truck, and I snatch them from his grip. "Do what you need. I'll get a ride home later."

"Are you sure? I can come pick you up afterward?"

"If I need a ride, I'll call you. Otherwise, don't worry."

"Okay," I say to Jake. Twisting around, I wave to Rylee and Nora. "It was nice to meet you both."

"You too," Nora says, nudging Rylee with her elbow. "I hope we see more of you."

"Me too." I turn on my heel and stroll out of Porter's.

Since I'm making it a habit of giving my perfectly good underwear to complete strangers, I bought some new ones while I was shopping, along with three pairs of jeans and a variety of tops and sweaters. It's so much cheaper to shop here than it is in Knoxville. No sales tax on clothing is a huge bonus. With no job, I need to save as much as I can. Sitting on a bench outside the food court at the mall, I tear off a piece of the soft pretzel and toss it in my mouth. It's warm, buttery, and oh-so salty. I close my eyes and savor the taste. Why is telling Jake I'm jobless so difficult, unlike the simple decision between a pretzel or a cinnamon bun? Something sweet or something savory? Tell Jake and have him be disappointed in me, or not tell Jake and let him live in blissful ignorance? I know which one I want, but I know which one I should do. Sadly, this isn't the first time I've been shit on. Before working for Pax, I co-owned a photography studio. Then, out of the blue, my business partner left without a word, cleaned out most of the bank account, and there wasn't anything I could do because her name was on the account too. Jake wasn't too thrilled when I took the last of the money, said fuck it, and had myself a fun weekend in Vegas. My motto was "damn the man." Eve needs fun. Needless to say, I didn't win big and save my failing business. Instead of fixing my problems, the trip created more, at least according to Jake. If I tell him I quit my job after being blindsided that my ex-boyfriend/boss is married, I'll get the how-can-I-be-so-irresponsible speech. That's the last thing I need right now.

I stare down at my empty pretzel bag and frown. All that's left are oversized grains of salt. Another one might be in order to help me decide. Crumpling the paper in my fist, I rise to my feet and collect my shopping bags before heading back to the pretzel stand for another magic eight ball pretzel to tell me what to do. While delicious, the second pretzel failed me in the future telling department. I still don't know what to tell Jake. I stand from the bench outside the food court and toss my garbage into the bin.

Porter's
ALE HOUSE

I stroll through the doorway to my temporary bedroom and unload everything onto the bed. These new clothes should make my trip to Harbor Highlands more believable. After removing all the tags, I shove everything into my suitcase. From another bag, I pull out two giant pink pillows and toss them on the bed. Now it feels less dead in here. My phone buzzes on the comforter with an incoming message. I glance at the screen and roll my eyes. Pax's name flashes at the top, and I get a preview of the message. It's basically the same thing he's sent me for the past fifty messages. How much he's sorry. He wants me to come back. If I want, he'll leave his wife for me. The last one makes me gag. I won't be someone's second choice. Or the other woman. My life has been full of one terrible decision after the other. Pax has been the biggest one of them all. I feel so stupid. How could I have been blind to the fact he's married? Maybe a background check will be a new requirement before I date a guy in the future. Anything to avoid this situation from happening again. I flop onto the comforter and drape my arm over my face. How did I end up here? But more importantly, how long can I keep it from Jake? He's the last person I want disappointed in me. And this will most definitely disappoint him. My phone buzzes again. One quick glance at the screen and roll my eyes. Even seeing his name makes me angry. I pick up my phone and unlock it. When I find his number, I hit edit and change his contact name. Then I put it on silent. I'll eventually need to talk to him to square away my last paycheck. For now, I need him to get the hint and leave me alone.

Rising off the bed, I pull my book out of my tote bag. Returning to the bed, I lay down, leaning against the headboard. I slide my finger through the pages where my bookmark is and start reading. I need the drama of someone else's life to give me an escape from my own.

I wake up with my cheek stuck to the pages of my open book. Once I started reading last night, I couldn't stop. On the one-year anniversary of losing her husband, the main character took a trip to a charming small town in the mountains where her husband took her every year for their anniversary. A two-day stay turned into four, then six. Eventually, she found a job at the local bed and breakfast, where she had many run-ins with the incredibly hot local handyman, including a very spicy scene when he fixed her shower. It inspired me. Not that I'll find my own handyman, but I won't turn down the idea either.

The clanking of pots and pans draws my attention. Jake is like a bull in the pots and pans aisle. I change my clothes and shove one of my new hoodies over my head before tying my hair back in a ponytail.

I pad into the kitchen and stop at the doorway. Jake's back is to me as he cracks an egg into a pan on the stove. The acrid scent of burnt toast wafts around the kitchen. Two pieces of almost-black toast pop up from the toaster.

"I see your culinary skills haven't improved."

Jake juggles half the eggshell before it falls into the pan. "Shit." He fishes out the eggshell and tosses it into the garbage. "Do you want breakfast?"

Rising to my tippy toes, I peer over his shoulder at what he's cooking and scrunch my nose. "I'll pass." It looks better than anything I could cook but also nothing like diner food.

"I promise it will taste better than how it currently looks."

"I'm okay."

"So, what are you going to do while you're here?"

"Um. I don't know exactly." I press my lips together, working up the courage to ask Jake for a job. Spinning around, I lean against the counter. "Maybe you could put me to work at the bar."

Jake stops stirring his eggs and stares at me. "Wait. You come for a visit, and you want to work at Porter's?"

I shrug my shoulders. "Sure, why not?" Telling him I technically don't have a job anymore and could use the money might not be the wisest decision. "It seems like my only chance to spend time with my brother." I flash him a smile and elbow him in his stomach. It's the truth. He eats, sleeps, and breathes his bar.

He shakes his head but says nothing because he knows I'm right. "You know what? Sure. I could actually use some help since Dessa's moving to part-time. I'll get you a couple of Porter's shirts, and I'll have Rylee, Nora, and Lach show you the ropes."

"Great! I can't wait to start." I spin around and twist

the dial left on the toaster. "Next time you won't have to eat charcoal." I flash him my megawatt smile. Perhaps my luck is finally turning the corner. I hope so anyway.

THIS IS GOING TO BE GOOD

Lach

I yank open the door to Porter's. My eyes need a moment to adapt to the shift from sunlight to fluorescent lighting. Nora's a few feet away, clearing empty beer bottles from a table on the left wall. My gaze drifts from her to behind the bar. A woman—who I don't recognize—wearing a black Porter's shirt with her blonde hair pulled back in a ponytail stands in front of a shelf of liquor bottles.

"Hey Nora, who's that?" I nod toward the bar.

Her gaze drifts from me to the woman behind the bar and back to me. A wide grin splits her face. "Oh, you don't know who that is?"

I study the woman for a beat longer. Did I hook up with her? From this side, I'd think I'd remember hooking up with her. My brows pinch together. "No. But you say that like I should."

She laughs. It's slightly sinister, but it's Nora, so it's a friendly sinister. "Oh, this is going to be good." She turns to the side. "Hey, Eve!"

The woman spins around. All the color drains from her face. The pint glass slips from her grasp, shattering on the hard floor with a loud clang.

"Oh shit," I mutter.

Nora holds an imaginary popcorn bucket in one hand and motions as if she's tossing kernels into her mouth. "This is better than any matinee."

I brush past Nora, and she chuckles behind me as I rush to the bar. I've come to grips that Kat would forever live only in my dreams, so to see her not only at my work but behind the bar is mildly shocking. Or a lot shocking. Her real name is Eve. Why does that name sound so familiar? "What are you doing here?" I grit through my teeth. The words come out harsher than I intended, but I'm in a current state of confusion. Or Panic? I'm not even sure.

"I could ask you the same thing," Eve whispers, eyes wide.

Nora sets a tray of empty bottles on the bar top. "This is Lach. And from what I hear, you two know each other."

My heart thumps in my chest. I tear my gaze away from Kat—or Eve—and settle on Nora. "What's going on?" All Nora does is smile brightly at me. She's useless in helping me solve this mystery.

"What are you doing here?" I ask Eve.

"I'm in town visiting my brother. And what are you doing here?" Her brows raise.

"I work here. But that doesn't explain why you're behind the bar wearing a Porter's shirt."

"What the hell?" Jake storms in from the hallway where his office is located. "I'm gone for five minutes, and shit's already breaking."

"I'm sorry. It bumped against the counter and fell from my hands. I'm such a klutz," Eve says to Jake.

Shit. Now I feel like an asshole. She's getting reprimanded for dropping the glass because of me.

Jake groans. "It's fine. You're not the first person to break a pint glass, and I'm sure you won't be the last. I'll get the mop." Before any of us can say anything, he retreats to the storage room.

I'm rooted in place, still unable to comprehend what the fuck is happening. The girl I had the most amazing night with, who I thought I would never see again, is standing before me at my job, looking as sexy as ever. My fingers twitch with the need to reach over the bar and haul her mouth to mine.

Nora grabs the small broom from next to the register. Jake returns and helps Nora clean up the mess. Eve and I stare at each other like two deer in headlights. Jake drops the mop in the bucket and turns to me. "Lach, this is my sister Everly."

Everly. As soon as he says the name, alarm bells flash in my head. Son of a bitch. She's Jake's sister. I was aware Jake had a younger sister, but I'd never met her. It's not like Jake to share a scrapbook of his life with all of us.

"Call me Eve." She holds out her hand to me from the other side of the bar.

My gaze jumps from hers to Jake's and back to hers. Slowly, I wrap my fingers around her soft ones. She gently squeezes, just like the night in the hotel room. Except it wasn't my hand she was squeezing. Fuck me. I drop her hand like it's on fire. I slept with my best friend's sister. My jaw clenches as I attempt to keep my facial expression neutral, though inside, I'm freaking the fuck out. Obviously, Nora knows. Did she tell anyone else? Did Eve tell anyone?

"Lach, can I talk to you in my office?" Jake's tone is stern.

Oh shit. He knows. He saw it from the way she gripped my hand. The way our eyes connected. He knows I ravished his sister's naked body, gave her multiple orgasms, all the while my dick was stretching her tight pussy. Beads of sweat pool at my hairline. "Yeah. I'll be right there."

He turns on his heel and strolls down the hallway.

I spare a glance at Eve. Her eyes connect with mine. Based on her face, she's just as confused as I am. I peel my gaze away. As much as I want answers from her right now, I'm more concerned with Jake and what he might know. When I cross through the doorway of his office, he's sitting behind his desk. I rap my knuckles against the wood door, and he glances up.

"Close the door behind you and have a seat." He points to the chair across from his desk.

Oh fuck, he knows. Rarely does he close the door, especially when alone with someone else. I do as he says. I bite the inside of my cheek, not wanting to spill in case he's still clueless. Based on his actions so far, he suspects something.

He clears his throat. "You're my best friend, and I trust you the most."

I nod along as I swallow the softball-sized lump in my throat. He's fairly calm for someone who might know I slept with his sister. Calm before the storm, maybe? My leg bounces on the ball of my foot.

He rests his elbows on the desk and links his fingers. "I want you to help me keep an eye on her."

My leg freezes. Her. Eve. The lump in my throat just became a boulder and catapults to the pit of my stomach.

"She tends to find trouble," he adds.

"Keep an eye on her?" I spit out.

"Yeah. She'll be in town for a little while, but she hasn't given me a definite answer for how long. She's said a week or two, but if I know my sister, there's something she's not telling me."

That I was balls-deep in her only a few days ago. That's probably what she's not telling you. Fuuuck.

I rub the back of my neck. "I don't know if that's such a great idea." In fact, this is the worst idea of all the ideas. Nothing good can come out of this.

"Please, man. I wouldn't ask if it wasn't important. I need an extra set of eyes on her to make sure she doesn't get herself in trouble."

I can't tell him the reason I can't, and I have no other reason not to. Outside of work, Jake hates depending on others, mostly because the ones who should have been there for him have always let him down. He only asks for favors when it's the absolute last resort. He's my best friend and has been at my side every time I needed him. I'd be a shit friend if I said no. I'm going to hate myself later, but I tell him, "Yeah. I can do that."

"Thanks, man." The creases in his forehead soften, and he rises to his feet. "While you're at it, maybe teach her a thing or two about bartending."

A bitter taste fills my mouth as the acid in my stomach churns, making me queasy. "Anything."

"I knew I could count on you."

With a curt nod, I manage a tight-lipped smile, my jaw muscles clenching. I'm afraid if I open my mouth, I'll say something stupid.

"I'm going to get back out there. Make sure she doesn't break anything else."

"I'll be right behind you." After Jake exits his office, I

blow out a deep breath. Resting my elbows on my knees, I rake my fingers through my hair. Of all the scenarios I considered, this one is the furthest from what I expected. Most of all, I don't know what the fuck I'm going to do.

Chapter 12

MESSY AND COMPLICATED

Lach

When I leave Jake's office and go back to the bar, I spot Eve and Jake at the opposite end. He's showing her the beer selection, what's on tap, and what's chilled. She looks even more gorgeous than I remember, her long legs and every curve of her delectable body underneath the Porter's shirt. Somehow, I'm supposed to watch out for her to honor Jake's wishes while not wanting to wrap her in my arms and kiss the hell out of her. I'm going to be in a constant state of blue balls while she's here.

I can't have both, though. I can't betray my best friend. That's when shit gets messy and complicated, and both are the last things I need.

"I knew that was going to be fun."

I glare down at Nora. "How did you know? And why didn't you give me a heads-up? A phone call or text would have been nice."

"And miss that exchange?" She throws her head back in laughter. "Never. And you damn well know you would have done the same thing if the situation were reversed."

I shrug. She's not wrong. I would have reveled in all the awkwardness, just like I had to endure.

"She's exactly how you described, but her tattoo gave it away. How many people have a sunflower tattoo on their neck? It was a carbon copy of the one you drew. But now you can get the girl you've been lusting after." She nudges me with her elbow.

I huff out a humorless laugh. "If only it was that easy."

"Why isn't it?"

"Did you miss the part where she's Jake's sister? I'm his best friend. I prefer my balls attached to my body. They work better that way," I murmur so only she can hear.

She rolls her eyes. "I think you're being a little dramatic."

"Have you met Jake?" I glance over my shoulder to make sure he's not standing behind me. "I slept with his little sister," I grit through my teeth.

"It's not like you knew who she was when it happened."

"But I know now, and there is no way I can pursue anything."

"So you're just going to ignore her the entire time she's here?" She props a hand on her hip. "If she's working here, that's going to be a little hard."

A manic laugh escapes me. "Wait. It gets better. Jake asked me to look after her." I rub my temples. The more I think about this, it's a terrible idea. Cinder blocks rest on my chest. It's going to take all my strength to keep my distance.

Now it's Nora's turn to laugh. "This is better than the

sitcoms my mom makes me watch with her. Plus, I get to watch it play out in front of me. Where's my popcorn?"

My gaze drifts down the bar to Eve. She's laughing and smiling with a couple of customers. She's completely at ease while I'm freaking the fuck out. "Who all knows?"

"Pretty much everyone but Jake," she says nonchalantly.

I glare at her.

"What?" She shrugs with her palms up. "Rylee was here when Eve first came in with Jake, and since it all started at Dessa's wedding, we had to tell her." Nora shrugs.

"Keep this between us for now."

She presses her lips together and motions like she's zipping them closed. Luckily, a customer draws her attention so I can have a few seconds to stew in my own thoughts. My fingers curl around the edge of the bar. From the corner of my eye, I catch sight of Eve. Jake has left her to her own devices for the past thirty minutes—but who's counting—and she's been doing a great job. She's a natural with the customers. Charismatic. She grabs a chilled pint glass from the cooler and sets it under the tap. She pulls the lever down but misjudges the flow before it's too late, and foam spills over the rim. Panic takes over her face, but she quickly recovers without spilling beer everywhere. My mouth twitches into a smile. Damn, she's cute but off limits.

"Okay, I'm going to take off."

At the sound of Jake's voice, I spin around, praying he didn't catch me staring at Eve.

"I have to open in the morning. Can you bring Eve home tonight?" he asks me.

Fuck. I was hoping I'd have a day or ten before Jake

started cashing in on me watching his sister. "Yeah. Of course."

"Thanks, man."

He strolls to the end of the bar and talks to Eve. I'm sure to let her know he's leaving, and she'll get a ride with me. Her gaze flits to mine, and a small smile spreads across her lips. Yep. That's exactly what he told her. Great. I push off the bar and storm to the storage room. There has to be something that needs to be organized back here.

For the rest of the night, I do my best to avoid Eve. Since she's been at Porter's, the space behind the bar shrank by fifty percent, and every ten seconds we're either bumping into each other or crossing each other's paths. She'll graze my arm or rest her hand on my back while she passes behind me. My heart leaps in my chest every time. I swear she purposely sticks out her ass every time I pass by. There's been three times now where her ass has brushed against my dick. Yes, I've been counting because each time another thread of my dwindling willpower snaps. Mix that with her sweet coconut scent invading my senses, and I'm on the brink of losing my shit. Even the sound of her voice has me on edge. Whenever she asks me a question, I either grunt a response, which she may or may not understand, or I give her a quick one-word response. Which aren't helpful, but I need to minimize the time I spend with her. Or near her.

By the end of the night, I'm exhausted, not because of work but from playing dodge-Eve. From the opposite end of the bar, I watch as she struggles with one of the beer taps.

"Nora, go help Eve." I nod in Eve's direction.

She glances to where I nodded and then back at me. "Why don't you go help her?"

"Because I'm doing my best to keep my distance."

She rolls her eyes. "You know, you're not going to be able to keep this up."

All attempts to push away thoughts of her have been futile. The only thing I can do is simply grit my teeth and suffer through the rest of this miserable night. "I'm trying not to think about that. I need to stay more than an arm's reach away from her. Otherwise, I might not be able to control myself."

Nora gives me a half smile. "It's kind of cute. I've never seen you like this with a girl."

I glare at her. "Me either. I'm at a loss on what to do about it."

"Since you're in distress—"

"I'm not in distress."

"Flare guns are launching into the sky all around you. I'll bail you out this time, but just know I'm not always going to be here." She shuffles down to the other end of the bar to help Eve.

She's right. Mayday. Mayday. This vessel is going down, and sinking into the dark abyss of the ocean is more appealing than dealing with Eve and Jake. Sadly, I'm not a boat, so I need to face this. Driving her home will be my first test.

After we finish cleaning and restocking the bar, Nora sets the alarm, and I turn to Eve. "Are you ready to go?"

Eve freezes before pivoting to face Nora and gasps. "He speaks," she says, sarcasm dripping from her voice.

"Yeah. Lach's just being dumb." Nora glares at me, and Eve laughs.

I motion for them to take the lead while I shut off the lights and lock the door. The parking lot is mostly empty. Only a few cars remain, left behind by customers who got rides home. Nora and Eve are a few steps ahead of me, chatting about the night. I keep my distance. As Eve struts in front of me, my gaze keeps drifting down to her round ass. It's certainly not an ass I should fantasize about. I can't help but think back to the night in the hotel room. My fingers digging into the soft skin of her ass as I pound into her while her nails claw at my thighs, her orgasm on the verge of exploding. My dick twitches in my jeans.

"This is me." Nora points to her car.

Fuck. I startle at the sound of her voice and shake the thoughts away. Nora glances my way and smirks. No doubt she caught me checking out Eve.

"Alright, you two kids have fun." She turns to Eve. "I'll see you later."

"Bye, Nora." Eve gives her a wave.

I unlock my truck and climb in without saying a word. Eve follows suit. I turn the key, and the engine roars to life. My seatbelt clicks into place, and Eve buckles hers. As I follow Nora's taillights out of the parking lot, silence fills the cab. I'm praying it can be like this the entire drive to Jake's.

But Eve breaks the silence. "So, are you going to just not talk to me?"

My fingers tighten on the steering wheel. I keep my gaze locked on the road in front of me. "That's my plan until I figure out what to say."

"Fine. I'll talk." Even in the dark car, I see her shift in her seat to face me. "It was a bit of a shock to see you again. Especially when I never expected to. Even more surprising that you work at my brother's bar. But I'm excited to see you. You helped me turn a really shitty situation into something fun. Definitely enjoyable. You made me feel like I could actually have something good in the world."

My grip tightens to the point my knuckles are almost white. But if I let go of the steering wheel, I'll want to reach over and touch her, and I can't. I shouldn't. She has all the same feelings I'm having.

She wrings her hands together in her lap. "I don't know how long I'm going to be in town. I need to figure some stuff out, but in the meantime, I'd like for us to at least talk. Get to know each other. Grunts and head nods don't count." A small laugh escapes her. "I certainly wouldn't be opposed to sharing another bed."

From the corner of my eye, I catch her staring at me. Maybe she's trying to read my expression. To determine whether this facade I'm giving her is fake or if, in fact, I want to explore more of this connection we share. But I can't. I blow out a deep breath. "You're my best friend's sister. That's how shit gets messy and complicated. And I can't do that to Jake."

"I see." Her face falls as she twists to face the dashboard. "I'm an adult, and you're an adult. I think we can make our own decisions."

"You don't understand. I just… I can't do that to Jake." Mostly, I'm afraid of what Jake would do to me. "He's one person in my life who's always had my back."

"So you're just going to ignore me. Got it." She crosses her arms over her chest and turns away to stare out the window as streetlights pass by. The rest of the car ride to Jake's house is silent. When I pull up to his short driveway from the alleyway, I know the gentlemanly thing to do would be to escort her to the door, but if I remove my hands from the steering wheel, I'll reach over and tug her to my lap because that's what I've wanted to do all night.

She turns to me, waiting to see if I'll say anything, but I keep my gaze locked on the closed garage door in front of me.

A small sigh escapes her. "Good night," she murmurs under her breath. She waits a beat for me to respond, but I don't. With a push, she opens the door and slams it closed, causing me to flinch.

I watch as she walks to the back door. Once she's inside and turns off the porch light, I throw my truck into reverse. My tires squeal as I stomp on the gas pedal. This is what I wanted. But why do I feel like an asshole?

Chapter 13

THE PLAN

Eve

I'm at a loss with Lach. Besides Jake, he's the only person I know here, and he wants nothing to do with me. For the past week, he's kept his distance whenever I've worked with him. When I tried to talk to him, he kept his replies to a minimum and went searching for anything to get away from me, which included alphabetizing the liquor shelf, picking up cigarette butts in the parking lot, and even removing all the broken tips out of the dartboard.

Now I'm pulling a play from Lach's playbook and trying to avoid Jake. He keeps prying into my life plans. I get he's being the protective older brother, but I don't even know what my life plans are. There are only so many places I can hide from him since I not only live with him but also work at his bar. Locking myself in my room only works for so long; he knows I'm not a recluse. Currently, I'm sitting in his office across from him, waiting for my interrogation.

"It's been a week. How long is your vacation? What's your plan?"

Indefinite. But I can't tell him that. "I don't know." Deflect. Deflect. Deflect. Sitting up straighter, I lean toward Jake. "What's your plan? You seem to be in the same place you were when I left town nine years ago. You're still single."

"This isn't about me."

"But we could make this about you."

His gaze meets mine. Concern etches his features. "Is something going on? Are you in trouble?"

The permanent scowl on his face fades away, and his soft tone guts me. It's rare for Jake to show his soft side. I can't continue to lie to him. My shoulders sag. "I'm not in trouble per se, but something did happen." His eyebrows raise, waiting for me to continue. The words are seconds from spewing out of my mouth, but I swallow them down. "As you know, I've been working as a photographer's assistant."

"Yeah." He nods.

"Well, my boss…" I inhale a sharp breath, and I meet Jake's gaze. For once, he's not scowling. There's genuine concern on his face. "He's been thinking about selling the business." The lie tumbles out of my mouth. I can't face the look of disappointment that would have followed if I told him the truth.

"Are you thinking about buying the business? If you need some money, I'd be happy to help you."

My shoulders sag. "I was thinking of trying something else. Or maybe a location change." Moving back to Harbor Highlands has jumped to the forefront of my mind since meeting Lach. At this point, there's nothing keeping me in Knoxville.

"Where would you move to?"

Damn Jake and all his questions. "Maybe back to Harbor Highlands. I would already have a job." I point at the Porter's t-shirt I'm wearing and wiggle my eyebrows.

"If you keep breaking everything, that job may be no longer."

"Hey! I've only broken a couple of things."

"Three. That I'm aware of. The last one being a bottle of vodka."

"I still maintain that the bottle broke itself. Companies really need to make those bottles out of thicker glass." Jake shakes his head, and I laugh.

He uncrosses his arms, resting his elbows on his desk. "If that's what you want, you know you are always welcome."

I nod. I certainly can't tell him I want to explore whatever is developing between me and his best friend.

"You okay with catching a ride home with Lach?"

And he's back to business. It would be better if Lach talked to me, but it's a ride. We can sit next to each other in fun, awkward silence. Again. "Yeah. That's perfect." I fake enthusiasm.

"Okay. But later, we'll talk more about your plan." Jake rises to his feet, and I follow suit.

"Looking forward to it." I flash him the most exaggerated fake smile I can muster. Truth be told, I'd rather stab myself in the eye with the broken vodka bottle than rehash my lack of life plan again.

Jake exits his office, and I trail a few steps behind until we reach the bar. He says a few words to Lach and waves at Nora before he's out the door. At least Nora's here, so I won't feel like I'm talking to a brick wall. As the night progresses, the customers get few and far between. Nora takes a seat on a stool on the customer's side of the bar. Her fingers dance over the screen of her phone.

"Ugh, this stupid app is going to drive me to drink." Nora drops her phone to the bar top.

I glance up from placing glasses in the under-the-counter dishwasher. "Well, you're in the perfect spot." I shrug. "What's the app?"

She rubs her temples. "I've been working on programming a dating app."

I freeze, glass midair. "Wait, you're programming an app? Like, you know how to do that?"

"Yeah. I went to college for computer programming."

"Impressive. Why are you working at Porter's, then? I feel like there would be more money in that than bartending."

She props her chin on her hand. "It's kind of a long story, but essentially, the hours are less demanding, so it works."

I nod. I don't want to pry into Nora's life, but there's more behind that answer than what she's telling me. "Aren't there a million dating apps?"

"Yes, but all those are 'find the love of your life' or 'hookup for a night of forgettable sex.' Mine's different. It's an app for people who need a date for a night and can't find one. Dessa gave me the idea last year when she needed a date for a wedding. There are no obligations besides being the date."

"That's kind of a cool idea."

"Mostly, it's for people who have to go to family gatherings and have to endure the countless 'Why are you still single?' 'You need to settle down,' or 'You're not getting any younger' questions," she says in a mocking tone. "This app will fix that. At least temporarily." She laughs.

"It could be useful for making someone jealous." The words tumble out without thought. It's not that I want to go on a date to make Lach—or anyone—jealous, but it could push someone into figuring out their feelings.

"Suuure." She eyes me wearily. "You could do that too. I have a spot to mention date specifics. Right now, I can't get this messaging feature to work properly. But when I get this last bug fixed, I'll need a beta tester." She flashes me a cheesy but hopeful smile. "You're new to town. Single. It's a great way to meet people with zero expectations."

Join a dating app? I am new to town. The single status is up for debate. Technically, I am, but I want to see what happens with Lach first. "I don't know about that."

"Well, think about it. Especially if," she nods her head toward Lach, "he's going to be a grumpy brute."

A laugh escapes me. That's him to a tee right now.

As expected, Lach spent the entire night saying as little as possible to me. If I happened to be within five feet of him, he'd find an excuse to go somewhere else. It was a quiet night. The cooler didn't need to be stocked eight times.

I spot Lach at the end of the bar with no escape besides jumping over the bar top. Now's my chance to demand answers. I'm no longer playing his game of dodgeball. I strut to where he's standing and cage him in with a hand on my hip.

"Why are you ignoring me? Every time I walk into the room, you walk to the other side. You barely say more than two words to me each time you see me." He freezes, and a moment of silence passes between us. Then it hits me like one of my imaginary dodgeballs. I lower my voice. "Do you regret what happened between us?"

He flinches as if my words stung him. He tilts his head to the ceiling and blows out a deep breath. "I don't regret it." His head falls and turns toward me. "In fact, I can't stop thinking about it."

Chapter 14

CONSEQUENCES BE DAMNED

Lach

When I'm with her, I'm thinking about her. When I'm not with her, I'm still thinking about her. Then Jake's angry scowl flashes in front of me like an annoying website pop-up, except there's no close button. She's Jake's sister. My best friend's sister.

She pops her hip. "Then what's your problem?"

"My two rules have always been don't date an ex's sibling or a best friend's sibling. It gets messy. And this," I point between me and her, "is going to get messy."

"This," she points between herself and me, "is fun." Her face softens. "You made me forget how shitty things have been lately. I just want more of that."

My heart thunders in my chest as I glance over my shoulder to make sure the coast is clear. "Me too."

Reaching up, I cup her cheek. I brush my thumb over her soft skin, running it back and forth. Her hazel eyes meet mine. I ache to bend down, press my lips to hers, and whisper how desperately I crave her. How much I need her. But I can't. Her plump pink lips part a fraction and her chin raises, waiting for my lips to touch hers. Instead, I drop my hand and retreat a step. Her shoulders slump.

"I'm sorry." I stride past Eve. She turns on her heel and follows me. As I pass through the threshold of the storage room, I flip the light switch. The fluorescent lights flicker to life, illuminating the space. When I reach the liquor shelf, Eve is next to me, resting her back against the metal. She swivels her head toward me.

"So, what are you going to do? Ignore me the entire time I'm here?"

I freeze with my hand on the neck of the bottle. "I don't know what else to do."

Her brows pinch together. "I don't know what that means."

Keeping my gaze trained on the bottle, I blow out a deep breath. "When I'm near you, all I want to do is haul you in my arms and kiss you."

"But I'm Jake's sister."

"Yeah."

"At this point, it's kind of late, isn't it? We've already kissed. In fact, we've already had sex."

I jerk my head to look over my shoulder to make sure no one else is around. "You have to be quiet."

She rolls her eyes. "Okay." She leans toward me and whispers, "You've already given me multiple orgasms."

I have, and I thoroughly enjoyed every single one. With a sigh, I release the bottle and push my hands through my hair.

"Look, I understand keeping secrets from Jake. Currently, he doesn't know I left Knoxville because I quit my job or about my ex being married. I wanted to tell him. I tried to tell him," her gaze drops to her feet, "but I didn't want to disappoint him." She inhales a deep breath and lifts her head. "But sometimes we need to take things for ourselves."

Every scenario that runs through my mind has Jake giving us his blessing, but that's only a fantasy. I've seen Jake punch people for less. And that's the reality.

"Because I want more of this," she purrs, taking a step closer and dragging her fingertip down my chest, sending shivers down my spine.

Fuck. I don't need this now. The proximity of her presence short circuits my brain. Every ounce of my rational thinking is shot to shit. Consequences be damned, I need to kiss her. I wrap my hand around the back of her neck, haul her to me, and crash my lips to hers. A small squeak escapes her, but within seconds, she melts against my body. I've missed this. I've missed her. Tilting my head, I deepen the kiss. Her soft lips move against mine, both of us getting lost in the kiss.

"I hate to kill the moment." Nora's voice echoes through the storage room.

My heart rate spikes as adrenaline shoots through my body. I jump away from Eve as if she's a blazing inferno. Together, we are. She's the gasoline, and I'm the matches. One strike, and we combust.

"It's getting busy out there," she hikes her thumb behind her, "and I need some help. You can finish making out later." She spins on her heel and disappears from the doorway.

"Fuck," I mutter.

"No—"

"I shouldn't have done that." Without sparing a glance at Eve, I swipe a bottle of rum off the shelf and storm out, leaving her alone in the storage room.

With a loud thud, I slam the bottle onto the bar. I can't

believe I did that. I wasn't thinking. What if Jake came back, and it was him instead of Nora? Plus, there are cameras. I doubt Jake sits around watching surveillance video, but he could. Fuck. I wasn't thinking. Instead, I got caught up in Eve.

"Sorry to interrupt your make-out session. I promise you can continue later, but those customers at the other end of the bar need drinks first." Nora pulls three bottles of beer from the cooler with one hand and pops the caps off each before sliding them across the bar.

"Got it." I don't address the kiss. It's best I don't. Maybe if I ignore that it happened, everyone else will too. But I should talk to Eve when I drive her home, and tell her we can't do this. Then I can do it with no prying eyes.

Eve returns and doesn't look my way once. Instead, she stays at the opposite end of the bar with Nora. For the rest of the evening, she does what I did to her. Avoids me.

After the bar closes and we clean up, I break the silence. "Eve, are you ready to go?"

Her hardened gaze meets mine. "Actually, Nora's going to give me a ride."

I fucked this up. All of it.

Chapter 15

IT'S A SECRET

Lach

Since Eve arrived, I've been avoiding Jake as much as possible without looking suspicious. It's hard to look your best friend in the face when your face has been between his sister's legs. There's no easy way to start that conversation without it ending in bloodshed. Most likely mine. Luckily, I don't have to work with Jake tonight but instead Nora, which is only slightly better.

"Why are you fighting this? Because of some stupid rule you made up?" Nora rests her hands on her hips. "After witnessing that kiss last night, it's hard to deny the chemistry you two have."

With a furtive glance over my shoulder, my heart pounds in my chest. Since the coast is clear, I turn my attention back to Nora. "Jake's my best friend, and he asked me to look out for her. I don't think having sex with her is what he had in mind." I rest my palms on the bar, locking my arms. "Jake, you, Dessa, and Rylee. You guys are all I have. You're my family. And if I fuck this up with Jake, he'll get you guys in the divorce, and I'll be left with nothing."

"I don't think Jake would divorce you."

I turn my head to face her. "I've seen him do a lot more for a lot less."

"I'd be thrilled if I had a sibling date my best friend."

"Too bad Eve can't be your sister instead of Jake's."

Nora's blonde braid whips around as she spins and rests her butt against the cooler. "So you're just going to deny yourself happiness? Because you've never talked about a girl like you have her." She leans in closer to me. "I've never seen you look at a girl like you look at her either. It's like your eyes fucking sparkle when she's within five feet of you. That doesn't happen with just anyone."

She's right. I've never felt this way with anyone else, but that's not the issue I'm most concerned about.

"Is it worth the risk?" She holds out her hands, palms up, moving them up and down like a balance scale. "Lose the girl and be miserable, or know that Jake will understand about the whole situation and be happy for you."

I shake my head. "'Jake' and 'happy' aren't necessarily two words that go hand in hand."

A sly grin takes over Nora's face. "You're aware you and Eve are closing the bar tonight, right?"

I blow out a deep breath and drop my head. "I saw it on the schedule yesterday. I was tempted to call in sick today."

"That seems unlike you."

"That's exactly why I'm here. Unknowingly, Jake's certainly not making this easy on me."

"What is his story, anyway?" She rests a hand on her

hip. "He's all business twenty-four seven. Can the muscles in his face do anything else besides scowl?"

"Jake's?" My brows lift. "It's complicated."

"Clearly. He's a ball of string knotted together. I'm going to go see if he wants to talk to me. Maybe I'll try to convince him to set up a profile on OneDate. Someone may need a grumpy brute to intimidate an ex or something." She pushes herself off the cooler.

I laugh. Jake on a dating app… That would be one cold day in hell. "Good luck."

"I'd ask you, but you're off the market and in love." She winks as she strolls past me.

"Hardly." I shake my head.

"So, Lach, I hear you're hooking up with—" Dessa strolls behind the bar.

She returned to Harbor Highlands from her honeymoon yesterday. Being the resident mixologist, she creates all the drink specials at Porter's. Since her now-husband is the catcher for the Seattle Warblers baseball team, she'll spend the off-season in Minnesota, spring training in Arizona, and Seattle during the regular season.

"Shhh!" I zip my fingers over my lips.

Dessa clamps her mouth shut. Leaning in, she whispers, "Oh, so we're keeping it a secret."

"You remember that 'I owe you' you owe me? I'm cashing in."

Last year, Dessa conned me into helping her go on a wild goose chase to find some tourist-trap machine where you put a penny in and turn a wheel, and it flattens the penny, imprinting it with an image. I spent my entire day rummaging through five fully crammed storage buildings to find it for Garrett, and now I'm asking for my favor in return.

"What is it?" She reaches for a shaker and tosses in a scoop of ice.

"You can't say anything to Jake."

She laughs. "You know this is going to blow up in your face, right? Big ol' explosion?"

"Probably." I scrub my hands down my face. "But I don't know what to do."

She rests a hand on her hip. "It's simple. You either stop fantasizing about sleeping with his sister, or you tell Jake you've slept with his sister and want to do it again."

I exhale a deep breath. "Honestly, both of those sound like terrible ideas."

"Continuing to sneak around behind his back is probably the worst idea yet." She quirks an eyebrow at me.

I hate that she's right. Fucking Dessa and her rational behavior. "We've only shared a kiss since she's been here."

"Doesn't mean you don't want more," she sing-songs.

I tilt my head and stare at the ceiling. This shouldn't be so hard. Quantum physics is hard. Telling your best friend you slept with his sister, and you want to continue sleeping with her isn't quantum physics. Why would I rather learn how to split an atom than tell Jake?

"I just need time to figure out my plan. So far, it's not working out so well. It's like the universe just keeps shoving us together, and my willpower—"

"Is non-existent," Dessa finishes for me.

"Pretty much."

Dessa grabs two bottles and pours the liquor into a shaker. "Alright, well, I'm not taking the heat for any of this, so if Jake says something to me, I'm blaming you."

"Fair."

Using the gun, she squirts cranberry juice into the shaker. "Also, your secret is safe with me." She shoves the cap on the shaker and tosses it back and forth. "For what it's worth, if you like her, which it seems like you do, go for it. She could be your one, and you don't want to miss your opportunity." She grabs three glasses and pours equal parts into each one.

Nora returns, a grin on her face. "He told me 'hell no,' which is better than 'fuck no,' so I think he's easing into the idea."

Both Dessa and I laugh.

"Here, try this." She slides one glass toward me and one to Nora.

I take a sip and frown. "Too sweet."

"Yeah, I agree with Lach," Nora adds. "Jake, try this." She holds out her glass to Jake as he passes behind us.

"I don't drink," Jake deadpans.

Nora whirls around. "Wait! You own a bar, and you don't drink?"

"That's what I said." He stops at the register and presses some buttons until it pops open.

"That's very *Cheers* of you. But also, how did I not know this?" Her gaze slides from me to Dessa, and we both shrug.

"I don't air my dirty laundry for everyone to see, unlike all of my bartenders." Jake closes the register with a heavy thud. "You're what? Twenty-five? How do you know about *Cheers*?"

"My mom watches a lot of reruns of old sitcoms. She has a lot of time on her hands, and I get sucked into watching when I'm with her." Nora crosses her arms over her chest.

Jake nods but adds nothing else to the conversation. "I'm going to the bank and then dropping the truck off for Eve, who'll be in shortly." He comes to a halt in front of me and leans in.

My body tenses. Can he smell my fear?

"Keep Eve away from the expensive liquor even if you have to tackle her. I don't want to write off any more bottles of Scotch," he says quietly so no one else can hear.

Tackle Eve. My body on top of her. Her tits pressed against my chest. Her soft, breathy moans at the shell of my ear. Fuck. Nope. There can't be any tackling happening tonight. "Sure thing," I choke out.

As the night carries on, Dessa leaves. Nora leaves. And I'm left with Eve. Who hasn't spared a single glance my way. Granted, the night has been busy as hell, so we haven't had time to chitchat. Every time she strolls past me, I get a whiff of her coconut shampoo, and all I want to do is grab her and bury my nose into the crook of her neck. It's agony to want something you can't have. When the clock rounds 12:30 a.m., the crowd settles down and I restock the coolers. The sooner the closing duties are done, the sooner we can leave.

Eve stretches on her tippy toes, and the hem of her shirt rides up, exposing a small patch of skin on her belly. I itch to lean down and drag my lips over her soft skin. My dick twitches in my pants. All she needs to do is exist, and I want her. She stretches a little more until her fingers brush against the bottle of Scotch. It inches closer and closer to the edge of the shelf. She changes her position, but her toe catches the edge of the rubber mat. Gravity takes over, and the bottle tumbles off the shelf. Her arms windmill as she tries to regain her balance while catching the bottle.

I abandon the drink in front of me, and in two leaping strides, I wrap an arm around her waist. With a loud smash, the bottle crashes to the floor, shattering into a thousand pieces. The spray of liquid soaks my jeans. The smokey aroma wafts around us. Her hand latches onto my bicep, and her eyes pinch shut, bracing for impact. A second later, her lashes flutter open. Her hazel eyes stare back at mine.

"You caught me." Her words are soft and breathy.

"Always."

Her nose scrunches, and her lips purse. "Jake's going to be so mad at me. He warned me about breaking any more bottles."

"I'll tell him I did it," I blurt.

"You don't have to do that."

"I don't, but I will."

Her pink lips curve into a soft smile. Fuck. I've missed her smile, especially when it's directed at me.

"Instead of those 'Number of Days without an Accident' signs, we should get one for you that says 'Number of Days without an Eve Accident.'" Fuck. I'm rambling. I don't ramble. But I want to keep talking to her. Just like this. With her in my arms.

"Today it would go back to zero." She smiles. "Um. Can you help me stand?"

Shit. I forgot she's still in my arms. It's easy to get lost in her. I hoist her to the standing position. I'm reluctant to let her go. Her touch and closeness are what I've missed.

She steps out of my grasp. Bending down, she collects the larger pieces of broken glass. "Your pants are soaked." She pulls a towel off the bar, brushing it over my shins and up my thighs, inching higher and higher.

My dick gets the wrong idea. I take a step back so I'm out of her reach. "It's alright. Why don't you get the mop? I'll clean up the glass." Mostly, I need her to stop touching me. She nods and rises to her feet. We work together to clean up the mess. For the rest of the night, there's a little less hate tension between us, but the palpable sexual tension is at an all-time high. Before we close for the night, I leave a note for Jake that I owe him a bottle of Scotch.

Chapter 16

HOLDING PINKIES

Lach

My phone rings next to me, and I glance at the screen. Jake's name flashes across the top. For the past couple of weeks, I've been doing my best to avoid him. Mostly because I'm trying to figure out all this shit with Eve. I fear I'll spill everything to him, and he'll split my lip. Losing my best friend isn't an option. He is one of the few constants in my life, and my life would be shit without him.

I press talk. "Hey, what's up?"

"The hockey game is on tonight. I ordered a couple of pizzas. Want to come over?"

"Yeah. Sure." Shit. Eve. I certainly can't ask if she'll be there, or it might look suspicious. Racking my brain, I try to remember if I saw her name on the schedule tonight. Either way, I hope she's working. "I'll be over in a little bit."

I park my truck at the curb at the front of the house. I should have driven around back to see if Jake's truck is here. After hiking up the few stairs, I rap my knuckles against the aged wood door, announcing my entrance before I twist the knob and step inside to the small entryway, catching the scent of tomato sauce and melted cheese. As I shrug out of my jacket, I glance around to see if Eve's here. Both the couch and chair are empty. No other voices can be heard, only the announcer on the TV. Jake strolls into the living room with a pizza box in one hand and a beer in the other. He tosses the unopened can in my direction. I juggle the beer before securing it between my hands.

"Just in time. It's about to start." Jake nods toward the TV.

"Great." I crack open the beer and take a long swig before throwing myself on the couch. Jake takes a seat on the opposite side. Asking him about Eve is on the tip of my tongue. But I shouldn't. Instead, I wait.

By the start of the second period, Eve's a no-show. I lean against the couch, sinking into the cushion. The rumble of an engine sounds from outside. My gaze shifts to Jake, and he's staring at the TV. I glance over my shoulder at the back door. After a few beats pass, my nerves settle. Then the door opens and clicks shut.

"Oh my god, you'll never believe what happened tonight." Eve steps through the doorway from the kitchen to the living room. "A couple came in and got a table. They had a few drinks and talked, even laughed. After a little while he slides—"

Our eyes lock, and she freezes. She bites her lips together, fighting her smile. My foot bounces. I want to jump up and kiss her. Tell her I'm an idiot and I don't regret our kiss from a few days ago. But Jake's next to me.

She hangs her jacket in the closet next to the front door. "Anyway, he slid divorce papers across the table.

Then he just got up and left. Who does that?" She saunters into the living room and shimmies past me. Her tight jeans that hug her hips are at my eye level. Hockey. Ice. Sweat. Pucks. I need to think of anything other than what color panties she's wearing underneath her jeans. Her gaze wanders from my knees, up my torso, past my chest, until we lock eyes for a few beats. I pray she's going to keep walking and sit in the armchair next to Jake.

She spins around, and the center cushion depresses as she takes a seat. "What are we watching?"

"Hockey," Jake says without taking his eyes off the TV.

"I love hockey. I'm down for some stick-in-the-net action. She tucks her feet under her, leaning closer to me.

"Puck. Puck in the net. Not the stick," Jake deadpans.

Eve's eyes lock with mine. "As long as something goes in my, I mean, the net."

"I'm going to get another." Jake lifts his can of non-alcoholic beer. "Want one?"

"I'm good." I wave him off.

"Eve?" Jake asks.

"No thanks. But I'll have some pizza." Reaching forward, she grabs a slice from the box on the coffee table. She lifts the slice to her mouth and takes a giant bite. "Mmm." She chews and swallows. "I wish I could make pizza this good. Hell, I wish I could cook anything this good. Cooking's not my forte."

Once Jake disappears behind the wall, I lean in so only she can hear. "What are you doing? You're not mad at me?"

She takes another bite, chews, and swallows before she says, "I talked with Nora. She said you're an idiot and don't know what you want. If I want this," she points between us, "I need to take matters into my own hands."

I'm relieved to know she's not mad at me because, fuck,

all I want to do is lay her down on this couch and kiss every inch of her naked body. The sound of the fridge door closing jerks me from the fantasy playing in my head. I drop my hand to my crotch and discretely adjust myself in my jeans, except it doesn't go unnoticed by Eve, who's currently smirking at me.

"What did I miss?" Jake says as he enters the living room.

"Nothing," we both say in unison.

Jake takes a seat on the couch. "What the hell? Nothing? Minnesota scored a goal."

"Oh yeah. That happened," Eve says.

During the rest of the period, I steal glances at Eve while also making sure Jake doesn't notice. I'm an asshole.

Eve wraps her arms around herself. "What temperature do you have it in here? Artic?"

"It's not that cold," Jake says.

"Easy for you to say when you're a natural radiator." Eve twists to face me. Reaching over my lap, her tits graze my arm. She peers up at me from under her lashes. A smile twitches on her lips. Her fingers wrap around the corner of a small fleece blanket, dragging it over me. She haphazardly unfolds it, a corner falling over my lap while she covers hers. I don't move the blanket and neither does she. Her hand dips underneath the fleece. She stares at the TV while her fingertips brush against my leg.

I peer at Jake, whose attention is on the game, and then I slide my hand under the blanket. I find Eve's hand and brush my thumb over the back. The touch is small, but it's exactly what I need. She makes all my worries disappear. Even when she's my biggest worry. My attention is no longer on the game, but instead, it's on Eve as I trail a fingertip over her palm. She adjusts herself on the couch, inching closer to me. I hook my pinky around hers. Her teeth sink into her lower lip, and she fights a smile. As much as I want to pull her to my lap and nuzzle her neck, I can't. Instead, I settle for her touch. She's tearing down my willpower, brick by brick, and soon I'll no longer be able to deny her. Or myself.

Chapter 17

BECAUSE OF YOU

Lach

Last night was reckless. It shouldn't have happened, especially with Jake sitting on the couch. He could have caught us. Maybe he did, and now he's plotting the perfect murder.

My willpower is disintegrating faster than a paper straw in a glass of water, especially after last night and now today. She has her golden hair pulled back in a ponytail, showing off her sunflower tattoo I love. All I want to do is brush my lips against her delicate skin, right below her ear next to the ink. Her sweet laughter floats down the length of the bar, making my dick twitch. The sound of her laughter, light and carefree, is utterly captivating. I could listen to it all night long. But instead, I'm stuck in the torture of having to work beside her and closing down the bar—just the two of us. I need to restrain myself from touching her because once I do, I won't be able to let go. Fuck. I need away from her so I can breathe. "Hey Eve, I have to run to the back for a second. Can you handle everything?"

She twists around, counting the five patrons sitting at the bar. "Yeah. I think I can handle it." She nods.

I storm down the hallway, shoving the bathroom door open. It clicks shut behind me. For the past six hours, I've been next to her or within feet of her. I'm in desperate need of a break. I've never been so caught up in someone before. She makes it hard. So fucking hard. My restraint is on the verge of snapping like an over-stretched rubber band. One more tug and it'll snap in two. Sadly, I have ninety minutes before I can relieve my misery. Until tomorrow, anyway. If I start closing duties early, maybe I can cut it to sixty. I blow out a deep breath and head back to the bar.

When I round the corner, I freeze. My gaze drifts down. The denim is perfectly molded to Eve's ass as she grabs a bottle of beer from the bottom of the cooler. I tear my gaze away. This is going to be the longest ninety minutes of my life.

Over the next hour, customers get fewer and farther between. I start the closing duties early, hoping to get out of here faster. Every time I turn around, Eve is right there, standing next to me, brushing past me, or reaching over me. The sly and playful upturn of her lips each time our gazes connect makes me suspect she's doing it on purpose.

When the last customer leaves, I lock the door. "I'm going to go to the storage room to restock the liquor shelf and coolers."

Eve tugs her hair from her ponytail. Her long hair cascades down her shoulders like a silken waterfall. "Okay. I'll start sweeping." She pulls a broom from the small nook next to the register and starts sweeping on the far side of the bar.

I flip the light switch, and the fluorescent lights flicker and hum to life. I stalk across the room, swipe two bottles of vodka, and tuck them under my arm. Footsteps echo across the storage room, and I glance over my shoulder. Eve stops within arm's reach of me.

"I never got to say this last night," she tucks a strand of hair behind her ear, "but I didn't stay to watch hockey. I stayed because of you," she murmurs. Her hand rests lightly on her chest, near her heart, the words a confession. Delicately, she trails her fingers over her chest and down the valley of her tits. "I went to bed thinking of you." My nostrils flare with every rise and fall of my chest. Her hand drags over her stomach. "Your mouth on mine. While your fingers dipped into the waistband of my sleep shorts. The same ones from the hotel room."

My gaze lingers on her fingers as she idly traces the waistband of her jeans. As seconds pass, my heart rate accelerates so fast it might burst through my rib cage.

Her lips fall open on a whispered gasp. "I closed my eyes, picturing your hand, your fingers as they slid inside the elastic and over my pussy."

"Eve," I growl, the rest of the words getting lodged in my throat. I'm torn between telling her to stop and that she can't stop until she finishes.

Her hand dips to between her legs. "The pad of your finger grazing over my clit before sliding down to my entrance."

"Eve." My deep voice is a warning. But it's not a warning to stop. All my restraints snap in half. This is the point of no return. In one long stride, I'm clasping her hand in mine. Her hooded eyes stretch wide as I tug her out of the storage room.

"Where are we going?" The clatter of her steps shuffle behind me, but she quickly regains her balance.

I don't answer her. Instead, I lead us into the employee room. Without turning on the light, I drag her to the far corner of the room. Spinning her around, her back smacks against the wall. My fingers dig into the soft skin of her waist as my other hand threads through her hair. I crash my lips to hers. She inhales a sharp breath before her lips mold to mine. It's a sweet and satisfying kiss. Her hands roam up my torso and rest on my chest while I tug her closer, my growing erection digging into her stomach. She moans into my mouth, and I swallow the sound.

I barely survived the last week not kissing her. Touching her. Because this is perfection. Her kisses are like a breath of fresh air, bringing me to life. Realization hits me—I hadn't been living until I met her.

She breaks away from the kiss. Her chest heaves as she collects her breath. "We're doing this?"

I press my lips to hers, giving her my answer.

"And Jake?"

I run the tip of my nose along hers. "Honestly, I don't even know anymore. The only thing I'm sure of is you. This. Kissing you. Touching you. It's the only thing I need."

A small smile flirts on her lips. "Me too." Her mouth crashes to mine. The kiss is just as frantic as earlier as if she needs me just as much as I need her.

My hand slides over the curve of her ass and to the back of her thigh. I hike her leg over my hip, grinding my rock-hard dick against her. A moan rumbles from the back of her throat, so I do it again, loving the noises she makes. Fuck, I miss this. Miss her. So damn much.

Chapter 18

IS THAT A REQUEST?

Eve

I pull Lach closer, grinding against his denim-covered cock. I'm seconds away from having an orgasm just from dry humping. His breathing hitches, a ragged, desperate sound as if he's about to lose control. In the few weeks I've known him, he's always appeared calm and collected, except when it comes to me. I'm the one he loses control over, and I fucking love it.

Breaking away from our kiss, I drop my leg to the floor. Using the wall, I slide down, feeling every ridge and valley of his abs as I drag my hand down until I'm eye level with his cock. He rests his palms against the wall, shadowing me from what little light shines in the break room, and peers down at me.

"What are you doing, Eve?" His voice is raspy.

My fingers trail along the waistband of his jeans. "I need something to suck on."

With one quick motion, I flick the button open and

peel back the denim, yanking it over his hips. I salivate at the sight of his thick cock stretching the cotton boxer briefs. Leaning in, I drag my lips over his bulge. He sucks in a sharp breath from the contact. One of his hands drops, and his fingers thread through my hair.

"Take me out. Show me how much you can take in that pretty mouth of yours."

"Is that a request?"

"No. It's a fucking demand." His voice is deep and gravelly.

Like a turkey thermometer, my nipples spring to life beneath my shirt. Lach going alpha male on me is the biggest turn-on ever. "I guess I better be a good girl and do what I'm told." With my fingers wrapped under the elastic, I pull down. His cock springs free. A bead of pre-cum glistens at the tip. I wrap my fingers around the silky-smooth base and swirl my tongue around the head. A deep groan sounds above me, spurring me to continue. I suck the crown into my mouth like a lollipop.

Lach's fingers tangle in my hair. "Show me how much you like my cock in your mouth."

With my hand still on the base of his shaft, I slowly slide my mouth down his length. When I'm about halfway, I pull back up.

"You can do better than that." His other hand drops from the wall, and he wraps his fingers around his cock. I release my grip, letting my hand fall away. The head of his cock glides across my mouth as he paints my lips with his pre-cum.

"Open," he commands, his voice sharp.

I part my lips.

"Stick your tongue out."

I do as he says, and he rests his cock on my tongue. Slowly, he tunnels himself in and out of my open mouth.

My scalp tingles as his grip on my hair tightens. "You look so fucking gorgeous with my dick in your mouth. Now be a good girl and suck."

I peer up at him through my lashes and close my mouth around his cock. My hands grip the outside of his thick thighs as he thrusts his hips, his cock sliding in and out of my mouth. I take over, bobbing up and down on his shaft. Removing a hand from his thigh, I curl my fingers around his length and slide up and down in tandem with my mouth.

His chest rumbles with a low, rough sound. "Keep going. Just like that."

His cock twitches in my mouth. I know he won't last much longer. With the flat of my tongue, I run it along the underside of his length. At the tip, I suck the crown into my mouth and release it with a pop. I wrap my lips around the silky skin and slide down. The tip hits the back of my throat, and I fight a gag. His leg trembles under my fingertips. His groans mix with my slurping sounds. I drag my mouth up his cock and back down while twisting my hand around his base.

"Fuck. Sunflower. Your mouth feels too fucking good. I'm going to come."

I love I make him lose control. The sex goddess, or mouth goddess, in this case, deserves a crown. But mostly I love the nickname. I double my efforts, and within seconds, his hot cum hits the back of my throat. He grunts and groans while his hips buck. I swallow every last drop of him. When he's finished, I pull off. His still semi-hard cock bobs in front of me. I wipe the corners of my mouth before rising to my feet.

"Oh fuck. That was… Can I keep you?"

I giggle. "As long as you promise to repay the favor."

"Name the time and place." He nuzzles my neck, pressing a kiss right below my ear.

I want to tell him right here, right now, but we need to finish cleaning the bar, or Jake will get suspicious about why I'm walking through the door so late. I doubt he'd appreciate me telling him his best friend offered orgasm services. With a light tug, I pull his boxer briefs and jeans up over his hips. He adjusts himself before pulling up the zipper and fastening the button.

"The time will come. But for now, I'll just go home and fuck myself with my vibrator while I imagine you calling me Sunflower."

"I wish I could be there to witness that." His soft lips press against my neck.

"Next time. But also, Sunflower?" I pull away and lift an eyebrow. "When did we create nicknames for each other?" I remember he used it the night in the hotel room, but I thought nothing of it, mostly because I never thought I'd hear it again.

"You started it, Kat. But I like Sunflower more." His lips press against the sunflower tattoo below my ear. "Because of this right here."

I lift my chin to give him better access. "Mmm. If you don't stop, I'll be pulling out my Go Directly to Pussy Licking card ."

"Time away makes the pussy grow fonder," he mumbles against my skin.

I laugh and shove at his chest. His step falters. "And with a line like that, my pussy has now retreated inside itself. Let's finish closing so we can get out of here."

I indeed spent the early morning hours with my vibrator, and I imagined Lach the entire time. I was on the verge of suffocating myself with a pillow while trying to keep quiet so Jake didn't hear me.

Yesterday, I checked the schedule, and I'm a little disappointed I won't be closing with Lach again. Oral sex in the break room part two would be a fun closing task to cross off the to-do list. Instead, I'm closing with Nora. I love her free spirit, and she's not afraid of my brother. That's the type of woman he needs in his life. Since I'm going in early with Jake, I'll get to see Lach before he leaves from working the early shift, though I doubt I'll get a few minutes alone with him.

I'm a few steps behind Jake as we enter Porter's. Before I'm fully through the doorway, my gaze shoots to behind the bar. My lips curve into a smile when I spot Lach. His back is to me, but as soon as he spins around, our eyes connect. He freezes for a brief moment. Even from across the bar, the crinkle in the corner of his eyes is noticeable. His gaze drifts next to me, and his smile falters. He offers Jake a chin lift before diverting his attention back to the customer across from him. I continue to follow Jake to his office. He takes a seat behind the desk, and I sit in the armchair across from him.

With my hands resting in my lap, I pick at my cuticles. It's time I stop sitting still and take some chances. Or a chance. I clear my throat. "I think I want to move back to Harbor Highlands." Jake lifts his head. His forehead wrinkles, unsure what I'm talking about. "At least for a while. A change of scenery might be good for me."

"Did you hear from your boss? Is he selling the business?"

My gaze drops to my lap. My heart hammers in my throat. I need to do this. Rip the band-aid off. "About that.

I don't have a job." I hold my breath in anticipation of what he's going to say to me.

"What do you mean?"

I inhale deeply, calming my nerves. "I lied. My boss isn't selling the business. But also, I no longer work for him."

"You got fired!"

I flinch. "Thanks for assuming the worst. No. I quit." I hold my head high and square my shoulders. Act confident. He'll believe I know what I'm doing.

"So you have another job lined up?"

"No. But I had a good reason."

He pinches the bridge of his nose. "What the hell, Eve? You quit and came here. Then what?"

I throw my hands in the air. "I don't know, but I'll figure something out."

"You need to do something with your life. I know you got the shit end of the deal with your business, but you need to pick yourself up and start again."

My blood boils. Yes, I made a couple of poor decisions, but they don't define me. "We all can't have a bar given to us when we hit rock bottom." Jake's shoulders slump. I sucker punched him in the gut. "I'm sorry. I didn't mean it. My life is floundering, and coming here seemed like the best option." My head drops forward, and I stare at my hands in my lap. "I quit because my boyfriend, who was also my boss, is married, and I just found out."

Silence fills the room.

"Why didn't you just tell me?" His once angry scowl morphs into a slightly less angry one.

Heat creeps up my neck and floods my cheeks. Being vulnerable is not in my nature. Deflection is more in my wheelhouse, but it's Jake. He deserves the truth. "Because

I'm embarrassed. Who doesn't know their boyfriend is married?"

"Eve. Look at me."

I lift my head and meet his gaze. Tears prick the corner of my eyes.

"It's not your fault."

I blow out a breath. "Truth be told, there's nothing keeping me in Knoxville anymore."

"I always have a room at my house for you."

The corner of my mouth twitches. "I'd hate to cramp your style."

"It's fine."

"If you have a girl over, just tell me and I'll disappear. Maybe put a sock on the doorknob." I smirk.

"That won't be necessary," he deadpans.

"Just in case. Keep that info in your pocket." I slide my hand over an imaginary shirt pocket.

"I'll make room in the garage for your car so you can have somewhere to park."

A humorless laugh bubbles out of me. "Well, about that… I don't have a car anymore." I hunch my shoulders and roll my lips together.

He glares at me. "Spill it, Eve."

"It was about a month back I got rear-ended. I'm fine. But the car, not so much. Insurance totaled it because of the expense to replace all the sensors and electronics. I've been able to get around with rides with friends or Uber. Grocery delivery has become my new best friend."

He pinches the bridge of his nose. "Alright, so no car. I'll find you one because I'm certainly not playing chauffeur."

"But I could get you one of those cute little golf hats." He narrows his eyes at me. "Fine. No hat. But will you come with me to move all my stuff?"

"Oh. Um." He rubs the back of his neck. "That's a tough ask. I have the bar."

"Maybe a few days away from the bar—"

A knock on the door interrupts us.

Lach appears in the doorway, looking like a snack. "Jake, the health inspector is here." He hikes his thumb behind him.

"Alright, thanks." Jake rises to his feet.

My gaze drifts to Lach. The corner of my mouth twitches into a smile. I spin around to face Jake. "Since you're busy with the bar, Lach can help me."

"Help with what?" Lach asks.

"Getting my stuff from Knoxville and bringing it back to Harbor Highlands."

His eyes widen. "I don't know." His words hang heavy in the air. "Shouldn't Jake help with that?"

Twisting in my chair, I face Lach. "He doesn't want to leave his bar. And some of my stuff is heavy. So, I could really use a guy's help." I give him a tight nod, praying he realizes this gives us an opportunity to spend time together, alone. No prying eyes. Just an orgasmic good time.

"You know what? I like that idea," Jake interrupts. "I'll rearrange the schedule with Rylee to get Lach a few days off. I'll even make it paid. That cool with you?"

I ping-pong between Jake and Lach.

"Yeah." Lach exhales a deep breath. "I can do that."

Jake rounds the corner of his desk and stops in front of Lach. He clasps him on the shoulder. "Thanks. I really appreciate it." Leaning in, he whispers, "I trust you'll keep her out of trouble." But he doesn't say it quietly enough so I don't hear.

I roll my eyes. The protective big brother doing what he does best. Little does he know Lach is a willing participant in my trouble. Between the sheets. On top of the sheets. Wrapped in the sheet. A lot of sheet action will be happening.

"Yeah. That's what I do," Lach says.

"Alright. I better get out there." Jake strolls out of the office and down the hallway.

Lach watches until he's out of sight, then he spins around. "What the hell was that?"

I stand and strut toward Lach. When the tips of my shoes touch his, I stop. "Now we get a few days alone while we move my stuff to Harbor Highlands. You're welcome." I bat my lashes and flash him a sultry smile.

He leans closer to me. "Wait. You're staying?"

I nod. A sexy smirk, the one that makes me clench my thighs together, flirts on his lips. Yes. This is the best idea I've ever had.

Chapter 19

CHARLIE CUMMING

Eve

I stare out the rectangular airplane window. We're still sitting on the tarmac of the tiny airport in Harbor Highlands while we wait for the rest of the passengers. Although it's labeled as international, the airport still only has four gates and a security line that takes ten minutes at most. It's been two weeks since my chat with Jake about moving back. We celebrated Beersgiving, which may be my new favorite holiday. There was so much food, laughter, and games, thanks to Nora. Jake's lips might have twitched slightly with amusement. As much as I wanted to wrap my arms around Lach and spend the entire night with him, I couldn't because my brother was there. Watching. He eventually rearranged everyone's schedule so Lach and I could get a few days off together to collect my belongings. I roll my head to the side an inch, my travel pillow preventing me from turning all the way. "Hopefully, this flight goes better than the last."

"I'm sitting next to you this time, and I have no plans on going anywhere."

"Like to the hospital."

"Yeah. But you have to admit, it worked out for us."

"It did." I reach over the armrest and wrap my hand around his, expecting him to move his hand to intertwine our fingers, but instead, he moves away. My heart plummets to the tarmac. I slide my hand to my lap. "Alright then," I murmur, mostly to myself. Twisting away from Lach, I cross my arms and stare out the window, watching them load the luggage onto the plane.

His shoulder lightly nudges mine. "I'm sorry. I'm not big on public displays of affection."

I peer at him from the corner of my eye. "But you made out with me at the resort bar with tons of people around. It doesn't get more public than that."

"That was a kiss."

"That's different from holding someone's hand, how?"

"You can kiss anyone. You can walk up to a stranger and kiss them, and it can mean nothing." He diverts his gaze away from me. "Holding hands with someone is more intimate, and it's not something I do."

"You can't walk up to anyone and kiss them. You need to watch for clues. When I kissed you, I didn't just kiss you. I warmed you up to the idea first and when you didn't say no, I went for it."

"You were caressing my thighs. I wasn't going to say no." He shrugs.

"Oh my god. That's why guys are so surface level." I laugh.

"What do you want? Long nights spent sharing our feelings and brushing each other's hair?"

I playfully backhand his bicep, and he laughs. "The first part is fine, but you can brush your own hair. Since I know you can't be serious for five minutes, let's circle back to the hand holding. Have you never held someone's hand?"

He's silent for several long seconds. When I think he's not going to give me an answer, he responds. "No."

"Never?"

He shakes his head. "Nope."

"Pinky holding doesn't count?"

"Pinkies don't count."

Another laugh escapes me. "It's different, but I respect it. One more question. Why do you consider holding hands more intimate than a kiss?"

He presses his lips together, contemplating his answer. "Because a kiss is just a stepping stone that leads to other things, like sex, which has the purpose of having an orgasm. But when you hold hands with someone, there's no ulterior motive other than to show your affection toward that person."

"So a kiss can't be affectionate?"

"No, it's just a different kind of affection."

"That's pretty deep, Dr. Phil." I bump Lach with my shoulder. Instead of pulling away, I stay where I am. I'm desperate to touch him, even if it's only my shoulder.

"But mostly, what if someone recognizes us and tells Jake?"

I glance around the cabin before my eyes fall on Lach. "We're on an airplane. I highly doubt anyone will recognize us."

"But they could. And I'm already toeing the line of being the asshole to my best friend."

I let out a huff. "I get it. I hate keeping this from Jake too. But also, I don't want to not do this because I really enjoy this."

His soft blue eyes meet mine. "Me too."

When he looks at me, I see the pain in his eyes, the yearning to hold me close and kiss me. It makes it hard to be mad at him. "Plus, I don't want to drop so many truth bombs on Jake. I can only handle so much of his disappointment in me."

"Hey, Lach. How's it going?"

Both of us peer up, and a guy with dark hair is staring down at us. His gaze darts from me to Lach. Slowly, I inch away from Lach, straightening my shoulders.

"Hey, Ben. Not too bad. How about yourself?" Lach responds.

"Good. I'm headed to Chicago for work. Seeing you reminds me I need to swing by the bar sometime and say hi to Jake. I heard his sister's in town, and she has a photography business. The wife keeps hounding me to get family portraits taken."

Shit. If I don't say anything now, he'll find out later. Leaning over Lach, I stretch out my hand. "I'm Eve. The sister. I'm taking a hiatus from the photography business for now."

His large palm grips mine. "Sorry to hear that, but it's nice to meet you. I'm Ben. I've known your brother for a long time."

I drop my hand to my lap. "He seems to be a very popular guy in Harbor Highlands."

"Are you two off to Chicago?" Ben asks.

"No, we're going to Knoxville to move all my stuff back to Harbor Highlands. Jake sent Lach to help me since he didn't want to leave the bar," I say with a chuckle.

Ben laughs. "That sounds like him. I'm sure he wouldn't even leave if it was on fire."

"That's what I'm learning," I add.

"Alright, I better go take my seat. It was good to see you, Lach. Eve, nice to meet you."

"You too," I say. I peer over my shoulder as Ben continues to stroll down the aisle to his seat. When I spin around, Lach's gaze bores into mine with a raised brow.

I roll my eyes. "Okay. Fine. I don't like it, but I'll go with it." I lean against the backrest and cross my arms over my chest.

Halfway into the flight, I feel something brush against my hand resting in my lap. Glancing down, Lach's arm lays across the armrest. His pinky extends and hooks with mine. An eruption of butterflies takes flight through my body. I peer at him. His eyelashes fan over his cheeks, but the corner of his mouth curves into a smile.

Porter's
ALE HOUSE

After our connecting flight from Chicago, our plane lands in Knoxville—well technically, Alcoa—and we order an Uber to the nearest U-Haul location, which is three miles away. From there we drive to my rented townhome in West Knoxville, and Lach parks the U-Haul out front.

Lach jumps out of the truck and shuts the door. He meets me at the curb. "This looks nice." He stands in front of the long, tan rectangular building. A few shrubs and rock landscaping decorate the exterior. Each unit is side by side, but all have their own entrance.

"It served its purpose. Now, it's time to move on to the next chapter. Shall we get started?"

Lach follows close behind while I unlock the door and push it open. I glance around. I've only been away for a month, but it feels like a lifetime. So much has changed since then.

"This shouldn't be so bad." Lach rubs his chin, assessing all my belongings.

Unlike Jake's bland interior, my townhouse is filled with

various art and photographs covering the walls. Furniture is minimal but heavy enough that I need a second person.

"No. But I didn't want to move all this myself. I'm happy it's you and not Jake helping me."

"Me too, Sunflower."

His arm wraps around my shoulder, and he tugs me to his chest. I sink into him, loving his warm body against mine. He presses a chaste kiss to my forehead. The sweet gesture makes me want to say "fuck it" to all the packing and we get our cardio in a different way. But he pulls away.

"I'll grab the stuff from the truck." Lach exits the front door and, a few minutes later, returns with a stack of boxes we picked up on our way over, along with our carry-on bags.

Luckily, most of my stuff can fit in the boxes, minus a few of the larger furniture items. We devise a plan to box up one room at a time and move it out. We save my bed for last so we have somewhere to sleep tonight.

After we box, tape shut, and label one room, we carry it to the moving truck, playing Tetris with all the items. A professional packer, I am not. I'm more of a "here's an open box, let me throw whatever is in arm's reach into it" person. Case in point, the box at my feet holds everything on and inside my nightstand, including a stack of books and self-care items, along with the laundry basket of clean clothes next to it.

The packing tape screeches as I run it over the closed flaps. With the box in hand, I push through the door with my back. The unseasonably hot sun beats down on me as it tries to burn me alive. Mix that with the beads of sweat already sliding down my temple from packing, and I'm a hot mess. Both physically and mentally. I juggle the box with one hand while attempting to rub my face against my shoulder.

"Eve!"

My entire body tenses from the familiar voice. I forget how to breathe. The box tumbles from my grip and crashes to the sidewalk, splitting the side. Two books, along with a variety of lingerie, scatter across the sidewalk. My bright pink vibrator rolls across the concrete and comes to a halt against a pair of brown loafers. I'm frozen in place, an icy dread gripping my heart. Not only is the last guy I wanted to see here, but anyone walking by gets a front-row view of my vibrator.

"You're back. I've been trying to get a hold of you," Pax says, his tone sharp.

Crouching down, I grab everything off the sidewalk and shove it back into the box while trying to make sure nothing else escapes.

"Pax, what are you doing here?" Stretching across the sidewalk, I reach for my vibrator, but Pax bends down and scoops it up before I can. My head drops. Son of a bitch.

"I've been driving past your house like every day. I sent you numerous messages." His arms flail through the air like an inflatable tube man.

I climb to my feet. "Yeah. I've been ignoring those." The outline of his body comes into focus. I shield my eyes from the sun and frown when I spot his fingers wrapped around my vibrator. My head throbs. I'm going to need to burn it now.

"There's a big wedding coming up. So I—"

"Pax, I quit," I say firmly.

His dark brows furrow. "What do you mean, you quit?"

"A month ago, when I left the hotel room in Florida, I said I quit." My gaze drops from his face to my vibrator, and I hold out my hand.

"Oh!" He drops it in my palm. "I thought you were just going on a vacation or something."

Rolling my eyes, I cross my arms over my chest. I tap the head of the vibrator against my bicep. "No. If you'd pull your head from your own ass for five seconds, you'd know that. I. Quit." I make sure to enunciate the last two words so he hears them correctly this time.

"Who are you?" Lach throws an arm around my shoulder and tugs me to his chest. I didn't hear him come outside over the beating of my heart in my ears.

"I'm her boss." Pax squares his shoulders as if he has any claim to me.

"Former boss," I add.

Pax's gaze drops to Lach's arm around my shoulder. "Who are you?"

"I'm her boyfriend," Lach says with no hesitation.

My heart soars from his words. We've never talked about what we are, but when questioned, he has no qualms about claiming me as his, and I will happily take it. Pax's jaw clenches. The satisfaction of his annoyance makes me snuggle deeper against Lach.

"After all this, you have a boyfriend," Pax spits.

"I don't owe you any explanation." I spin out of Lach's grasp. "Hold Charlie Cumming." I smack the vibrator against his chest with a thud. He catches it before it hits the cement. I stomp toward Pax. "And you have zero grounds to confront me about a boyfriend because you. Are. Married."

He shakes his head in disbelief. "I can't believe you would do this. We had something special. I was ready to start a new life with you. But you had a boyfriend the whole time. Does he know about us?"

My nostrils flare. A box of rocks has more intelligence than he does. "He is well aware of this fucked-up situation. But is your wife? Maybe I should call her." I reach for my phone in my back pocket. "Tit for tat."

He frowns.

I slide my phone back into my pocket. He's not worth the even larger headache. I just want to finish packing and get out of town. I point down the sidewalk. "You need to leave. I'm done with you. Done with the job. I'm moving on. In fact, I'm leaving Knoxville. Now, I need to pack so I can get the hell away from you!" Pivoting on my heel, I stomp past Lach, who's still holding my vibrator, and back into the townhouse.

"Eve! Wait!" Pax's desperate voice echoes behind me.

"I think it's best you leave," Lach says.

When I'm inside, I brush the curtain back and peek out the window. Lach's still talking to Pax. Based on the glower on Pax's face, Lach is reiterating what I told him. I don't know whether I want to kiss the hell out of him or giggle because he's wielding Charlie Cumming. Since he's slaying my dragon, I'll make sure to return the favor. My teeth sink into my bottom lip. Stay on task. Sex later. Packing now.

Finally, Pax retreats down the sidewalk. Lach crosses his arms, watching him until he's out of sight. He tucks the vibrator in his back pocket before picking up the box I left behind and sliding it into the back of the moving truck. I meet him in the doorway, leaning against the doorframe as he strolls up the sidewalk. The gray t-shirt molds perfectly to his sculpted chest. I nibble on my bottom lip. The sleeves of his shirt stretch taut, straining against the bulging muscles of his biceps. Unsure of what I ever did to deserve this man, I know I'm never letting him go. I can't hide the smile that spreads across my lips. He comes to a stop in front of me.

"What's that smile for?"

"Thank you." I clasp his cheeks and lean in, pressing my lips to his. I pull away but don't remove my hands. "For everything. I was afraid if I stayed out there a second longer, I'd end up strangling him. And I wouldn't survive prison." Dropping my hands, I huff out a laugh.

"It was nothing. That guy's an asshole."

"I don't have many regrets in life, but he's in the top three."

He shoves his hands in his front pockets. "I hope I didn't cross the line by saying I was your boyfriend. It seemed like the easiest way to get rid of him."

A pang of disappointment hits me in the gut. He said it so Pax would leave. "No." I wave him off. "It's fine. Do you know you still have Charlie Cumming in your back pocket?"

"You mean your vibrator? Yep." The corner of his mouth curves into a smile.

"Are you going to give it back?"

"Eventually. But also, Charlie Cumming, as in…"

"Charlie has me coming all night long." I shrug as if it's the only logical answer.

He laughs but doesn't say anything as he sidesteps me and walks down the short hallway toward my bedroom.

A part of me wants to pester him about why he wants to keep Charlie, but also, I'm curious about what he has up his sleeve or, in this case, his back pocket.

Shortly after midnight, we flop onto the mattress on the floor. We cleared my entire townhouse except for the mattress, a couple of pillows, and a blanket. My eyelids drop as if sandbags are glued to my lashes. Both of us are still in our clothes from the day, and I don't think either of us cares. Lach drapes an arm around my waist and tugs me to his chest. I snuggle against him, loving the proximity.

"Night, Sunflower," he murmurs. He presses a kiss to the top of my head. Seconds later, his breathing evens out to soft snores. After a few minutes, his breathing lulls me to sleep.

Chapter 20

THE ANGRY BEAVER

Lach

I stir awake. Every muscle in my body hurts as if I moved an entire townhouse into a moving truck. Oh. Wait. I did. Then my muscles grew more tense when Pax unexpectedly appeared. It took everything in me not to break his nose with Eve's vibrator.

Eve stretches, pressing her ass into my dick.

I pull her closer to me, running my nose over her cheek. "Don't start something if you don't intend to finish," I whisper.

"Mmm. I want nothing more, but I hurt. Everywhere."

I laugh. "Same. What do you say we finish packing and hit the road? If there's no traffic and we drive straight through, it's only a fourteen-and-a-half-hour drive."

"Ugh. Wishful thinking. Probably closer to seventeen or eighteen."

"Either way, the sooner we get moving, the sooner we can get coffee and food."

"You really know the way to my heart, but it has to be at some small roadside diner. Those are my favorite."

"Deal." I press a kiss to her cheek before rolling off the mattress.

After we're ready for the day, we pack the last of the items into the truck. Eve stands at the end of the sidewalk, staring at her townhouse. I'm not sure if she's sad she's leaving or if it's a different emotion. I move to stand next to her. My arm brushes against hers, and she peers up at me.

"Are you ready to go?"

She nods. "Yeah. I am. Take me home, Lach."

Wordlessly, I round the rear of the truck, and Eve takes the passenger side. We both climb in, and I start the engine. I type the address into my GPS and shift into drive. Eve twists away from the side window to face me with a wide grin. It's one of her bright, genuine smiles. I'm glad I get to spend this time with her. It almost feels as if we could be real. Then I remember she's my best friend's sister. I turn my attention to the road and step on the gas.

An hour into our drive on I-75 North, Eve turns down the radio and faces me. "I'm ready to cash in on your promise of coffee and food."

I glance at her. "Yeah. Where do you want to stop?"

She pulls out her phone and types on the screen. I glance from her to the road while she scrolls.

"Oh, I got it! It's about fifteen minutes up the road. The Angry Beaver Diner."

"That's an interesting name."

"It reminds me of the cartoon when I was a kid. Did you ever watch it?"

I shake my head. "Nope. I didn't watch a lot of television growing up. So that's where you want to stop?" I change the subject, not wanting her to ask questions about my childhood. I closed that door a long time ago, and I'd rather not open it up again.

"Yeah. It looks charming." She holds out her phone toward me.

I peel my gaze off the road and look at her screen. It's a picture of a diner with black-and-white checkered flooring, red booths, and a counter that runs half the length of the room.

"You like places like that?"

She lowers her phone. "I do. I like the small-town vibe. Plus, I guarantee this is the type of place only the locals frequent. There's always some woman with curly white hair named Betty serving coffee. There's the chatter of cooks calling out orders and servers carrying plates full of short stacks. It's my happy place."

I glance at her from the corner of my eye. As she stares out the window, I can't fight the smile that tickles my lips. If a diner will make her happy, I'll give her all the diners from here back to Harbor Highlands.

I spot the oversized cartoon beaver sign from half a mile away. I pull into the full parking lot of The Angry Beaver. If all the locals are here, I suspect it's the entire town. Luckily, I find a parking spot in the far corner which may or may not be an actual parking spot. I jump out and round the rear, meeting Eve. We stroll side by side to the glass double doors. With my hand on the metal handle, I hold the door open for Eve to lead the way, and I follow a step behind her. Servers hustle past us with plates lining their arms as we wait next to the Please Wait To Be Seated sign. This place is exactly how Eve described. Bacon grease and maple syrup aromas fill the diner. Cooks yell orders back and forth.

"Look!" Eve elbows me, pure elation written on her

face like a kid given free rein in a toy store. "They have t-shirts. I need the Angry Beaver or Bust one."

"Welcome to The Angry Beaver," An older woman wearing a red apron tied around her waist and salt-and-pepper hair tied back into a bun greets us. "Just the two of you?"

"Yes," Eve says.

She grabs two menus and waves for us to follow her. Families, couples, and friends fill practically every table, chatting over breakfast. We meander through the crowded diner until she stops at a booth along the far wall. Eve slides into one side, and I take the other. The server places a laminated menu in front of each of us. I glance at her name tag. It's not Betty, but Mary Lou.

"What can I get y'all to drink?"

"I'll have a coffee," Eve says.

"And I'll have an orange juice. And a water. Thanks, Mary Lou," I say.

She saunters off to help a table a few feet away. We both peruse the menu in silence.

"I think I know what I'm going to order," Eve says.

"Let me guess. The fluffy pancake stack with bananas."

She drops her menu to the table. "Now why do you think that would be my order?"

"It's sweet, and you seem like a pancake kind of girl."

"Let me guess, you're going to order the steak and eggs because it's meaty and manly." She squares her shoulders and puffs out her chest.

A smile spreads across my face. "Actually, I'm getting the fluffy pancakes with extra bananas."

A sweet laugh, the one I love, bubbles out of her. "I never expected you to be a fluffy pancake kind of girl."

"I can never make them like they do at a diner. They just don't turn out the same."

Mary Lou returns a few minutes later with Eve's coffee in one hand and expertly holds my water and orange juice in the other.

"Have y'all had a chance to look over the menu?" Mary Lou asks.

"Yes. I'll have the omelet super deluxe with extra crispy bacon. Not like extra crispy, but extra bacon, and make it crispy," Eve says. She lowers her menu. "I once asked for extra crispy bacon, and I basically got bacon dust. No one wants bacon dust."

I give Mary Lou my order for pancakes with a side of sausage links before she collects our menus and tucks them under her arm. She saunters to the next table without missing a beat.

"I wonder how long she's been working here. On the menu, it said they opened in nineteen seventy-eight. By the way she floats around with ease, I bet she's been here since they opened. Could you imagine working in the same job for that many years? Even if I had my photo studio, I don't know if I'd want to do that for the rest of my life."

I strum my fingers on the tabletop. "My plan is to never leave Porter's."

"Really?" She taps her chin before dropping her arm to the table. "I mean, I get working for Jake. He's great because he's my brother and all, but serving drinks for the rest of your life?"

The "J" word. The elephant looming over me who told me to watch out for his little sister. For the past day, I forgot how our relationships weaved together and pretended we were just Eve and Lach. In another twenty-four hours, our bubble will burst, and I'll snap back to reality.

"It's more than serving drinks. It's something new every day. Plus, it's like a second home to me."

Her shoulders sag, and her smile turns upside down.

"Can I just say," she blows out a breath, her gaze dropping to the table, "I'm envious of the friendships you and everyone have at the bar. Everyone has each other's back, no matter what. I never had that."

I tug at the paper strip securing the rolled silverware. "Now you do."

She peers up at me through her lashes. A smile tugs on her lips. I'm not sure if she believes me or not, but it's true. She's only been working at the bar for a month, but she fits right in. All the girls love working with her, and I certainly enjoy her company.

Under the table, my leg bounces. All I want to do is slide out of my side of the booth and join her on hers, wrap my arm around her, and never let her go. Before I rise from my seat, Mary Lou returns to our table with a row of plates lining her arm and another in her hand. Someone can only perform that juggling act with years of experience. She places the omelet in front of Eve, whose eyes widen as if she didn't realize her omelet would be the size of a newborn baby. Mary Lou places a plate of the extra crispy bacon next to it. Then she sets a stack of pancakes with bananas in front of me. After Mary Lou leaves to help the next table, both of us continue to stare in disbelief.

I break the silence. "That's like a two-pound omelet. Are you going to be able to eat all that?"

Her eyes slowly drift to mine. "You underestimate my love of diner food. I will leave here with an omelet baby in my belly." She rubs her stomach and wiggles her eyebrows. "But I'm having serious food envy over your pancakes."

I love that regardless of the situation, she's always herself. I've been with women who conform to be someone they think I want, but not Eve. You get what you see. With her fork, she slices into the corner of her omelet and stabs it with the tines. She shoves the giant bite into her mouth and chews. Her eyes roll back as she sinks into the booth.

"Where has this been all my life?" She presses the napkin against her lips.

I drizzle the maple syrup over the top of my pancakes before cutting off a chunk and putting it in my mouth.

Eve goes in for another bite. "If I didn't start a photography studio, I would have wanted to run a diner. But I'm a terrible cook. I once caught a pot of water on fire."

"That takes talent." I nod between bites. "How would you run a diner then?"

She laughs. "Oh, I wouldn't be in the kitchen. I'd be like Mary Lou." She nods at Mary Lou as she chats with customers. "I'd be in the dining room, charming the customers and telling others what to do."

"Well, you'd certainly be good at that. But did you know ninety percent of restaurants fail within the first year?" I cut a chunk of my pancakes off, stab a slice of banana, and shove it into my mouth.

"Apparently, so do photography studios, so it sounds right up my alley." She shrugs before taking a sip of her coffee. She grabs a piece of bacon and stops halfway to her mouth. "I'll trade you this strip of bacon for a bite of your pancakes with a slice of banana."

I laugh. "No deal. These pancakes are like gold. I share with no one."

"Okay. Two strips of bacon." She plucks another piece off her plate, waving the salt-cured pork in the air. "And half a sausage link."

Shit. The bacon does smell good. "You drive a hard bargain, but deal."

She smiles triumphantly as we exchange food. I take a

bite of bacon while she chews a mouthful of fluffy pancakes and my last slice of banana.

When she swallows, she rests her chin on her hand. "Tell me, Lach, how is a guy like you single?"

I take a drink of my orange juice, needing a few seconds to figure out how I answer. Do I give her the real, honest answer or the fabricated one?

"Is it because you haven't found the one or something like that?"

"I haven't had a desire to find the one. Relationships always end in heartbreak. Why go through all the trouble?"

She rests her elbows on the table. "Sure, some do, but not all of them. Look at your coworkers. Rylee found Trey, and Dessa reunited with Garrett."

"They're the outliers. Also, each of them went through a lot of shit before they found each other. I want to avoid the shit. I've had enough heartbreak in my life." My body stiffens. The last sentence just tumbled out. It's not something I readily talk about. Eve doesn't need to know how fucked up my life has been. Hoping to keep her from asking any other questions, I add, "I'm very content with where I'm at right now."

Her lips press together as she contemplates my answer. "But is content really happiness?"

I shrug. "For me it is."

Her gaze drops to her plate of food as she nods.

Clearly, it's not the answer she's looking for, but it's the only one I have. The closest thing I've found to happiness is when I started working at Porter's. Jake welcomed me into his small, tight-knit family that later included Rylee and Dessa, eventually Nora, Garrett, and Trey. I owe everything to Jake, and I'm sure fantasizing about his little sister isn't what he had in mind.

Chapter 21

CAPTURE THE PERFECT MOMENT

Eve

I thought this could be different. Maybe something would develop between me and Lach. Obviously, he isn't looking for a serious relationship. Another Dead End sign flashes in front of me. But he seemed so excited, practically bouncing on his feet, when I said I was moving. Perhaps I'm overanalyzing this. I just left a relationship where I was the other woman. Granted, I know I'm not the other woman in this relationship or fling, but I felt a connection. I should just have fun while it lasts so I don't set myself up for heartbreak.

We continue eating our breakfast in silence. After a few bites, I set down my fork. A wave of nausea crashes into me. I lean back and rest my hand on my stomach.

Lach stops with his fork halfway to his mouth and meets my gaze. "Is something wrong with your omelet?"

"No. It tastes great."

He drops his fork to his plate. His attention is now fully

on me. "The crease in your forehead tells me otherwise. Are you feeling okay?"

"My stomach's a little queasy."

"Have some water." He slides his glass across the table for me.

"Thanks." I give him a tight-lipped smile before I swallow a big gulp.

Lach finishes his pancakes while I pick at my bacon. Everything else I leave untouched. When we're finished, he pays for our breakfast, and we continue on the road.

While Lach drives for the next two hours, we make small talk about the various businesses we pass and funny billboards like the one that read "Quality Erections" for a construction company. At the three-hour mark, my eyelids drift closed.

Porter's
ALE HOUSE

I stir awake and stretch my limbs as much as I can while my eyes adjust to the light. We're parked at a gas station, but when I turn toward the driver's seat, it's empty. A second later, Lach steps through the glass double doors with a plastic bag in hand. I can't keep my eyes off him as he strolls toward the truck. He runs a hand through his hair. His gaze connects with mine through the windshield, and a flutter floats through my body. His gaze, unlike any other, makes me feel seen, understood, and cherished. It's soft and gentle but also screams, "I want to rip your clothes off and have my way with you." And I greenlight that idea.

Lach opens the door and climbs into the cab. He sets a plastic bag on the center console before tilting his head toward me. "You're awake. How are you feeling?" His words are soft. Comforting.

"Good." I adjust myself in my seat, hoping my cheeks

aren't as red as they feel from fantasizing about Lach stripping me naked. "I don't know what it was, but the nap certainly helped."

"I didn't want to wake you, but since you're awake I got you some water, snacks, and a turkey sandwich. In case you were up for eating since you didn't have much of your breakfast."

My heart swells at his thoughtfulness. "Thank you."

"I wasn't sure if you liked mayo or mustard, so I got both." He holds up the two condiment packets.

"Actually, both are perfect. Mayo on top and mustard on the bottom."

"I like the bottom. Mustard is what I meant. I also like mustard on the bottom."

A laugh bubbles out of me.

A pink blush fills his scruff-covered cheeks. "Also, I got sour gummy worms."

My eyes widen, and I snatch the bag from his grasp and rip the top off. "How did you know my favorite road snack?" I reach inside and pull out a brightly colored worm-shaped candy. My lips press together when the sweet and tart hit my tastebuds.

The corner of his mouth curves into a smile. "I didn't. But they're my favorite too."

I grab another sour gummy worm from the bag and pass it to him. He takes it and pops it into his mouth. When he's done chewing, he says, "On that note—you want to use the bathroom before we get back on the road?"

"Yeah, that's a good idea." I unbuckle my seat belt and climb out of the truck. A few minutes later, I return, and Lach has the water bottles in the cup holders and my sandwich laid out on the center console. I can't help but smile as I climb into the passenger seat. "How far did we get?"

"Not as far as I'd like. There was a car accident south of Indianapolis. Traffic was at a standstill for a while until they were able to re-route us. I'm thinking we'll maybe stop outside of Chicago for the night and finish the rest of the drive tomorrow."

I take a drink of my water. "Yeah, that sounds good." I won't complain about spending another night alone with Lach because I don't know what's going to happen once we get back to Harbor Highlands. He may be reluctant to pursue anything between us, but I know he wants this as much as I do. I just need to convince him how amazing we can be.

I pull my camera from my bag and stare out the window, looking for inspiration. Almost a month has passed since I've been able to exercise this creative outlet. I've missed it. I lift the camera, closing one eye. A sense of calm washes over me every time I look through a lens. I twist to face Lach. His profile fills the viewfinder. A strong, scruff-covered jaw. His nose is perfectly straight, with a narrow bridge and a refined tip. His long, dark lashes blink once. Twice.

He twists his head toward me. "What are you doing?"

"Taking your picture."

"Out of everything surrounding us, there has to be a better view than me."

I scrunch my nose, pretending to volley his words around. "I beg to differ." The soft click of the camera fills the cab, capturing this moment.

With a chuckle, he reaches across the seat, his fingers brushing against the camera. I lean away. Now it's my turn to laugh. Everything with Lach is so easy. Carefree. Fun. All the things that have been missing from my life in the past... all my life.

He drops his hand, and it falls to my thigh. His fingers

splay over the denim, its warmth radiating through my jeans. I don't know if he purposely put his hand there, but I'm afraid if I move, he'll remove it, and I don't want him to.

Turning toward me, a smirk on his lips, he says, "As soon as we're out of this truck, it'll be my turn to take pictures of you."

I drop the camera on my lap and bite my lower lip. "What kind of photos?" I drag a finger across my collarbone and down my chest. His eyes follow the same path.

He clears his throat before turning his attention back to the road. I lift the camera and snap a picture, wanting to capture the slight pink that dusts his cheeks.

"Are you going to take pictures of me for the rest of the drive?"

"Maybe."

He laughs again, and I snap another picture. I zoom in on his long fingers as his hand drapes over the steering wheel and take another. Panning the camera to the left, I focus on his face. He meets my gaze from the corner of his eyes, a flicker of something unreadable in their depths, but he doesn't move. I snap another picture.

"So, what do you love about photography?" he asks.

"It's like little moments frozen in time. Captured memories."

"You ever worry about spending too much time trying to capture the memories versus just living them?"

His fingers flex on my thigh, causing butterflies to erupt in my belly. This right here is everything I want. This is precisely the perfect moment I want captured for eternity. Raising the camera, I press the button, taking a picture of his hand on my thigh. "There's definitely a balance between the two."

"Think of all the people who spend their time taking pictures, capturing the memories, instead of living them. How many pictures do you have on your phone that you've taken but you never look at? Who knows if you ever will? They just sit there, taking up space until you run out of room and delete them."

"That's certainly one way to think of it. But if you're taking pictures with purpose, it's different because when you look back at all the photos, and if they invoke an emotion, you know you've captured the perfect moment. They may be happy, sad, scary, frightening, or a deep love. If you feel any of those, you've captured the right moment."

His soft gaze drifts to mine, and his lips twitch into a smile. He removes his hand from my thigh, and I frown at the loss.

"Come here." He lifts his chin, motioning me over. "Bring your camera. Let's capture the perfect moment."

I lift the armrest on my side, and he does the same to his. Setting my camera in my bag, I grab my cell phone instead. Selfies with a regular camera don't work. I slide to the center seat—it's more of a child seat, but it's a seat, nonetheless. He wraps an arm over my shoulders. I hook my pinky with his, hold out my phone, and snap several photos. Some where he's smiling with me and others where he's in profile. Perfect memories in case it's the only thing I'll have. After I finish taking pictures, I move to slide to my seat, but Lach tightens his grip, stopping me.

"Stay."

A small smile curves across my lips. "In the middle seat? What am I supposed to do? Straddle the center console?"

He peers at me from the corner of his eyes. "I'll give you something to straddle later."

"Promise?"

He laughs and pulls me closer. "You certainly like to challenge me, don't you?"

I smirk and shrug. Lach shakes his head and laughs. The constant shift of hot and cold with Lach is giving me whiplash. I'm going to go into shock one of these times. Tomorrow, we're back in Harbor Highlands, and I need an answer by then. I can't continue doing this back and forth any longer. In the meantime, I'll savor this time I have curled against his side in case it's all I'll get. We sit mostly in comfortable silence, which is out of character for me. But with Lach, everything is different. My world seems brighter and more vibrant. The sounds sharper and more alive. There are no words to describe it. Almost as if we know each other without knowing each other. Two lost souls reunited. I wonder if he feels it too.

After an hour passes, my phone buzzes. I glance at the screen, and my body stiffens. Lach peers down at me.

"It's Jake. He's wondering how far we are."

Lach nods, lifts his arm from my shoulder, and pulls away. A pang of disappointment washes over me. Jake's not even here, yet he still ruins things. Now feeling foolish for sitting in the middle seat, I sit up, unbuckle my seatbelt, and slide to the passenger seat. I reply to Jake before tucking my phone away in my purse. I shift my body toward the door, cross my arms over my chest, and stare out the window as we pass by flat fields and the sporadic patches of trees.

Soon, the bright sky turns to dusk and eventually nightfall as we pull into the parking lot of a hotel outside Chicago. With traffic and detours, the GPS-estimated eight-hour drive turned into twelve. I'm beyond ready to get out of this truck. Once we're parked, Lach grabs his backpack and my small rolling suitcase, and we stroll into the hotel together. He gets us our room keys and escorts me to the elevator. Our room on the third floor is a standard king-size room with a small pull-out couch next to the bathroom that has a tub and shower. There's a desk against the far wall by the window. It'll be our little sanctuary for the next twelve hours.

"I'm going to jump in the shower." Lach sets his backpack on a chair and stands my suitcase next to it. He grabs a couple of items from his backpack before going into the bathroom. The door softly clicks behind him.

I hear the shower turn on, and I plop down on the bed and grab my phone. I send a quick message to Jake and let him know where we are and that we'll be back tomorrow. Several messages from Mr. Shart draw my attention. After the third "Don't leave, I miss you" text, I delete all the others without even reading them. I send him a text with Jake's address for my paycheck, then block his number. I'm slamming the door and throwing away the key on that chapter of my life.

I drop my phone to the comforter. I bite my lower lip, contemplating if I should just join Lach in the shower. Water conservation and all. He wants this as much as I do. His eyes tell me everything I need to know. Every time he looks at me, it's like he has to fight with himself to not clasp my cheeks and kiss me. He's given in a few times, and he beats himself up afterward. What we are doing isn't wrong. I need him to understand that. I roll off the bed and rise to my feet as the water shuts off. A few minutes later, the door opens, and Lach emerges wearing only a pair of gray sweatpants that hang dangerously low on his hips. Water droplets slide from his neck and disappear into the light smattering of hair on his chest. He runs a towel through his hair, causing his reddish-brown hair to sprout in all directions. His tattoos, a collection of bold designs and intricate patterns, are fully visible. I'm mesmerized by the way the ink slowly dances on his skin as his muscles flex with every twist and turn. In an instant, a flood of naughty ideas converge between my legs. I clench my thighs together to relieve the ache. His eyes meet mine, darkening to indigo with each passing second. All my thoughts are a jumbled mess when he looks at me like that, and instead of ducks, I need my thoughts in a row in order to navigate this. Also, I need the shower to have a removable showerhead to help me clear my mind.

Chapter 22

YOU'LL GET IT. I PROMISE.

Lach

Why is it the one woman who I actually enjoy spending time with and want to always be around has to be my best friend's sister? Does the universe hate me that much? I rest my hand on the shower wall as the water stings my back. Throughout my twenty-nine years of life, I know I've done things I'm not proud of, most of them in my younger years. Ditching school, running from the cops, and stealing Christmas wreaths from one neighbor only to turn around and sell them to another neighbor. Being older and wiser, I don't deserve punishment now.

I rise to my full height. The water beating down on me, I blow out a deep breath and scrub my hands down my face. It's like I have an angel on one shoulder and the devil on the other, except I have Eve on one shoulder, looking sexy as hell like the temptress she is. Fuck. I want it. I want her. All of her. Then on my other shoulder I have Jake, arms crossed, glowering at me like he's five seconds away from ripping my head off Mortal-Combat style. I'm torn because I can't have both, and I kind of like my head attached to my body. Why couldn't she be anyone else's sister? In the cab of the truck, with her tucked against my side, it felt real. Natural. Like we're destined to be together, our souls intertwining, our hearts beating as one. For once, a chance at happiness was within my reach. Then Jake happened.

Turning off the water, I step out and half-ass dry off before tugging on a pair of sweats. As I open the door, I run the towel through my hair. I come to a halt when I notice Eve staring at me, lips slightly parted. Lust swirls in her irises as her gaze wanders from my face, down my chest, and to the waistband of my sweats before repeating the same perusal in reverse. The desire in her eyes tells me everything I need to know. My willpower dissipates into a cloud of dust.

Eve saunters past me, her coconut scent lingering in the air before she disappears into the bathroom. The door closes behind her, giving me a few minutes to collect myself. I blow out a deep breath as I walk across the room. I toss the towel on the back of the desk chair. Turning around, I flop back-first onto the comforter. My legs hang over the end of the bed, and I throw my forearm over my eyes.

We only have one more night alone together, then our little make-believe fantasy bubble bursts, and it's back to reality. I've already crossed the line with Eve, so it's not like I can take it back. One more night with her wouldn't make things worse; instead, maybe it will rid her from my system. Several minutes pass, and I'm still lying on the bed. The hairs on my arms rise. I feel her before I see her. Sitting up,

I lean back on my elbows. She's standing a few feet away. Her wet hair drapes over her shoulders. Nothing but a towel is wrapped around her. Fuck me. I didn't even hear the water shut off or the door open. In a few short steps, I could be standing before her, pressing my lips to hers. With a small tug, the towel would fall to the floor. For the rest of the night, I can pretend she's mine. But that's all it can be. Pretend.

Before I can speak, she stalks toward me. Her heated gaze locks onto mine, unwavering and intense, the silence punctuated only by the rapid beat of my heart. The towel shifts back and forth with every sway of her hips. She stops between my legs, her hands on her waist, a slight smile playing on her lips as our eyes meet.

"Tonight's our last night together before we're back in Harbor Highlands. What does that mean for us?"

I rest my hands on her hips. The towel is rough beneath my fingers. Her soft, bare skin would feel so much better. "That's the million-dollar question." I bow my head. The weight of uncertainty is heavy in the air.

Her fingers softly comb through my hair. "Then let's have one more night."

I want nothing more, but it's not that simple. I peer up at her. "As long as you're around, I don't think it can be only one more night." My heart thunders in my chest.

"It doesn't have to be." Her fingers slide from my hair down to my cheek. I lean into her warmth.

"But—"

"Don't say Jake. For once, I want my brother out of the equation. This is about you and me."

My grip on her waist tightens, and I peer up at her, swallowing. Hard. "And what do you want?" My tone is low and deliberate, each word measured and precise.

"I think it's obvious what I want. I want you. I want to

be with you. I want to continue this with you." She motions between us.

I can't keep lying to myself. "I want you too, so fucking bad."

"So it's settled." She inches herself closer. Her teeth sink into her bottom lip as she drags a finger down the seam of the towel wrapped around her. "We keep doing this."

I drop my hands to my sides, and she freezes.

She rolls her eyes. "Then there's Jake," she says with an exasperated sigh. "We're both adults. We're capable of making adult decisions, and this is one of those."

"I know you're right, but—"

"He's your best friend," she finishes. "Let me ask you this: do I make you happy?"

I ponder her words, their weight settling heavily on my chest. Right now, at this moment, she's my only happiness. I nod.

"If Jake is a friend, wouldn't he approve of your happiness?"

She's not wrong. He should be thrilled about my happiness, no matter the source, even if it is his little sister. "I know, but I need to tell him. This has already gone further than it should have."

Bending over, she slides her hand up my thighs just like the night at the hotel bar, the sultry gleam in her eyes included. "You want to stop until you get Jake's approval?" Her tongue peeks out, swiping across her bottom lip. My gaze follows hers, a slow descent from my eyes to my lips, lingering before the return journey. Fuck me. All it takes is one look from Eve—those piercing hazel eyes—and my logic short circuits, a wave of inexplicable attraction washing over me.

"We do this on one condition. We don't tell Jake. Not yet, anyway. Not until I can figure out how to handle it."

"The secret's safe with me." She lifts her leg. The bed dips as her knee sinks into the mattress. Then the same thing happens on the other side until she's straddling my lap. All the blood rushes to my dick as she lightly runs the pad of her finger across my chest. "There's only one other thing I want." Her voice is low and seductive.

I curl my arms around her, holding her to me. "What's that?"

"I want you to fuck me." With a flick of her wrist, her towel falls open. Her plump tits are on full display. I'm definitely not telling Jake about any of this.

"I'm going to do more…" I suck one of her hard nipples into my mouth before releasing it with a pop, "than fuck you, Sunflower." Wrapping my arms around her waist, I lift her as I rise to my feet. A soft giggle escapes her. The towel pools at my waist where we're touching.

"Where are we going? The bed is behind you."

I move forward a few steps. With one hand, I hold Eve close to me as I reach down and remove my backpack from the chair with the other. "Right here." Eve softly lands on the cushion. With a tug, I pull the towel off her lap, exposing her delectable naked body. How did I get so fucking lucky? My eyes linger on her ample tits before trailing down to where her knees are slightly parted. My erection strains against the cotton of my sweatpants. Reaching down, I adjust myself. Eve sinks her teeth into her bottom lip as she tracks my movement. I'm seconds away from coming in my pants just from that look. Crouching down to the floor, I slide my hand up the back of her smooth calf. At her knee, I hike her leg over my shoulder, revealing her glistening pussy to me. She gasps above me as the cool air hits her. The light stubble on my cheeks scrapes against her skin as I press my lips along the inside of one thigh. Her fingers lightly graze my scalp as she weaves them through my hair while I do the same on her opposite thigh.

"Oh. Lach." Her words are breathy as she bucks her hips, silently telling me she wants more. I'll give her more. I'll give her everything, even if it's just for tonight.

With my thumb, I spread her open and slide my tongue up her center. Her nails scrape against my scalp, sending a shiver down my spine as her fingers tighten in my hair. I give her another lick, only harder, teasing her sensitive skin with my tongue.

"Mmm. More. I need more." She directs my head exactly where she wants me, pushing her pussy against my mouth. If she wasn't chasing an orgasm, I'd think she's trying to suffocate me. I run the tip of my tongue up her center, tasting her sweet honey. Again, she moans. I love her moans. I love that I'm the one she's moaning for. It's only me who gives her pleasure. I keep licking her, consumed by desire and hunger like a starving animal. And maybe I am. Starved for her.

I slide my hand along the smooth skin of her thigh, hooking my thumb beneath the curve. I push until her knee hits her chest. "Hold this, Sunflower." She releases the grasp on my hair and clasps the back of her knee, following my directions. I swirl the tip of my tongue around her opening, teasing her and keeping her on edge.

Her hips shimmy beneath me. "Right there. Fuck me. With your tongue." Her words come out in breathy pants.

I nip at her thigh. "Patience. You'll get it. I promise." With my other hand, I press against her thigh, spreading her even wider. I flick the tip of my tongue over her clit before wrapping my lips around the tight bud.

"Oh! Oh! Yes! I need you. In me. Now."

"I have a better idea." Leaning back, I reach inside my backpack.

Peering down at me between her legs, her brows pinch together. "What are you doing?" Her words are breathy.

"Giving this back."

Chapter 23

JUST ENJOY THE RIDE

Eve

The head of a pink vibrator emerges from between my legs. Charlie Cumming! He's no longer kidnapped! My nipples pebble from excitement. I've used him many times on myself, but I've never had someone else use him on me.

"Don't worry, I sanitized it."

I flinch when the cool silicone makes contact as he slides the tip up and down my slit, coating it with my arousal. Within seconds, all thoughts of the cold vanish, replaced with a fiery inferno starting at my toes and rising throughout my body. My head falls against the chair as a slow moan falls from my lips. It's a blissful out-of-body experience.

"Should I lick your pussy while fucking you with this? Would my greedy sunflower like that?" He presses the tip into my opening, only half an inch, and stops.

"Yes. Yes. Yes," I chant. I rock my hips, trying to fuck the vibrator.

"So fucking greedy." He tugs on the vibrator, keeping me from taking the pleasure for myself.

I whimper at the loss. A second later, he pushes the vibrator in a little farther, then pulls out after an inch before pushing back in. Leisurely, he continues to fuck me. A spark ignites, shooting through my entire body. I watch as the pink disappears inside of me. Each time he pulls out, it glistens with more of my arousal. His tongue swipes across his lips as if he wants, no needs, to savor every last drop. Under his hooded eyes, his irises burn with lust. He bends down and slides his tongue over my opening. A moan escapes me, and my back arches. My nails dig into the armrest while he continues to eat me out while spearing me with the vibrator. Reaching up with my other hand, I cup my breast, alternating between kneading the tender skin and pinching my nipple. My breathing becomes shallow as my moans and pants echo around us. "This feels so good."

He pulls away. My arousal coats his lips. "You like when I fuck you with your vibrator?"

"Yes."

"You certainly take it like a good girl."

I curl my fingers around his hair and move his head exactly where I want it. He understands the assignment, and instead of using his mouth for talking, he puts it to better use. His tongue slides up my center, getting harder and rougher with each pass while he spears me with the vibrator. I squirm in the chair, savoring all the pleasure. His lips wrap around my clit and suck.

"Ah! Lach!" My back arches off the chair. My toes curl. "Oh fuck. It feels so good. I want to…" My pussy clenches around the vibrator, but I wish it was Lach's cock instead.

His heated gaze fixates on my throbbing pussy as he thrusts the vibrator in and out. The pad of his thumb circles my clit as his mouth descends on me again. Between his mouth, his thumb, and the vibrator, it becomes too much. A white-hot heat erupts inside me and floods my body.

"Ah!" I roll my hips, needing more, needing him. "Oh! I can't—" Words fail me as my pussy spasms around the vibrator. All I can do is feel.

"Come for me, Sunflower. All over my tongue. I want to taste you."

My hand falls to his head, fingers clawing at his hair, as my orgasm rips through me. My chest heaves as I collect my breath. Lach sits up, my orgasm glistening on his mouth. He pulls out the vibrator and drags the tip across my inner thigh, leaving behind a trail of wetness.

"Let me clean you up." He bends down and slides his tongue up my slit and over my still swollen clit.

"Oh! Lach! I can't. I'm going to. Pass out." I work to collect my breath, but it's useless as my clit vibrates with pleasure. It's like a rollercoaster ride that's nothing but nonstop hills. As soon as I hit the bottom, I'm shot right back up. I don't even get a second to breathe.

"I got you, Sunflower. Just enjoy the ride." He continues to lick, suck, and nibble on my swollen clit.

"Yes! More!"

He flicks the tip of his tongue over my tight bud and my back arches. My hand slaps the chair's armrest. I need something to keep me grounded before I shoot off like a rocket. My knuckles turn white as I grip the fabric of the armrest for dear life. There's a good chance he's going to bruise my clit. But it's never felt this good before. A slow heat builds in my belly, and without notice, it bursts into an explosion. My eyes roll back in my head, and another orgasm consumes me. Lach continues to lick my pussy until my body stops shuddering. Slowly, he sits back on his haunches. He swipes the back of his hand over his mouth.

"Don't tell me you have to clean me up again. That would just be a vicious, while pleasurable, cycle that would never break. But now it's my turn." I stand on wobbly legs and Lach does the same, hands on my hips to help my balance. "One of us is wearing entirely too many clothes."

My gaze slides down his chest and to his cock, tenting his sweats. A smile flits over my lips as I slide my fingers under the waistband and tug them over his thighs. His cock springs free, bobbing up and down, the tip glistening with a bead of pre-cum. After the sweats drop to the floor, he steps out of them. With a tight grip on his thick girth, I slide my hand over the head. A deep groan rumbles from his chest. His gaze drops to me. With his cock still in my hand, I pivot us so his knees hit the back of the chair. I release him from my grip and shove at his shoulders until he falls to the cushion. With my hands on his knees, I lower myself between his legs, but he stops me when I'm halfway.

"As much as I want your lips wrapped around me, I won't last, and I want to be inside you."

Slowly, I rise to my feet and glance over my shoulder. My bag with the condoms I picked up at the convenience store is on the nightstand next to the bed. Which would be a more favorable place for sex, but that's too easy. I spin around, walk the few steps, and swipe the bag. While I make my way back to Lach, the plastic bag rustles as I blindly dig inside. My fingers wrap around the cardboard box. I pull it out and discard the bag on the floor. Sliding my finger under the flap, the glue releases, and I yank out an accordion of three foil packets. The box joins the bag on the floor. I toss the condoms at Lach, and they smack against his chest and slide down to his waist.

"Did you know these work better outside the foil?"

"Then I suggest you get to work because, in about five seconds, I'm going to mount you like a wild stallion."

A smile curves his lips. He rips the foil pack and pulls out the condom. He rolls it over his cock and pinches the tip. The chair is small, but I manage to climb on his lap with my knees tucked outside his. Reaching behind me, I curl my fingers around the base of his cock, lining him up with my entrance. There's no more foreplay. I'm primed for him. As soon as the head breaches my opening, I slide down until I'm fully seated. My mouth falls open on a gasp as he stretches me wide.

"Ah fuck." Lach groans out. His fingers dimple my waist, holding me still.

Slowly, I rock my hips, loving how he feels inside me. One of his hands skates up my ribs until he's cupping my breast. His thumb brushes over my stiff nipple, alternating between pinching and caressing.

I moan out his name as I continue to ride his cock. My nails dig into his shoulder muscles, creating half-moon craters in his skin. My head falls back, and my lips part. His hands grip my waist, halting my movement.

"What's wrong?" I peer at him.

"Sit up and turn around."

I quirk an eyebrow. "Bossy."

He leans in, his teeth nipping at my tender breast. "It will be in your best interest to listen."

I roll my eyes but do as he asks. With my back to Lach, he guides me backward.

"Reverse cowgirl me."

I step between his spread legs. His hand moves from my waist to his cock, holding himself while I sink down. My fingers clench his muscular thighs as I take him all the way.

"You're so tight like this."

Just as I'm about to move, a ringing fills the room, and I freeze.

"Your phone's ringing."

"Yep." He slides his hands over my rib cage. A wave of goosebumps washes over me. His lips brush across my shoulder blade before he places a kiss there.

"Are you going to answer it?"

His mouth stills, then it's replaced with his warm breath. "Do you want me to stop what I'm doing right now to answer my phone?"

"No. Don't stop."

"Okay," he laughs, "that's what I figured."

I'm used to dating the dingleberry, Pax. Several times, while we were in the middle of making out, he'd answer his phone, claiming it was a client or on many occasions, his sister. Given what I know now, it was his wife every time.

Lach's warm breath grazes my skin as his lips brush against me, the pressure of his hands firm but gentle on my waist, urging me to move. So I do. His nose trails across my shoulder blades as I slide up and down his cock. It's the perfect mix of sweet and filthy. My back arches. The new angle causes a spark to ignite inside my belly. His calloused fingers skate across my chest and pinch my hard nipple. The spark bursts into a fireball.

"Ah! Yes!" A bolt of pleasure courses through my body. From every fingertip to the tips of my toes. Everywhere. He continues to pepper kisses across my back while I fuck his cock. The faint sound of my phone rings in the room. I ignore it, but Lach freezes.

His lips graze the shell of my ear as he whispers, "Your phone's ringing. Do you want me to stop so you can answer that?"

"Hell no! If you stop, I'll shank you." My body shakes from his laughter.

"It's kind of what I figured. But the shanking is new. Lean back, Sunflower. Put your feet on the armrest. Can you do that?"

With him still inside me, I lean back. He slides down the chair slightly to a half-sitting, half-lying position. Spreading my knees, I stretch to rest my feet on the armrest. My muscles pull tight and burn with exertion. I need to do more yoga. He slips out, and I hate the loss of him. Reaching between my legs, I wrap my hand around his girth and guide him to my opening. In one swift thrust, he's stuffing me full.

"Ah!" My shriek quickly turns to a moan as he pounds into me from below.

My fingers claw at the armrest, trying to keep a fraction of control. But he feels too good. I'm already on the brink of explosion. His fingers go between my legs and circle my clit.

"Oh god!" My back arches.

My moans create a melody with his grunts. He continues to pump his hips in and out. A burst of white, sultry heat soars through my body.

"Yes! Yes! Yes!" His hand claps over my mouth.

His lips graze my ear as he whispers, "Shhh. The entire hotel can hear you milking my cock." He pounds into me from below, and his hand muffles my screams of pleasure.

"Fuck. Sunflower. I won't last much longer. You feel too fucking good."

My orgasm rips through me, my pussy clenching around him. On one last, hard thrust, his orgasm roars through him. His movements slow to a stop. All the tension escapes my body, and I collapse against his chest. He slides out of me and wraps his arms around my stomach. He presses a kiss just below my ear where I have my sunflower tattoo. Something about the gesture is so sweet. He could kiss me anywhere else, but he always picks that spot.

"What do you say we move this party to the bed? Plus, I need to dispose of the condom." He presses another kiss to my neck as his calloused fingers slide down my thighs.

Once again, my heart flutters. "If I must."

Reluctantly, I drop my feet to the floor and stand. Sauntering to the bed, I throw back the covers, crawling underneath, while Lach tugs the condom off and strolls to the bathroom. A few seconds later, he emerges. I can't help but stare at how his tattoos dance over his skin as he moves. It's mesmerizing. He climbs into the bed and instantly pulls me to him, nuzzling my neck as we lean against the headboard.

"So why me? What makes me different from all the other girls?"

He chuckles. "Are you fishing for compliments?"

"No, you just seem to be the type of guy who wouldn't have any issues attracting a girl. Yet you're here with me, even when I'm the last person you should really be with." For a magnitude of reasons. Some his. Some mine.

He's silent for a few minutes. For a moment, I think he's fallen asleep, but he says, "You challenge me. It's not every day I have a girl ghost me."

"So you've always been the one to leave?"

"No, there's always just been a mutual understanding. Same question. Why me?"

I don't need to consider it. "You make me feel safe. The moment I met you, it felt different. I think it was part of the reason I bolted from the hotel room. What I was feeling was new, something I never experienced before, and fight or flight kicked in. Flight seemed like the easier choice."

"If you run, you never have to face those feelings."

"Exactly."

"Did I ever tell you I like your tattoo? It reminds me of the sun. Bright and full of life. You are my sunshine. You make me miss you when you're away," he softly sings.

A laugh burst out of me. "Oh, that's really cheesy."

"Okay, well, how about this? You are my sunshine. You make me horny when you are near."

"That's even worse!"

"Both are very true statements." He chuckles.

"It's actually my favorite flower. That's why I got it." I drag my finger up and down his arm, watching the hairs slowly stand on end. "Why does this feel so different with you? I've been in my fair share of relationships, but none of them have felt like this. And if I'm being honest, it's slightly terrifying." I pinch my eyes shut at using the word "relationship." We've never talked about what this is, and who knows what it will be once we get back to Harbor Highlands. "I'm not saying that this is a relationship per se, but you know, we're together talking about relationships."

"No, I feel it too. I've not had my fair share of relationships, but it's been by choice. I do like being here with you. Just like this."

I trace the colorful ink on his arm. "So, what about your tattoos? Any special meaning behind them?"

His muscles tense under my touch. "Um. I drew them."

I glance at him, and his gaze is directed at the ceiling. There's more behind his answer, but clearly, he doesn't want to talk about it. "They're amazing. You're an amazing artist."

All the tension releases from his shoulders. His warm palm rests against my cheek. He directs me to meet his eyes for a beat before he leans in, pressing his lips to mine.

There's no way he could be ready for round two, but if he is, count me in. Lach's phone dings, and he freezes for a second.

"That's right. Someone's been blowing up my phone." He twists to pick up his phone from the nightstand. After unlocking it, he scans whatever's on the screen. He rips off the blanket and swivels to the side of the bed, his back facing me.

My brows pinch together. "What's wrong?"

"There was a fire."

Chapter 24

MY SUNSHINE

Lach

"Where? Porter's? Is everyone okay?" Eve's frantic voice sounds behind me as she moves to sit next to me. She tucks the blanket around her and under her arms.

"My apartment. All the messages earlier were from Rylee." I pull up her number and press talk. It rings a few times before she picks up.

"Oh my god, Lach. We've been trying to reach you. Jake's been trying to get a hold of Eve." Panic laces her voice.

I rub the back of my neck. "Oh, um, sorry we were busy... eating dinner." I certainly can't say I was fucking Eve. Rylee wouldn't care, but I'm more concerned about Jake. By the echo in the background, she has me on speakerphone, and anyone could be listening. Drawing the attention away from Eve and me, I ask, "There was a fire at my apartment? What happened? Is the building a loss?"

The mattress rises as Eve stands to get her phone from the other nightstand.

"Some people at the bar were talking about it, and Jake went and checked it out. He determined that the fire was mostly contained to the building's north side, but fire trucks were everywhere."

I exhale a deep breath. "Okay. My apartment's on the south side, so maybe it's not a total loss." If it is, that's all my stuff. What I'm worried about most is all my artwork. The clothes and furniture are replaceable, but fuck, the art isn't. Living my life as a bachelor, I didn't have much because I didn't need it. All the major appliances came with the apartment along with a small dining room table that I use as a desk. All my dishes are old and need replacing anyway, along with my TV. From the corner of my eye, I glance at Eve standing a few feet away from me. Concern etches her face.

"It's hard to say. But the north side is almost gone. I'm kind of glad you're helping Eve instead of here; otherwise, you could have been home during the fire."

Shit. That never crossed my mind. More than likely, I would have been home. "Thanks for letting me know. We're just outside of Chicago, so we'll be back tomorrow. Then I'll have to call my landlord and figure out what's happening."

"Of course. Anytime."

I hang up.

The bed dips as Eve sits next to me and rests a comforting hand on my arm. "All my messages were from Jake saying there was a fire."

"Yeah." I throw my phone onto the bed and rest my elbows on my knees, scrubbing my hands down my face. "It was my apartment building. Jake said the damage was mostly contained to the north side, but who knows, the water and smoke might have destroyed the whole place."

"And all your things."

"Yeah. I guess I'm kind of lucky I wasn't there." Though I feel like shit for the couple of small families who live there. It's a week before Christmas, and they're without a home. I'll call Seth. He, along with his wife Parisa, run the Lilith House. It's a non-profit that helps community members in need. They'll certainly have clothes and toiletries, maybe even some toys in case they have nothing.

She rests her head on my shoulders.

I wrap my arm around her and press a kiss to the top of her head. Just having her by my side is comforting. Scenarios of what could have happened flash through my mind. What if it was my neighbor's apartment? What if I was home? What if I couldn't escape? All of this with Eve would be for naught. Even though I've known her for a short amount of time, I can't imagine not having her in my life.

I exhale a deep breath. "What do you say we go to bed so we can get an early start tomorrow? Then I can sort through the fire situation."

Eve nods and scoots to the other side of the bed. She lifts the blanket, inviting me in. I click the button to turn off the lamp and snuggle against her. Right now, she's the only comfort I have in a world of uncertainty. Knowing that I drift off to a semi-restless night.

The next morning, both of us dress for the day. Before we hit the road, I talk to my landlord, and he confirms the fire started on the second floor on the north side. They're still determining the cause of the fire, but they suspect it was an electric heater. The structural engineer is still assessing how sound the building is to determine whether anyone will be able to collect their belongings—or collect what's not ruined from smoke or water damage. For now, no one is allowed in, so it's a waiting game.

The drive back to Harbor Highlands is mostly quiet. Eve is in the passenger seat reading a book, and I can't understand how someone can read in a moving vehicle. Motion sickness would smack me upside the head before I finished the first page. With her sitting cross-legged in the seat, immersed in a fictional world, she's the most beautiful woman in my world. Just like the sunflower tattooed below her ear, always searching for the sun. She's my sun, and I find myself always searching for her. I've always kept my circle small. The only logical reason why I want to open up to her is she's Jake's sister, so it's like I already know her. Reaching across the seat, I rest my hand on her thigh. Her gaze drifts to me over the pages of her book. A smile flits across her lips. It's sweet and sexy and everything in between.

"You're my sun."

"Huh?" She closes the book and sets it on her lap.

"My sunshine. The thing that makes my day brighter. I want to continue exploring whatever this is with you."

"The sex?"

I laugh. "Well, that too. But also, more than that. I want to get to know you. All of you."

"So, like a relationship? The thing you don't do?" She lifts an eyebrow.

"I'm not one for labels, but if that's what you want to call it. All I know is I want you to be in my life, but—" Her body tenses under my fingertips.

"The dreaded but." Her shoulders sag.

I wish it could be different, but I need to figure out the

best way to tell Jake that not only did I watch out for his sister, but I also did it while she's been under me, on top of me, and even as I had her pinned against the wall moaning my name. "I told your brother I'd watch out for you, and I doubt this is what he had in mind. Until I can figure out what to tell him, can we keep this between us?"

"Under normal circumstances, I'd think you're embarrassed to be seen—"

"Never. I want nothing more than to tell the entire world you picked me."

Her cheeks turn a dusty rose. "Okay. I'll agree to your terms on one condition." Her hazel eyes meet mine as her lips tug into a smile.

"What's that?"

Her teeth sink into her bottom lip. It's sexy as fuck. I wish I was the one biting her lip. "We use Charlie Cumming again."

I exhale a laugh and squeeze her thigh. "I think that can be arranged. But maybe he can get a new name?"

She laughs, the sweet and sexy one that makes me smile. "Yeah. I don't think so."

One of the weights lifts off my shoulders. Eve is fucking gorgeous, and even more important, she's smart, funny, and down to earth. There's no way she'd stay single in Harbor Highlands, especially working at Porter's. Someone would charm their way into her life. That's not fucking happening. She's mine. I never imagined those would be two words I'd use, but with her, I want to get it tattooed on my knuckles so I could punch it into any guy who gets close to her. With her I'm in over my head, nearly drowning, but I don't want to come up for air. The other weights will have to wait until I'm back in Harbor Highlands.

Eight hours later, with minimal stops, we arrive at

Jake's house. With an extra set of hands, we unload the U-Haul. All the larger items like her bed, a dresser, and boxes of kitchen stuff, go into the basement, while her clothes and everything else go to her bedroom. Every time Eve bends over, I fight the urge to stare at her ass in case Jake's watching. Outing myself only a few hours into our secret relationship, which I'm still getting acclimated to, is not part of the plan.

After I move the last box, I plop down on a stool at the kitchen island, resting my elbows on top. Jake stands across from me. His expression is unreadable. Does he know? Does he have some sort of brotherly intuition? Is he five seconds away from reaching across the counter to pull me over by the throat? I lean back to give myself a few extra inches, just in case.

"Hey man, I want to let you know…"

Shit. Here we go.

"You're welcome to crash here. It's not the Hilton, but I do have a couch in the basement, so you'll kind of have your own space just until after everything gets situated with the fire."

I blow out a deep breath. "Thanks. But I'll just check into a hotel. Hopefully, it won't take too long to find a new place."

"The basement is going to be better than any hotel. Plus, it's free."

I know Jake's wanting to be a good friend, but he doesn't realize the situation he's putting me in. Not only am I sleeping with his sister, but he's now wanting to house me under the same roof as her. The temptation is always strong, but being in such close proximity to her all the time would snap my last restraint to not out myself to Jake.

Eve enters the kitchen, wiping the back of her hand

over her forehead before collapsing into the stool next to me.

"Moving sucks. Remind me never to do this again. Or at least moving halfway across the country. Because I certainly don't intend on living with my brother for the rest of my life."

"Good to know," Jake says. "Speaking of living arrangements, Lach will stay in the basement until he can figure out a new place to live."

"You know what, I think that's an excellent idea." She swings her gaze to mine. Something brushes over my ankle. Glancing down, Eve slides her sock-covered toes over my jeans. I snap my head up and meet her eyes. Luckily, the island is blocking Jake's view.

"We get to be roomies." Her plump lips curve into the sexiest smile.

I'm definitely fucked.

Chapter 25

YOU HAVE TO BE QUIET

Lach

Jake leads me toward the back entrance of the house where the basement door is located. I've been downstairs on many occasions but never slept. He flips on the light, and a single light bulb illuminates the white stairwell. When he lands on the bottom step, he turns on another set of lights that fill the open space. Stud partitions create the bones of rooms, and the insulation on the exterior walls but no sheetrock gives it a half-dressed look. In the bar corner is a small bar in front of a pool table. To the right is a long couch with a TV sitting on top of an entertainment center.

"For the most part, you'll have the entire space to yourself." He waves his hand to the other side of the room where a chest freezer and washer and dryer sit.

"This is perfect."

"And the couch pulls out to a bed."

I huff out a laugh. "I remember helping you move that

thing down here. That was a bitch."

"And this is probably where it's staying. Feel free to move things around how you see fit. I have extra pillows and blankets upstairs I'll bring down for you. This might be a good reason to put that second bathroom in."

"I don't have plans to stay that long."

He clasps my shoulder. "Stay as long as you need."

"Thanks. Since it's still light out, I'm going to drive past my apartment and check out the damage."

He digs in his pocket, pulls out a key, and passes it to me. "Since you're staying here."

I nod. Shit. Maybe this whole secret relationship isn't a good idea.

Since I left my truck at Jake's house when we left for Knoxville, I jump inside. A few minutes later, I'm on the west side of town and pulling into the parking lot of my apartment. It's mostly empty except for a few abandoned vehicles and a couple of work trucks parked near the front entrance that's covered in yellow caution tape. The acrid stench of burned plastic wafts through the air. Even as the sun shines down, it does nothing to curb the chill in the air. For the most part, the building looks normal. Nothing fancy. A brick, three-story rectangular building.

My shoes crunch on the leaves scattered on the ground as I make my way to the back of the building, which tells a different story. The windows on the north side are shattered. Black streaks climb to the roof, staining the brick. My side of the building looks untouched.

When I approach the front of the building again, my landlord and a couple of other people step through the door and over the tape. When he's finished, I wave to get his attention. He tells me the structural engineer is still determining whether it's safe to enter and collect any belongings. He'll call me in a couple of days with an answer.

I have a few toiletries and clothes from the trip, but I'll need more in case it's longer than two days or if everything is ruined. At the store, I shop for essentials—socks, underwear, toiletries. I'll snag a few Porter's shirts from Jake. Something to get me by until I can get my things.

When I arrive back at Jake's, it's quiet. I dump the shopping bags in the basement, grab the bottle of shampoo and bar of soap, and head upstairs to jump in the shower. Turning on the hot water, steam billows from the top and fills the small room. I strip out of my clothes and peel the curtain back. Climbing in, the water beats down on my tense muscles and rolls down my body. It's been one hell of a day already.

If anyone deserves an Asshole of the Year award, it's me. Jake was at my side, lifting me up when I hit rock bottom and showed me my life doesn't have to be the dumpster fire it was becoming. I owe him my life, and how do I repay him? I fuck his sister. My shoulders sag as I lift my face to the water raining down on me. The droplets sting my skin. I'm torn between happiness and my best friend, and it's the worst fucking place to be. After running the bar of soap over my body and shampoo through my hair, I rinse. Slowly, I turn the faucet handle until the water turns icy. The frigid temperature reminds me this is real. I really need to figure out this shit with Jake so I can stop being an asshole friend. I finish turning the handle until the water stops. I step out and grab the last towel from the rack. I'll have to ask Jake where he keeps the extras. The coarse fibers scrape against my body. Shit. I didn't bring a change of clothes with me. Normally, I don't need to worry about it, but now I have roommates. After I finish drying, I wrap the towel around my waist and forgo dressing in my dirty clothes. A cloud of steam billows out behind me as I open the door. I'm only a few steps down the hallway when a door swings open, and I'm yanked inside.

"Jesus." My back slams against the door, closing it with a click. My jeans and T-shirt fall to the floor with a thud. Instantly, Eve's lips are on mine in a bruising kiss. She pulls away; her warm fingertips caress the edge of the towel that rests on my hips.

"I really think this roommate situation is going to work out great."

Her low-cut tank top kisses the top of her tits, and her hard nipples stretch the pink cotton fabric. "It does make things incredibly convenient. Where's your brother?"

She leans back to arm's length. "You're thinking of my brother right now?"

I slide my hands from her waist to her hips, afraid if I let go, she might leave. "I don't want to be, but given the circumstances, I think it's important we know where he is."

"He said he had to run to the bar."

"But he's not scheduled to work."

"You know Jake, he'll find something to do while he's there."

I shrug because she's not wrong. "We haven't even been back for twelve hours. Are you sure you want to do this here? Now?"

"Would you rather go outside? It's kind of cold, but I guess with our body heat, we'd stay warm." She runs her fingertips over my chest, tracing my tattoos like she always does. And like every other time she touches me, my dick twitches.

"You have a smart mouth. Anyone ever tell you that?"

She smirks. "You better find a way to shut me up, then."

I'll never tire of her sass. Bending down, I wrap my

arms under her butt and lift. I spin us around, pin her against the door, and slam my lips to hers. My tongue sweeps across the seam of her mouth, and she opens. Small moans escape her throat as I stroke my tongue over hers. I'll never grow tired of her. I'm drowning in her kisses. Her every touch consumes me. It's both terrifying and exhilarating. I press my lips along her jaw until I reach my favorite spot. Her head falls back against the door, giving me better access. A soft moan falls from her lips as I place open-mouth kisses on her tattoo. She wiggles against me. Her hips loosening the towel around my waist until she's able to grab the edge and fling it to the side.

"Much better." She grinds her cotton-covered pussy against me, practically fucking me over the sleep shorts. Her cheek grazes mine until her lips brush against the shell of my ear. "I want your cock inside me." Her warm breath whispers against my ear.

All the blood rushes to my dick. Holding her to me, I spin around. In a few short steps, I'm at the edge of the bed. A half giggle, half squeal escapes her as I toss her to the mattress. I hook my thumb under the waistband of her shorts and yank them down while she frantically pulls the top over her head. The bed dips as I kneel on the mattress, covering her body with mine. My dick presses at the apex of her thighs.

She slaps at the nightstand until she finds the handle and pulls open the drawer. Pushing myself up, I reach over and grab a condom out of the box. In one swift motion, I tear the foil packet open and pull out the condom. Rising to my knees, I slide it down my length. Eve's hooded eyes are on me the entire time. With my fingers wrapped around the base, I direct the head over her pussy. Swiping the head over her clit, the glistening tip confirms what I already know.

"You're already so fucking wet for me." I tease her opening with the head of my dick.

Her back arches. "Mmm. I was touching myself while you were in the shower." She lifts her fingers to my lips.

Her sweet scent lingers on them. My mouth falls open, and she pushes her fingers inside. My dick throbs just from the taste of her. I swirl my tongue, cleaning her fingers. At her opening, I push in without warning.

"Ah!" She pulls her hand away, and it drops to the comforter. Her back arches off the bed as her moans fill the room.

I pinch my eyes shut, savoring her tight pussy gripping me for a few seconds. "We have to make this quick." Slowly, I rock my hips.

"I don't care. Just fuck me." She reaches up and cups her tit, kneading the soft flesh. Her thumb and finger pinch her nipple, and her pink lips fall open on a gasp.

I love that she pleasures herself while I do the same. Placing my hand behind her knee, I push her leg up, widening her even more. I drive deeper, thrusting in and out. My mouth falls open. She feels incredible with the new angle.

"Oh god. Right there. Don't stop." Her nails claw at the sheets while the other hand still plays with her nipple.

I drive into her. Our skin slapping together. The headboard taps against the wall.

"Oh! Yes!" Her words come out in short pants, followed by a long moan.

Bending over her, I clamp my hand over her mouth. "You have to be quiet," I whisper. I grind my hips against hers, and she moans again. The headboard smacks against the wall with another loud thud followed by a bang.

A second later, there's a knock on the door.

Chapter 26

FIRST OF ALL, I'M A DELIGHT

Eve

"Eve, is everything okay?" Jake's voice sounds from the other side of the door.

Lach freezes, still inside me. My eyes widen, and my body tenses, causing my pussy to contract around him involuntarily. His eyes pinch shut, and he bites back a moan.

I scrunch my face and mouth, "Sorry," to Lach. I twist to face the door, answering Jake. "Um. Yeah. Everything is fine."

"Okay," Jake says. "I heard some banging, so I wanted to make sure."

My heart hammers in my throat. Lach scrambles to pull out of me. With the blanket wrapped around his other leg, he slams his foot to the floor with a hard thud. He hobbles around while being as quiet as possible, which isn't very quiet.

"Oh. Sorry. I was just… watching… porn, and I hit… the nightstand."

Lach stops searching for his towel and turns to me. "What the fuck?" he mouths while trying to contain his laughter.

I shrug, pinching my lips together to keep my own laugh from bursting out. I yank the blanket from him, and he stumbles backward.

"Didn't need an explanation. Have you seen Lach?" Jake asks.

"No!" I spit out entirely too fast to be casual. "I haven't. Why?" My gaze shoots to Lach. "Hide," I mouth.

He scans the room. "Where?" he whispers.

"I don't know. Anywhere." My voice is low so only he can hear.

He eyes the space between the floor and the box spring but, within seconds, realizes he won't fit underneath. He spins around to face the closet. With the speed of a camera flash, Lach's naked, pale ass disappears behind the door.

Jumping to my feet, I grab my bathrobe draped over the back of my desk chair. I shrug it over my shoulders and secure it closed with the rope. I finger comb my hair to make it look like I hadn't been on the verge of an orgasm.

"His truck's here, but I don't know where he is," Jake says through the door.

"I think he went out for a run."

A mop of chestnut hair peeks out from the edge of the closet doorframe. Lach's forehead wrinkles as he mouths, "A run?"

I shrug my shoulders. "I mean… run to the basement… so he could take a nap."

He rolls his eyes, but he smiles before disappearing into the closet again.

I stroll to the door and glance over my shoulder one last time to confirm it doesn't look like a sex party behind me. When it's clear, I crack the door open just enough for my head to fit through. "Maybe he's wearing his noise-canceling headphones. He does that sometimes." I scan Jake's face to make sure he isn't suspicious of Lach hiding in my closet.

"I glanced in the basement and didn't see him. I bet Rachel picked him up."

My heart twists into a painful knot in my chest, even though that's not the case since he's currently naked, hiding in my room. I don't know who she is, but the urge to kill Rachel is strong. "Yeah. Maybe." I fight to keep my tone neutral.

"Alright. I'm going to jump in the shower."

"Okay," I say a little too eagerly.

Jake walks the rest of the way down the hall and into the bathroom. When the door closes behind him, I race to the closet. I glare at Lach.

"What?" His brows pinch together.

"Who's Rachel?" I cross my arms over my chest.

"A girl from the bar. You want to discuss this now?"

I pop my hip. "Do you want to give me a better time?"

"Anytime when I'm not naked and hiding behind your closet door would be great." When I continue to glare at him without moving, he spits out, "She means nothing to me. You're the only one I want." He grips my chin and leans in, pressing his lips to mine.

My body softens, and I drop my arms to my side. "Good answer." I step out from in front of the closet. "Jake's in the shower. You should leave." I point toward the door.

"Did you find my towel?"

"No. I didn't prepare for proper towel placement in case of a quick getaway."

"My clothes?"

I twist around and scan the floor but come up empty-handed. "I don't know where they went."

He emerges from the closet, holding one of my cotton t-shirts over his cock. My gaze drops to the pink shirt with an opossum that says *First of all, I'm a delight.* I won't lie. What's hiding behind the shirt is a delight. Back at the bedroom door, I pull it open and peer into the hallway. The bathroom door is still closed.

"Now's your chance to get out."

"Alright." He stalks toward me as he rotates the shirt to cover both sides. "Have I told you I like it when you boss me around?" He comes to a stop when he's next to me. Bending down, he presses his lips to mine.

I melt against him. Now is not the time, Eve. "You can do more with that later," I murmur against his lips.

When he has one foot in the hall, the bathroom door opens. I palm his chest and shove him back into my room. With a grunt, all the air escapes his lungs. For a second time, he stumbles backward. I grab the doorknob and pull it so I'm trapped between the door and the doorframe.

"We're out of towels. I have a laundry basket full in my room." Jake strolls past me and to his room.

A few seconds later, he emerges with a stack of towels and goes back into the bathroom. I stand perfectly still, listening intently for the telltale sound of the shower turning on. After a few seconds to make sure he doesn't come back out, I open my bedroom door again.

Lach meets me in the middle of the room, my shirt still wrapped around his waist. "Fuck, that was close."

"Too close." I collapse on the bed.

The bed dips as he takes a seat next to me. "So, tell me about this porn you like to watch."

I playfully backhand him in the stomach.

He flinches. "Or not."

"If we just tell Jake, we won't have to do all this sneaking around."

"You're right. We wouldn't because I'd be dead."

Sitting up, I blow out a heavy sigh. "When do we tell him?"

"Not right now. There's just a lot going on with you moving back, me moving in." He runs a hand across my shoulders and down my arm. "I'll tell him. I promise."

I bite my lips together and nod. "Yeah, okay. Now is your time to escape. You better go."

His lips press against my forehead. Without another word, he rises off the bed, twists the knob, and peeks around the doorframe before disappearing behind the wood door.

I flop back on the bed. The roommate situation isn't panning out like I hoped. I should be screaming Lach's name while he gives me orgasm after orgasm, but instead I'm lying on my bed, alone, horny, and orgasmless since we were rudely interrupted. At least I can fix a couple of those things. I roll my head to the side. A chuckle escapes me as I spot Lach's towel on the floor between my suitcase and the wall, and his jeans peek out from behind a cardboard box. Never thought to look there.

Shortly after Jake's shower, the rumble of his truck sounds from outside as it disappears from the driveway. Reaching over to my nightstand, I yank open the drawer and pull out Charlie Cumming. With the silicone cock in hand, I slide it between my legs. Since Lach isn't going to provide the orgasm, this will have to do, and I'm going to make sure he hears every moan and scream.

For the rest of the night, I stay in my room, read my book, and pretend my life doesn't involve falling for my brother's best friend—instead, I'm in a fake relationship with a billionaire. It seems less complicated. When Jake gets back, I hear him talk to Lach, but I don't bother to join them. Instead, I fall into a restless sleep.

Porter's
ALE HOUSE

The following morning, I stir awake. The aroma of freshly brewed coffee wafts through the air. My nose pulls me out of bed. I secure my robe around me since I fell asleep wearing it last night. As soon as I open the door, Jake and Lach's voices carry down the hallway from the kitchen. Before heading that way, I make a pit stop in the bathroom. When I reach the kitchen, I stop in the doorway, the hairs on my arms standing at attention. Like a beacon, I instantly spot Lach, who looks up at me at the same time as if he knew I was going to be there. His eyes soften, and I fight to tear my gaze away.

"Good morning," I say to no one in particular as I stroll past them and beeline it to the coffeepot. I pull out a mug from the cupboard and grab the creamer from the fridge. I pour a splash of the creamer into the mug and then my coffee, letting the stream mix the two. I inhale the heavenly scent before taking a sip. A plate of cooked sausage links sits on the counter. I grab a link and take a bite. As soon as it hits my stomach, it revolts. I choke down a gag. That's odd. "Is this creamer expired or something?" Frowning, I peer inside the mug, but it's not curdling.

"I just bought it the other day," Jake says.

I take another bite of the sausage, chasing it with coffee, and the same thing happens. Only this time, I can barely swallow it. "Alright, well, I guess it's a no-coffee day for me." I dump the mug out in the sink and toss the last of the sausage link into the garbage.

"I have you and Lach working the closing shift tonight.

That way Lach can drive you. Also, I have a mechanic checking out a used car for you. It's nothing fancy, but it drives," Jake adds.

"Great. Thank you." I walk to where Jake's sitting and wrap my arms around his shoulders from behind. He freezes for a brief second but then relaxes and pats my arm. He's never been one for hugs, but since I'll be around more, he'll have to get used to it. Plus, he's kind of warming up to the touch. As I retreat to the opposite side of the counter, I shift my gaze to Lach to read his expression. But he's like a statue, not giving anything away. Tonight will be interesting. Jake rises to his feet and exits the kitchen, leaving Lach and me alone. From under the table, his leg bounces on the ball of his foot. A few seconds pass before he stands. With a quick glance over his shoulder, he stalks toward me. He stands behind me, his hands on the counter, caging me in. With him so close, my heart flutters in my chest.

"Are you feeling okay?" His warm breath skates across the shell of my ear.

I nod, unable to find words because that's what Lach, in close proximity, does to me. "Yeah." I eventually spit out. "It must be the creamer. I'll buy some to make sure it's good."

The tip of his nose brushes across my cheek. "Good."

I'm seconds away from spinning around and kissing him, but he pushes off and stands to his full height. Before I can turn around, he's strolling out of the kitchen and toward the basement. I blow out a deep breath.

We don't speak to each other for the rest of the afternoon, not even in his truck. I'm convinced Jake almost catching us scared him away. In a weird way, I found it thrilling. We're doing something forbidden. Naughty. It's like telling a child no, but it only makes them want to do it more. I'm most definitely down for more. I hate that it's my brother we're keeping the secret from, but it's Lach's choice, so I will let him handle it. Now, I wonder if he regrets it.

After we arrive at Porter's, Lach immediately busies himself serving customers on the far end of the bar, away from me and Nora. A few hours later, the night settles down a little. I run to the back to grab a case of beer. When I return to the bar, Lach's standing in front of the cooler I need to refill. I stroll behind him and set the box on the edge.

He glances at me. "I know what you were doing."

"What are you talking about?"

"Yesterday after I left your room." His forearms flex as he grips the edge of the bar. "You were in your room pleasuring yourself."

Heat rushes to my cheeks. "Oh, you heard me," I said, a playful lilt in my voice.

"You wanted me to hear."

"I needed to finish what you started." I shrug, then I lean closer to him, my arm brushing against his. "Let me ask you this." My eyes meet his. "What did you do while you heard me?"

Lust, thick and palpable, swirls within the dark pools of his eyes. "Wrapped my fist around my dick, pretending it was your tight pussy I was fucking. There was no comparison, though."

His hand rests on my lower back, sending tingles of excitement through me. I don't know how he does it, but every touch sends my body ablaze. His hand slides down the curve of my ass before walking behind me to the other end of the bar. With my head on a swivel, my gaze drops to his muscular ass confined in his tight jeans. When did a guy's walk become so sexy? He has a certain confident, masculine swagger about him. When I peel my gaze away, movement to my right catches my attention. Nora's hand rests on her waist, staring at me with a cat-caught-the-canary smirk on her face. I jerk my head away, hoping to hide the blush covering my cheeks.

She struts toward me, stopping a foot away, and props her hip against the cooler. "So I'm almost done with my dating app."

I peer at her and smile. "That's awesome."

"I could use some beta testers. What do you say? Want to help me out?"

"Oh. Um." Shit. What do I tell her? "Like, set up a profile?"

"Yeah. And match with others to test out those features. You're single, right?" She lifts a brow, waiting for an answer.

Fuck, what do I say?

She leans in so only I can hear. "I know there's something going on with you and Lach."

My heart hammers in my chest. Deny. Deny. Deny. "What are you talking about?"

She barks out a laugh. "You can't play me for a fool. Neither of you are Houdini hiding all the touching you've been doing tonight. Plus, every time you two lock eyes, I'm convinced you're going to start dry humping each other on the bar. I'm slightly jealous." She shrugs. "I would die to have a man look at me the way Lach looks at you. The best I get is a middle-aged drunk guy who's excited when I pass him a new beer. Anyway, anyone with a set of eyes can see it."

My shoulders slump. "Damn, I thought we were being inconspicuous."

"No. You definitely need to toss out the 'in' in inconspicuous. But I still need beta testers. I mean, you could help me out as a friend, and then Lach can do the same. Then you two can go out on a date," she lifts her hands, giving air quotes, "'as friends' while helping another friend."

I bite my lips together. It's a solid idea for us to have a date. "If Lach's in, I'm in."

"What am I doing?" Lach says from behind us.

Nora fills him in about knowing about us, how the app works, and needing our help as beta testers.

Lach rubs his chin. "So it's like an organized foodie call."

"No. Well, I suppose it could be. But that's not the intended purpose. Plus, how do you know what a foodie call is?" Both Nora and I stare at Lach, waiting for his answer.

"I fell down the rabbit hole of online videos. They just kept playing, and I just kept watching." He shrugs.

Nora waves him off. "Either way, not all dates require dinner. Or food."

"That should be a required question. Will there be food on this date? Someone might need to know if they need to eat before or not. Or what if there is food, and their date has an allergy? No one wants to go on a date that ends in the emergency room."

Nora sighs. "Dammit, you have a good point. I'll add the question."

Lach fake pops his collar. "I'm not all brawn. I have some brain too. Add the question, and I'll do it under one stipulation."

"What's that?" Nora asks.

"Jake can't know what you know about us." He waves a hand between me and him.

"Well, you guys can't keep your paws off each other, so it's only a matter of time before you out yourself, anyway.

Regardless, your secret is safe with me." Nora motions as if she's zipping her lips. "But the longer you keep it from Jake, the harder it's going to be telling him."

"So I've been told." Lach rubs at his temples.

Nora gives us instructions on downloading the app and setting up a profile. She then emails us a feedback form to give to her after our date. "And obviously, the sooner the better."

I pat Lach's chest. "This shall be a fun date." I flash him a bright smile before brushing past him to help a customer at the other end of the bar. We're going on a date. A real date. This is starting to feel real.

Chapter 27

YOU GOT IT BAD

Lach

Yesterday was brutal, especially for my willpower, as she fucked herself to orgasm. Am I jealous of her vibrator I refuse to call by the name she gave it? Absofuckinglutely. I was supposed to be the one who made her come, not some pink vibrator, and she knows it. My gaze drifts to Eve as she disappears to the opposite end of the bar. And now I'm taking her on a date. A part of me is thrilled, but the other half of me is screaming, "What the hell are you doing?" Dates are not keeping our relationship secret. That's exposing us to the entire world. But fuck, I'd be an idiot to turn down a date with Eve. To the world, it will be pretend. For us, it will be real.

From behind me, Nora blows out a low whistle. "You got it bad."

Slowly, I turn my head toward her. "I know. I should stay away, but I can't. It physically pains me to be away from her, and I don't know what to do."

She rests a comforting hand on my arm. "I'm happy for you. If she truly makes you happy, you should be with her. Jake will have to get over it."

I wish her words were true, but "Jake" and "getting over it" don't exactly work in the same sentence. Jake's fist meeting my face seems more likely. I rake my hand through my hair. "Every scenario has flashed through my head so many times. The optimistic ones are Jake telling me he's happy for me. I deserve to be with someone who makes me happy. I deserve to be with his sister. But I doubt those will be the words I get."

"Don't focus on that. Instead, focus on your date."

I huff out a laugh. "Is it sad to admit I've never been on a date?"

"I mean, I'm not surprised based on the fact that I've never seen you with another girl."

Glancing over my shoulder, I spot Eve chatting with a couple of customers. She throws her head back in laughter. I don't know what I did to deserve her, but I don't want to fuck it up. Turning to Nora, I ask, "What kind of date do I give her?"

She taps her chin. "I'm not sure. But whatever you do, don't do dinner and a movie. It's way too cliché."

Shit. That was the obvious choice.

"What are her interests?"

"Besides me?" I wiggle my eyebrows.

"If that's her only interest, I feel sorry for her. That would get boring pretty fast." She playfully winks.

"Hey! I've kept her interested this long. In fact, she keeps coming back for more."

She fake gags. "I don't need details on how you keep her interested. No, I mean, she has to have a hobby. She's a photographer, right?"

"Yeah." I rub the back of my neck. "But what do I do?

Take her somewhere to shoot photos?" Silence floats between us while I think. "I know she enjoys reading."

Nora straightens her shoulders. "There you go! You have your date."

I pinch my eyebrows together. "Reading?"

She rolls her eyes and exhales a heavy sigh. "Take her to a bookstore. Buy her some books."

"People do that?"

"If she loves reading, she'll love going to a bookstore. Trust me."

"I'm not sure." This seems like the too-obvious choice. It can't be that easy, can it?

"Says the guy who doesn't date. Just trust me. If she hates the date, I'll give you a hundred dollars. But if she loves it, you owe me." She rests a hand on her hip and smirks.

"Okay. It's a bet." She holds out her hand, and we shake on it.

"What am I going to spend my hundred dollars on?" She taps her finger to her lips.

The house is dark when we enter. Eve flips on the kitchen light while we do our best to be quiet and not disturb Jake. Eve shrugs out of her coat and yawns. She stretches, causing the hem of her shirt to ride up, exposing a tiny sliver of bare skin. I itch to lift her up on the counter and run my tongue over the exposed spot. Instead of turning my fantasy into reality, I stroll into the living room, hoping to get a few extra minutes with Eve. I flop down on the couch, turning on a lamp. A soft glow fills the room as Eve enters a few steps behind me. She sits on the cushion next to me and crosses her legs pretzel style.

"Have you filled out your profile yet?"

"I haven't. Have you?"

"No." She pulls her phone from her pocket. "I'll do that now."

I dig my phone out of my pocket and do the same.

A few minutes pass while we type on our phones. The couch dips, and Eve's arm brushes against mine as she leans over to see my screen. "What are you putting on your profile?"

I tilt my phone away from her so she can't peek. "Stuff."

She laughs and rolls her eyes. "Yeah, but what are you adding?"

"It's supposed to be a surprise. Then we'll know if we match."

"We're already a match." She beams at me.

"Then it shouldn't matter." I lean away, lifting my phone so the back is to her, and continue typing.

"Ugh! You're so infuriating," Eve pouts while she continues creating her profile.

When we're finished, we both hit submit and wait for approval. Within a few minutes, both our phones chime with a message from OneDate.

"Oh, look at that. Not even in the app for five minutes, and I already have a date." She flashes me a smirk.

"Me too. Do you think she'll be attracted to my good looks and dazzling charm?" I tease.

"Hmm." She taps her chin before shaking her head. "I don't think so."

A laugh bursts from me. "I thought the same." I lean toward her, so close I get a whiff of her coconut shampoo, and whisper, "Just so you know, whoever your date is, you are way too good for him."

Slowly, her head turns to face me. A soft smile tugs at

her lips. An electric charge arcs between us. I feel it every time I'm near her.

"I have something for you." Her words are soft. Almost seductive.

"Is that so?" I lean away and stretch my arm over the back of the couch, wiggling my eyebrows.

She laughs and playfully smacks my chest. "Unfortunately, that," she glances at my crotch, "is staying in your pants tonight. Let me grab it. I'll be right back." She rises to her feet and rounds the couch before strolling to her bedroom. When she returns, she has a hand behind her back. "I know we're not really in the gift-giving portion of this," she waves a hand between us, "but I saw this and thought of you. And it's Christmas." She swings her hand from behind her back and holds out a red and gold-wrapped present.

My back goes rigid as I sit up. "You got me a present?"

"Yeah. I mean, it's nothing special."

She places it on my lap. I stare at it, waiting for the gotcha prank because people don't buy me presents. Fuck. I don't remember the last time anyone bought me anything. Especially out of the blue because they saw it and thought of me.

"Please say something," she whispers. "The longer you stare at it, the more foolish I feel."

I peer up at Eve. "Shit. I don't know what to say."

"Well, for starters, you can open it." She bites her lips together.

I turn it over and slide my finger under the paper, releasing the tape. She takes a seat next to me as I carefully peel away the wrapping paper. It's a hardback, but it's not the traditional fiction size. I flip the book over and stare down at the colorful picture of a short stack of pancakes.

"It's a sketchbook for you to draw in." She shifts back and forth on the couch.

I can't take my eyes off the sketchbook. She bought me a sketchbook. She bought me a present, and it's a sketchbook. Warmth radiates through my chest.

"You hate it." She buries her head in her hands. "It's a dumb gift."

The wrapping paper floats to the floor as I spin to face her. I brush her hands away from her face, wanting to see her. "This is probably the best gift anyone's ever given me."

Her eyes widen. "Really?"

"I never got a lot of gifts, so this is great. I'll definitely make use of it."

A pained expression spreads over her features before she quickly recovers. "I'm glad you like it," she says softly.

Fuck. Now I feel like the asshole. "I didn't get you anything."

She rests a hand on mine. "I didn't get it for you with the expectation of something in return."

"But still." My gaze falls.

She sits up, inching closer to me. "How about this? You can make it up to me with the date." She grins. "Is it weird that I'm excited about going on a date with you?" She lifts her leg, tucking it under her as she turns to face me.

"Nah." I rest my hand on her thigh. Touching her grounds me, which tells me this is real. Right now, that trumps being scared. Mostly scared of what Jake will do to me, but I'm willing to pay the consequences because I don't think I can give Eve up. "I'm excited too."

She flips my hand over. With a feather-light touch, she drags her fingertips across my palm. "What do you have planned for our date?"

"Oh. I'm supposed to plan the date? I thought you were." I smirk.

"I can. How do you feel about mani-pedis?"

"It doesn't matter what we do as long as I get to do it with you." I lean closer, and she does the same. Even though we've been in the bar all night, her sweet scent invades my senses. Her eyes drift closed as our mouths inch closer together. A door creaks open, and we jump away from each other like a couple of teenagers on the verge of getting caught by a parent. My heart pounds in my chest as Eve does her best to put space between us. A couple more inches, and she'll be sitting on the armrest. A second later, Jake emerges from the hallway and enters the living room.

He scrubs the sleep from his eyes. "I thought I heard someone out here."

"Sorry we woke you," Eve blurts out.

I'm sorry too because I was seconds away from pulling Eve to my lap and kissing the hell out of her, then convincing her to stay in the basement with me so I could continue kissing her. Everywhere.

"No problem. How did the night go?" Jake stops behind the couch, crossing his arms over his bare chest.

"Good," I answer.

"The usual," Eve says at the same time.

Jake nods. "I'm going to get some water and go back to bed." Both of us stare as Jake strolls in the kitchen and back through the living room with a bottle of water. We're silent until his door clicks shut.

My shoulders drop, and I huff out a laugh. "How many close calls are we going to have before we get caught?"

"I think we have one or two more times left in us." A smile curves across her lips.

I shake my head and laugh. "Good night, Eve."

"Good night, Lach. Sweet dreams. I know mine will be." She flashes me a sultry smile.

My dick twitches in my jeans, and I exhale a deep groan. There's a good chance I won't be falling asleep for at least another hour while I lie awake, thinking of all the sweet dreams we could be having together.

Porter's
ALE HOUSE

The next day, I'm back at Porter's while Eve has the day off, but I'd much rather be with Eve. Playing dodge-Jake is cramping my style. He said I could stay as long as I needed, but I'm thinking time is up if I'm going to get any alone time with Eve. Better yet, I should just tell him I'm falling for his sister. Not falling, but fallen. I've fallen hard for her, which is just as terrifying as telling Jake. Maybe if I tell him while at the bar, with witnesses, he won't physically hurt me. It's an option.

Jake strolls down the bar with a case of beer in his hands. He stops a few feet shy of me and is definitely out of reach. Resting the edge of the box against the cooler, he flips open the top, grabs three bottles with one hand, and transfers them inside.

I wipe my palms on my jeans and swallow. Hard. "So, Jake." Without stopping, he peers up at me. "I wanted to—"

A crash on the opposite side of the bar startles us. "Fuck," Jake murmurs under his breath.

He shoves the box to the top of the cooler and stomps to where two guys are currently in a shoving match. I'm a few steps behind him. One thing Jake doesn't tolerate is fights in his bar. He wrangles one guy while I take the other. We toss them both onto the sidewalk, and their friends follow. We return to behind the bar, and Jake goes back to filling the cooler as if nothing happened.

"What were you going to say?"

Shit. Later. I'll tell him later. He has adrenaline racing through his veins. There's no doubt he'll do more than throw me out on the sidewalk. "I wanted to say, let me know when you want to start the bathroom renovation."

"I will."

I walk to the other end of the bar to serve customers mostly so I don't have to look Jake in the face. I lied to my best friend. Truth be told, I've *been* lying to him. Lying by omission. I'm a terrible fucking friend.

Chapter 28

PEE STICK

Eve

I wake up to a message from Lach.

> LACH
>
> I tried to tell him.

> LACH
>
> I couldn't do it.

A rock crashes in the pit of my stomach. I hate the sneaking around. I hate not wrapping my arms around him in public. I hate we're lying to Jake. I understand why. The last thing I want to be is in the middle of Lach and my brother's friendship. All of it is exhausting. After our date, we can regroup and finally draft a plan to tell Jake. The longer this goes on, the worse it's going to get. When I exit my bedroom, the house is quiet. In the kitchen, I peel back the curtain, only to see the driveway is empty. I prep the coffeemaker to brew half a pot, then return to my bedroom. As the coffee brews, I grab my phone from the nightstand and send a text to Lach.

EVE

If you need me to tell him, I will. You don't have to be the one to tell him.

A few minutes pass, and I don't get a response. I stroll back into the kitchen and pour myself a cup of coffee. My phone chimes with an incoming message.

LACH

He's my best friend. I feel like I owe it to him to tell him myself.

EVE

He's also my brother. He can't really hate me forever. We could tell him together too.

LACH

I'll try again.

EVE

Okay. But know I'm always here.

LACH

I know, Sunflower.

EVE

Also, where are you? Jake's gone, and I thought we could take advantage of the alone time.

LACH

My landlord called and said I could come by and see what's salvageable from the fire.

EVE

That's great! How is everything?

LACH

Almost everything is good. A lot of smoke
damage to the furniture and mattress. I
should be able to wash it out of my clothes.
Luckily, my computer, TV, and drawings are
undamaged.

EVE

I'm so happy to hear your art was spared.

LACH

Me too. Everything else is replaceable. I
doubt I'll be back before you leave for work.
Have a good night.

EVE

Thanks.

Over the next few hours, I lounge around and read my
book before I get ready for work. When I arrive at Porter's,
I find the bar packed. There isn't an empty chair or stool
in the entire place. Halfway through my shift, it finally
quiets down long enough for us to catch our breaths. I pull
my phone from my back pocket, hoping to see a message
from Lach, but nothing.

Nora chugs a glass of water before resting her palm on
the bar. "I'm having the worst cramps right now. It's like
my uterus is trying to Mike Tyson its way out of my
stomach." She sucks in a deep breath as if she's practicing
Lamaze.

Rylee stops next to Nora. "I have some air-activated
hand warmers in my purse. You tuck it in your waistband,
and it works wonders."

"Give me all of them. These period cramps can go kick
rocks," Nora says, whipping her braid over her shoulder.

My body tenses. Oh shit. My eyes widen, and I forget
how to breathe. When was my last period? I haven't had it

yet this month. Surely, I had it last month. It was spotty. I've never had a super heavy flow. But I still had it. Or was that the month before? Fuck. Static erupts between my ears, increasing in volume as if someone is turning the knob on a stereo to ten. Flashes of white flood my vision. Through all the sparkles, I can faintly see Nora's face. Her mouth is moving, but I can't make out her muffled words. It's as if I'm underwater.

"Eve? Eve, are you okay?" Her voice faintly pierces through the static. "Here. Sit down." She guides me to an unfolded footstool. "You're ghostly white. Are you okay?"

"Yeah," I shake my head. "I'm fine," I stutter.

"Are you sure? You don't look fine." Nora passes me a cup of water.

I take a sip and swallow hard. "I don't want to jump to conclusions, but I might be pregnant." My gaze flits between Nora and Rylee. Both their jaws are agape.

Rylee breaks the silence first. "How do you know?"

"I'm not entirely sure when I had my last period, and then there's been a couple of times where I just randomly get nauseous. I thought nothing of it until now."

Her eyes light up, and she rushes past us. She pulls out a jar of pickles from the cooler and twists off the top, then returns to where I'm sitting. She holds it under my nose like smelling salts. "Inhale."

So I do.

"That make you sick?" Rylee asks.

I shake my head.

"Damn. When I was pregnant with Kaelyn, pickles made me nauseous." Rylee screws the lid back on the pickle jar.

Nora rubs her hand on my shoulder in comfort. "It's quiet right now. Why don't you run to the convenience store a few blocks away? And find out for sure?"

Do I want to know? I have to find out eventually, but now? Right now? This second? I'm not mentally prepared to handle whatever the answer may be. Okay. That's a lie. I'm not mentally prepared to handle if the answer is pregnant. "Oh, I don't know. I'd hate to leave work."

"Rylee and I got it. Unless you want to agonize about it for the rest of the night?" She lifts an eyebrow.

Ugh. I hate that she's right. This will nag at me all night. I spare a glance at Nora and then at Rylee, and she nods.

"It's better to know sooner than later," Rylee says.

I blow out a deep breath. I wish Lach was here with me. Then again, I'd also need to tell him about the possible baby situation. "Okay, I'll be right back."

Fifteen minutes later, I return to Porter's with two pregnancy test boxes. Four tests total. Pushing through the bathroom door, I lock myself into a stall. The Porter's bathroom isn't my first choice to find out if I'm pregnant, but at least it could make for a funny story later. I tear into the first box and read the instructions carefully. Front and back. Twice. Peeing on a stick shouldn't be difficult, but leave it to me to screw it up. I slide my jeans to my ankles and sit on the toilet. With all the tests in one hand, I pluck one from the bouquet and hold it between my legs. I continue with each test until they're all thoroughly peed on, with the exception of the fourth. That one only has a few dribbles. My bladder can only hold so much pee, and three tests were my max. Carefully, I place the tests on the back of the toilet before I flush and wash my hands. Returning to the stall, I wait.

Anything and everything races through my mind all at once. It's streaks of thoughts. Nothing is clear. I rest my shoulder against the cool metal stall. My head flops to the side, hitting the metal with a thud. What if I am pregnant? I'd have to tell Lach that he's going to be a dad. I'd have to tell my brother he's going to be an uncle. But the biggest bomb is the dad is his best friend. This is certainly not the way I wanted to tell him. Two birds, I suppose. I check the time on my phone. Three minutes have passed. My heart thunders in my chest as I finally work up the courage to look at the tests. Thankfully, I got the ones that say "pregnant" or "not pregnant" for easy deciphering. I march down the line. Pregnant. Pregnant. Not pregnant. Pregnant. Fuck. Of course, I wasn't paying attention and don't know if the not pregnant is the last one that only got a few drops. I don't know what's worse. I don't know if this makes me more or less anxious because I still may be pregnant. Or not pregnant. It's like I'm jumping back on the merry-go-round.

The outside door opens and softly closes. "Hey, is everything okay?" Nora asks.

I step out of the stall, pregnancy tests in hand, and I fan them out in front of her. She scans each one. Her eyes light up as she moves down each one until she gets to the last.

"There is a three out of four chance I'm pregnant."

"Oh. What are you going to do?" Nora glances up at me, eyes soft with concern.

Everything in my stomach turns sour. "I'm not sure. I don't want to say anything to Lach, just in case I'm not. But I don't want to not tell him if I am."

"I'm sorry, Eve, that's definitely a tough position to be in." Her hand rests on my forearm.

It's soft and comforting. I can't imagine if I had to go through this alone. Surely, that's how it would be if I were still in Knoxville. Then there's our non-date tomorrow. There's no reason to alarm him with news I may be pregnant if I'm not. "I should go to the doctor and just find out for sure."

"That might be for the best."

I rip off a piece of paper towel and wrap up the pregnancy tests. Nora exits the bathroom, and I follow behind her. Before going back to the bar, I stop in the employee room and shove the tests in my purse. I gently push the metal locker door closed. It latches with a click. I've always wanted kids. But I also wanted to be married and living in a house, not shacked up in my brother's spare bedroom. Right now is certainly not the ideal time. I rest a hand on my stomach. If I am, I'll make the best out of it.

I push everything about being pregnant to the side. I don't know what to say or how to say it because I'm not one hundred percent sure how he's going to react. And that's what terrifies me the most. Right after having to tell Jake I'm pregnant with his best friend's baby. Tomorrow before our date, I'll schedule an appointment with a doctor to confirm the pregnancy or not. I never thought our first date would technically be a fake date. But everything else about our relationship has been unconventional, so... Why not this?

Chapter 29

STFUATTDLAGG

Lach

My leg bounces as I sit on the couch, waiting for Eve. I never expected to be this nervous to go on a date. Granted, this is the first date I've ever been on. It was never my thing. Mostly because I never made it my thing. I hope she enjoys what I have planned. The clicking of heels on the wood floor draws my attention. When I glance over my shoulder, my heart stops. Holy shit. I wipe my hands on my jeans before rising to my feet and spinning around. Eve saunters into the living room and rounds the end of the couch. Her rust-colored dress sways to the rhythm of her hips.

"Is this okay for our date?" She twirls. The hem of her dress flares around her knees, the fabric light and airy against her skin.

My gaze drops from her blonde hair draped over her shoulder, over the curve of her hips, to her toned legs and high-heeled boots. After picking my jaw off the floor, I meet her gaze. "You look absolutely stunning."

She smiles. "I'm assuming we're not going for a hike through the woods or anything."

I laugh. "No. Not this time. But maybe the next."

"Oh. You think you'll get another date?" She quirks an eyebrow.

"With the date I have planned, you'll be begging me for another before it's even over."

She rolls her eyes but can't keep the smile off her face. "Those are some big words. You better live up to them. Also, is this too much? I didn't know what to wear." She slides her hands down her torso, smoothing out her dress.

"It's perfect. If anything, I'm underdressed." I glance down at my white t-shirt, maroon hoodie, and jeans.

"It fits you." She brushes her hand down my chest, twirling the hood string around her finger. "So, it's perfect." She lifts her chin, her bright hazel eyes meeting mine.

Warmth radiates through my entire body. With a single look, she can bring me to my knees. What is happening? And why do I never want it to end? I want to touch her. Feel her warm, silky skin against mine. My fingers twitch with the need to pull her to my chest. I lift my hand—

"What are you two doing tonight?" Jake strolls into the living room.

I drop my hand and jump away from Eve. "Oh, um…" I push my hand through my hair.

"We have a date," Eve interrupts. "Nora asked us if we could beta test her new app to ensure everything runs smoothly. She said it would be more authentic if we actually went out."

Jake's silent for a few beats. I slide my palms over my

jeans. I hope he buys it even though it is kind of the truth. Though we are treating our fake date like a real one.

"What are you two going to do?" He looks from Eve to me.

"Yeah, Lach. What are we going to do?" Eve crosses her arms over her chest and tilts her head, a smirk teasing her lips.

"Um… Get a bite to eat. I was thinking fast food." My gaze meets hers, and I give her the same teasing smirk. "The burger place has a really great value menu. Also, I was thinking we should go dutch."

A laugh bubbles out of her. "Oh, you're a real charmer."

"That's not all. While eating our two-dollar hamburgers because dollar menus don't exist anymore, I'll tell you about all my prior hookups and then ask you if you have a best friend you could introduce me to."

"Well, this seems like the best. Date. Ever." Eve claps along like a cheerleader at the last words.

"I thought so." The corner of my mouth tips up into a half smile.

"Alright, well, yeah, you guys have fun with that." Jake walks past us, takes a seat on the couch, and reaches for the remote.

I escort Eve to the back door. I grab her coat and hold it up for her as she slides her arms inside.

"Such the gentleman." She untucks her hair from the collar.

"I figured I should do something nice before this date goes sideways." I twist the doorknob.

"Wait." She stares at me, then the door, and back at me. "Are you going to get a coat? It's like twenty degrees outside."

I tug at the collar of my hoodie. "That's what this is for?"

"Oh, that's right. I'm in Minnesota." She points at my jeans. "I'm surprised you're not wearing shorts right now, seeing that it's above zero."

"I can change if you want." I lift my brows. It's not uncommon to see mostly guys in shorts and occasionally sandals in the dead of winter. Sometimes, we'll go weeks with subzero temperatures, so when there isn't a negative sign in front of the number and your nostrils don't freeze on the first inhale, it can feel like a heat wave.

She shakes her head, fighting the smile that pulls at her lips. "Let's go, my little penguin. Our date awaits."

I pull the door open, and as she walks past me, I whisper, "This will be the best date ever."

Her head snaps to me, and she smiles. When we reach my truck, I open the door for her. Might as well continue with the chivalry. Once she's seated, I round the hood before getting into the driver's seat.

After I start the engine, she twists to face me. "So seriously, where are we going?"

"Don't like surprises?"

"I didn't know it was supposed to be a surprise."

I reach across the center console and hook my pinky around hers, resting on her lap. "Well, if you must know, we're going to—"

"No! Keep it a surprise." I glance at her. Even in the dark cab, her smile shines brightly. I can no longer hold back my own smile.

After driving for fifteen minutes, we arrive on the other side of town. I park my truck in an empty parking spot on the street. Eve peers out the side window and then back at me, her brows furrowed. At the same time, both our phones chime with an incoming message. I check the notifications, and it's from the OneDate app.

"It's asking me if I want to turn on my location." Eve turns to face me.

"Mine too."

Which one did you pick?" she asks.

"I said no. I don't want them to know where I'm taking you. What did you pick?"

"Yes. We're parked outside a hardware store." She hikes her thumb at the window. "I've watched a lot of *Criminal Minds*." She flashes me a smile.

"Alright. That's fair. But I'll have you know our date isn't to the hardware store. I save that for my second dates." I exit the truck and meet her on the sidewalk.

A gust of icy wind blows past us. Eve tightens her coat around her. "So now it's time I ask, where are we going? Because I'm certainly not dressed for the outdoor temps."

I don't say anything, still wanting to keep the secret a few seconds longer. Instead, I wrap my arm around her shoulder and tuck her into my side. One: to keep her warm, and two: I love having her next to me. We pass the window display of fake snow and shovels at the hardware store and come to a festive display of Christmas lights, a tree, and stocking filled to the brim with books. We walk side by side for a few steps until I release her, grab the cold metal bar, and open the door.

She freezes, and then her eyes grow wide. "Okay, this is starting off to be the best date ever."

"I told you."

Illuminated by a soft glow, a large sign hanging on the wall in front of us reads The Book Bar. A crisp scent mixed with vanilla lingers in the air. Luckily, it's a quiet evening, and we might get the place to ourselves. Less prying eyes means I can treat this like a real date.

Leaning down, I whisper, "Get whatever you'd like. My treat."

"Wait!" Her head snaps to me. "Our date is to a bookstore? And you're buying me whatever I want?"

"Yeah." I panic. She hates it. It's the worst date idea ever. Fucking Nora and her stupid ideas. "Is that a terrible date idea?"

"This truly is the best. Date. Ever!" she squeals before yanking on my hand, dragging me behind her as we hustle toward a shelf labeled New Releases. She peruses several shelves before reading the back of a few books. After the new release section, we wander down a few aisles until Eve stops at another bookshelf. Again, she picks one up and thumbs through it.

I lean against the shelf next to her. "Do you read a lot of books?"

She replaces the book and grabs another. "Depends. I probably get through like four or five a month. How about you?" Her gaze meets mine.

"I can't say I do a lot of reading. I just never got into it."

"I started reading in high school and then got into reading romance. I'm a sucker for a happily ever after. Although my actual love life suggests otherwise." She chuckles softly.

"What are those books about?" I nod to the stack of books tucked against her body.

"This one," she holds up the book with a blue cover, "is a workplace romance where two coworkers end up on a dating app, and they don't know that they're talking to each other. But eventually, he finds out before she does, and it blows up from there." She holds up another with a yellow cover. "This one is about two coworkers who hate each other because they are competing for the same promotion but get stranded together while on a work trip. They work out their differences. In bed. And the best part —he ties her up using his bow ties."

"That sounds hot." I spin to face her and grab the stack of books from her hands. Placing them on the floor, I stand in front of her. Bending down, I run the tip of my nose over her cheek until my lips are at the shell of her ear. "Does it go something like this?" I say so only she can hear. I slide a hand down her waist and onto her hip. Her breath hitches as she waits for my next move. I grab her hand and slowly lift it above her head. Once it's exactly where I want it, I secure it against the bookshelf with my fingers wrapped around her delicate wrist. I drag my bottom lip across her cheek, not kissing her but light enough so she knows I'm here. I extend my pinky until I reach hers, wrapping it underneath. Her breath hitches.

She peers up at me through her lashes. Her chest rises and falls with each passing second, her breath hitching with every inhale. "Almost." Her warm breath fans across my cheek. "You're missing the bow ties."

"I don't need bow ties." Still pinning her hand to the bookcase, I inch closer. My chest grazes hers. I drag my lips across her cheek until I reach the shell of her ear. "All I need are my hands, and I'd have you moaning in pleasure." Flashbacks of the night in the hotel room flit through my mind. I could hike her leg over my hip and slide my hand under the hem of her dress. My fingers would slide against her dripping wet, bare pussy until I reach her opening and thrust inside her. Her moans and whimpers would fill the entire store. Shit. Store. We're in a store. I drop her hand. "I'm going to go find the bathroom."

She blows out a slow breath. "To take care of that?"

She nods at my crotch, where my hard dick is straining against the zipper of my jeans.

"Something like that."

"Okay." A smile plays on her lips. "Come find me when you're finished."

I press my lips to hers in a chaste kiss, even though I'd much rather never let go. Pulling away, I glance over my shoulder to confirm we're still alone before reaching down and adjusting myself not only for comfort but in case I run into anyone. Having a hard-on is never a good way to introduce yourself. I wander around the outer perimeter of the store until I find the restroom sign. After washing my hands, I return to the same spot I left Eve, but the aisle's empty. I meander through the store, scanning all the rows until I find her perusing a row of books on the shelf. Slowly and carefully, I tiptoe down the aisle until I'm right behind her. I whisper, "What are you looking for?"

She jumps and spins around, clutching her chest. "Oh! Nothing!" She exhales a deep breath. "I—I was just walking around, waiting for you."

I glance up at the sign above the bookshelves. "In parenting?"

Her gaze follows mine before falling. A dusting of pink covers her cheeks. "Oh, is that where I am? I guess I got lost trying to find photography. I'm ready to check out." She holds up the stack of books she found.

I grab the books from her and carry them to the counter. Eve gets distracted and stops at a table of more books and a variety of knickknacks. I can't help the smile that takes over. She makes me so fucking happy. When I reach the counter, an older woman with light gray hair greets me with a friendly smile of her own. The name on her nametag reads Sandy.

She glances at Eve and then back at me. "At the risk of

sounding presumptuous, have you ever thought about proposing in a bookstore?" She beams up at me, her eyes crinkling in the corners.

I freeze, unsure if I heard her right. "Um. This is our first date."

"Oh gosh. I'm sorry. By the way you two have interacted with each other for the past hour, I would have thought you'd known each other for years." She grabs the books and starts scanning them. The beeping from the scanner matches the steady thump of my heartbeat.

"Yeah. It's complicated."

She stops and meets my gaze. "The best love stories that last usually are."

Is that what we are? A love story? Love has never been on my radar. Never something I tried to find. Something I always considered unattainable. At least for me. Fuck.

The beeping resumes, pulling me from my thoughts. "If you ever consider proposing, I have the perfect spot." She points to a sign behind me.

I turn around, following the invisible line. Sure enough, on the wall hangs a sign with giant script letters that reads Love Blooms Here.

"I also give a twenty percent discount on an engaged couple's purchase."

"Thanks. I'll consider that," I say because what else am I supposed to say? I came here for a date, and now this woman is talking about love and engagements.

"Oh, can I get this too?" Eve stands next to me, holding up a bookmark with bold, black letters printed on it. STFUATTDLAGG.

"Yeah." I take the bookmark and slide it across the counter.

"Thank you." Eve beams up at me.

"What does that mean, anyway?"

"I'll let you know later." Eve runs her hand down my arm.

"It stands for shut the fuck up and take this dick like a good girl," the woman behind the counter nonchalantly spouts out.

My eyes widen, along with Eve's. Not only was I not expecting it to mean that, but hearing it come from a woman who's someone's grandma was completely unexpected. I laugh/cough into my fist while Eve bites her lips together. The woman finishes ringing up the purchase, and I pass her my credit card. She drops the receipt into the bag and wishes us a great night.

Once we're outside, both of us burst out laughing.

"I can't believe that just happened. That made my entire day. No, week." Eve rests a hand on her stomach as she continues to laugh.

"Oddly enough, it wasn't the only bizarre thing she said to me."

She turns to face me, walking backward. "Do share."

"First, she asked me if I was going to propose because they have a section dedicated for proposals. And that I'd get a twenty-percent discount if I did."

Eve stops dead in her tracks, and I almost crash into her. "What's wrong?"

"Why didn't you get down on one knee?"

My heart stops beating.

"You could have saved yourself twenty percent?"

And my heart starts again. "Do you want to go back?" I hike my thumb behind us. "I don't have a ring, but maybe I can fashion one together. There's the hardware store next door."

She spins back around and leans against me. "Maybe next time. The spontaneity is over now."

When we reach my truck, I open her door. She climbs

in, and I pass her the bag. Before closing it, I lean in. "I know you had your heart set on fast food, but I hope you enjoyed the date."

Her cold fingertips caress my cheeks. "Best. Date. Ever." She leans in and kisses me. She pulls away a fraction. Her lips move against mine as she says, "There's always the drive-thru."

I laugh. "I knew you wanted a hamburger."

"Someone forgot to check if the date included food or not."

I shrug. "You got me. Let's go get you a hamburger."

"Can we make it a cheeseburger?"

"Sure." I close the door and a muffled "And fries!" sounds from inside my truck.

On the drive back to Jake's we dig into our fast food. I purposely take the long way so I can have a few extra minutes with Eve. When we return to the house, I throw away our garbage and flop down on the couch, taking the middle cushion. Eve takes the spot next to me. With her back against the armrest, she throws her legs across my lap.

"So, what did you think of the app?"

I run my hands over her smooth bare legs. "I think this is a really great idea."

"Me too. We have so many hookup apps. It's nice that there's something for when you need a legitimate date for a one-off event."

"I think this will do really well."

"I think so too."

"Have you tried any of those hookup apps?"

She shakes her head. "No. I never had a reason to try them. For the most part, I always had a boyfriend. Even between my previous ex and Pax, I would go out on sporadic dates. Some lasted longer than others. What about you?"

"Late-night booty calls through an app… I didn't need them."

She sits up, laughing. "Of course you didn't."

"And I wasn't sleeping with anyone who talked to me either if that's what you're wondering."

"And Rachel?" She lifts a brow.

"I never slept with Rachel. On many occasions, she tried, but I was never interested." I inch my hand under the hem of her dress and up her thigh. "Now, I have you."

She throws her head back in laughter. "Nice save. Either way, your past is your past. No judgment. But I'm excited to be part of your present." Her fingers play with a crease in her cotton dress. "Speaking of the future," she scoots closer to me, her eyes fixed on her lap, "There's something I need—"

Rustling from the back door sounds through the house. Eve scampers off my lap, kicking me in the thigh in the process. I flinch and rub the spot. She cringes and mouths "sorry" before sitting on the opposite end of the couch, crossing her leg away from me. I jump up and scoot to the other side, leaning away from her.

Jake enters the living room. The recliner glides forward as he leans against the back. "How was your non-date date?"

"Good," Eve replies.

"Great," I say at the same time.

He waits for us to elaborate, but all we give him is silence. "Thanks for sparing me the details." He pushes himself to his full height. "I'm going to jump in the shower and go to bed."

"Okay. Good night," Eve says.

Both of us track Jake as he exits the living room. Once he's out of sight, my shoulders deflate. I turn my head to face Eve. "Another close call." She nods. "What did you want to say earlier? Before Jake came home."

"Oh. Um." She sits up on the couch, lifting her legs onto the cushion and crawling toward me. She glances over the back of the couch to make sure Jake isn't standing there. When she's next to me, she stops and clasps her hands across my cheeks and presses her lips to mine in a soft kiss. She backs away a fraction of an inch. "I wanted to say thank you for the most amazing date."

"You're welcome. The next one will be for real." As long as I can tell Jake, I might possibly be, a tiny bit, in love with his sister. Fuck me.

Chapter 30

DAMN YOU, TWO PERCENT

Eve

People say your life flashes before your eyes when you're in a life-or-death situation. I'm going on record to say the same thing happens while you're waiting on the results to confirm a pregnancy. The only difference is instead of a flash, you get a several-minute montage of everything you did wrong in your life, and somehow, you need to teach your child not to make the same mistakes. It's not very encouraging. Especially as I lay on the cold vinyl pad with paper that crinkles every time I breathe.

Sofia, the middle-aged obstetrician with sleek black hair cut at her shoulders, glances up at me. "The urine test says you're pregnant, but let's do a transvaginal ultrasound to confirm."

My heart jumps to my throat. The home pregnancy tests I took told me I'm pregnant, except for the rogue one, which I was secretly hoping was the one telling the truth. Lach and I have always used protection. But the box says they're only ninety-eight percent effective. Damn you, two percent.

"Will you be able to tell how far along I am?"

"The ultrasound will give us a clearer picture of what's happening." She passes me a paper gown. "I need you to change into this. You can keep your shirt on but remove everything else. I'll be back in a few minutes."

I nod. She exits the room, and the door clicks shut behind her. I strip out of my pants and underwear and tie the gown around my back. I hoist myself onto the exam bed. The paper crinkles under my weight. Glancing around the room, posters of babies and fetuses fill my vision. I wish Lach was here with me right now, holding my hand and reassuring me everything will be okay. My head snaps up when there's a knock, and Sofia returns.

"Are you ready?"

"Yes." The nervousness in my voice is palpable.

I watch as she turns a machine on, and it springs to life. She holds a white wand in the air and rolls a condom down its length. When it's secure, she squirts gel on the shaft and rubs it around. "This might be a little cold."

I flinch as she inserts the wand. It is nothing like Charlie Cumming. Can't they put that shit in the microwave or something? They make warming lube; surely, they can make warming gel. There's a slight pressure as she moves the wand around. Then I hear it. A steady, whooshing sound fills the room. I roll my head to the side. All thoughts of Sofia between my legs with a wand shoved up my vagina dissipate. The grainy black-and-white screen shows a tiny, kidney-bean-shaped baby. My baby. I'm going to be a mom.

"It looks like you're about twelve weeks." Sofia continues to stir the wand inside me.

Quickly, I do the math in my head. Twelve weeks.

That's three months. Son of a bitch. I count and recount the weeks in my head because I don't want the math to be mathing. A lead weight drops in the pit of my stomach. It's not Lach's. I've only known him for almost two. There were only two times we got caught up in the moment and didn't use a condom, and one of those times was right before leaving for Florida.

"Is everything okay?" Sofia asks. She must have noticed my body tense or my expression gave it away.

"Yeah. Just nervous. It's a lot to take in right now." I'm on the verge of a slight panic attack because Lach is not the father. Bag of Dicks is.

"That's understandable."

Her warm smile does nothing to soothe the five-alarm freak-out I'm having inside.

Sofia continues to talk, but I'm not listening. I can't listen. There are too many thoughts racing through my mind, mostly that I'm pregnant with Fuckface's baby. My former boss. My married ex-boyfriend. Shit's going to get messier than an explosive dirty diaper. I have to tell Lach, the man I've fallen head over heels for, that I'm pregnant with someone else's baby. He has every right to leave because who wants to be with a woman who's pregnant with another man's baby? Tears well up in the corners of my eyes. Thoughts of him leaving rush through my head and slam into my heart like a freight train. I blink to keep them from falling. On top of telling Lach, I need to tell Jake. I don't know whether to be disappointed or relieved. I'm disappointed that I have to tell Lach it's not his, and on the other hand, I'm relieved I don't have to tell Jake I'm pregnant with his best friend's child. But telling him I'm pregnant with my cheating asshole ex's child isn't any better. The entire situation is a hundred times worse.

I finish the appointment and schedule another

ultrasound for twenty weeks. Sofia said I should hear in about twenty-four hours if there are any concerns. From the clinic back to the house, I'm on autopilot. I knew things were going to be hard, but this puts hard to shame. I park my car at the back of the house, and zombie walk inside. If anyone was home and spoke to me, I wouldn't have noticed. When I reach my room, I close the door and flop down on my bed. Is it too much to ask for the universe to stop shitting on me for five minutes? Every time I take a step forward, life pushes me back ten. And each time it gets harder and harder to claw myself back.

I can't string Lach along now that I know for sure, especially since it's not his. It's not fair to him. Jake's working the closing shift tonight, and Lach should be home in a couple of hours. That gives me one hundred and twenty minutes to stew on how I'm going to tell him. I sit on the couch, my knee bouncing a mile a minute. I check the time on my phone for the fiftieth time. It's 6:24 p.m. The drive from Porter's to here is only about ten minutes. The backdoor creaks open, the sound barely audible over the thumping in my ears. I jump to my feet and spin around. With a hand still on the doorknob, Lach glances up, and our eyes connect. He drops his hand, and instead of going to the basement, he struts into the living room.

"What's wrong?" His eyes soften with concern as he runs his hand over my shoulder and down my arm. His touch is gentle and soft and more than I deserve right now.

I exhale the air from my cheeks. "I don't know if you want to sit for this." I motion at the couch. "Maybe stand. I don't know."

"Eve. What's wrong?" He wraps an arm around my waist and pulls me toward him, but I spin out of his grasp. His hand falls to his side, and his brows pinch together.

I wrap my arms around myself. "I need to tell you

something, and I don't know how to tell you, so I'm just going to say it." My heart is a jackhammer in my chest, each beat a drum against my ribs as my palms grow slick with sweat.

"Eve. What is it?" His forehead wrinkles.

Slowly, I lift my chin and meet his gaze. "I'm pregnant."

Chapter 31

A UNITED FRONT

Lach

I can't move. Fifty-ton concrete blocks are strapped to my feet. She's pregnant. I'm going to be a dad. Diaper changes. Late-night feedings. This isn't something I ever expected to happen. It certainly wasn't planned. Oddly enough, I don't have the urge to flee. I'm more excited than apprehensive, maybe because it's with Eve.

"Shit, that came out wrong."

Eve's voice yanks me back to reality.

"You're not the father."

All the previous hope and excitement plummets off a cliff. I rear back, needing space between us.

Her eyes widen in terror. "Oh god, I'm ruining this." She pauses, pressing her lips together. "I'm pregnant. And I got pregnant before I met you. It's my ex-boyfriend's."

Fuck. She said words, but I'm still fully digesting them. "The married boss?"

She nods slowly, her eyes glistening with unshed tears.

She's pregnant with her ex's baby. What does that mean for us? "Are you getting back together with him?"

"Hell no. There is no chance Pax and I will ever be a thing again. I haven't even told him yet." Her gaze drops to the floor, and she wrings her fingers together. "I know this isn't what you signed up for. Hell, it isn't what I signed up for." Slowly, her chin lifts, and her eyes connect with mine. "But there's nothing I can do about it. I know this is a lot, and this baby isn't your responsibility, so I want to give you an out. A clean break. No judgment."

Do I abandon the woman who's become my anchor, the only person who truly sees me, or do I stay and give her everything she needs, knowing I need her just as desperately? The silence of the decision weighs heavily. It's obvious there's only one choice. I grab her hand, running my fingers over her soft ones. Tears well in the corners of her bright hazel eyes as she looks up, meeting my gaze. I raise my other hand and cup her cheek. A lone tear tracks down her cheek, and I brush it away with my thumb.

"What if… I don't want an out?" Her eyes drift closed, and she leans into my palm. "I'm not going anywhere. I need you just as much as the baby needs you. My life would be nothing without you in it. It has been nothing without you."

Tears roll down her cheeks like an open faucet, and I wipe them away with my fingers. "I need you too, Lach. I need you so much," she whispers, her voice trembling with desperation. She throws her arms around my neck and buries her head against my chest.

I wrap one arm around her waist and the other around her shoulder. My fingertips brush over her silky strands. "We got this, Sunflower. We got this." I press a kiss to the top of her head and just hold her in my arms, giving her all the comfort because I finally found my place in the world. With a finger under her chin, I force her to meet my gaze. "I want to be with you, no matter the circumstances."

Her mouth curves into a smile, her body shaking with quiet hiccups as she dries her tears. "What did I do to deserve you?"

"I could ask the same." My palms rest against her cheeks. She releases a deep exhale, and her shoulders drop. I thought we were in a good spot. How many more truth bombs does she have left to drop?

"Alright, so not only do we have to tell Jake we're seeing each other, but I also have to tell him I'm pregnant with my ex-boyfriend's baby. Should we dump it on him all at once? Or sprinkle it on him in tiny doses? Technically, it would be two sprinkles."

If I would have just told Jake about me and Eve, we would only be in half this situation.

"I'm really thinking this should be a tag-team effort now. A united front."

I nod. "I agree. You got my back. I got yours."

"Always. The next question is when? Because there will come a time when I won't be able to conceal anything under a baggy t-shirt." She rests a hand on her flat belly.

If she didn't say anything, I would have never known she was pregnant. She's going to be an amazing mom. Her patience at the bar far exceeds mine. There isn't anywhere else, besides by her side, that I'd rather be.

She slides her hand down my arm, drawing my attention. "We still have a few hours alone." She jerks her head toward her room.

"You don't need to tell me twice."

I lean against the headboard, the blanket draped over my waist, and I have Eve tucked against my side, her head resting against my stomach. I'm still half comatose from the orgasm. Sex with Eve is like a fine wine. It gets better the longer we're together. Is what we're doing reckless? Absofuckinglutely. Right now, I have no desire to leave her bed. She has a door. The basement doesn't. I'll sneak out in the morning, but in the meantime, I'm going to enjoy having her warm body snuggled against mine. It's something we rarely get, but hopefully, that will change. First, I need to get a few things in order. As Eve softly snores, I grab my phone and pull up the web browser. With one hand, since Eve currently holds my other captive, I type on my phone and scroll through several pages before blonde hair tickles my side.

Eve groans before peering up at me. "What are you doing? And why are you still awake?" Her warm breath skates across my bare skin.

"Looking for jobs."

Her brows pinch together. "Why?"

"I'm preparing for the aftermath of when we tell Jake about us."

Eve sits up, stifling a yawn. She leans against the headboard next to me, linking her arm with mine and resting her head against my shoulder. "You think he's going to fire you?"

I want this all the time. Snuggled in bed with Eve next to me. Not this sneaking-around, teenager bullshit. I only have myself to blame when I've had many opportunities to tell Jake but failed. Miserably. "It's a possibility. I'll definitely have to search for a new place to live sooner rather than later. That's next on my agenda."

"You're his best friend. He's not going to fire you."

I set my phone down on the bed next to me. "Yeah, I'm not confident he won't."

"Look, I know he's going to be a little angry." I raise an eyebrow. She huffs. "Maybe a lot angry. But there's no way he's going to fire you. I'll make sure of that."

"I appreciate you looking out for me." I press a kiss to the top of her head. The coconut scent of her shampoo is the only thing comforting to me. "I should have told Jake about us weeks ago."

"I could have easily told him too. He means a lot to both of us, and neither of us wants to hurt him."

"I guess we'll just have to wait and see how it plays out."

"What kind of apartment are you looking for?"

"I don't know. Dessa once mentioned there are some nice two-bedroom townhomes in her neighborhood that even include a yard."

Eve's body tenses next to me. "Why do you need two bedrooms and a yard?"

I glance down at her, and she meets my gaze. Curiosity swirls in her irises. "Because if we're doing this, I want to do it right."

All the color drains from her face. "You want me to move in with you?"

Never in my life have I lived with a woman. I've always liked my space, but deep in my gut, this feels right. Not only would I get to spend all my nights falling asleep next to her, but I can be there and take care of her and the baby. And that feels right. I know what it's like to grow up without parents. To not have a stable home. If I can help it, I want to make sure Eve's baby doesn't have to endure half of that. "Only if you want to. Unless you have your heart set on living with Jake, but I want to give you options."

She taps her chin. Cold air rushes under the blanket as she lifts the corner to straddle my lap. Her fingers run up my chest and over my shoulders. "Live with my ultra-grumpy brother or with his amazing, smart, incredibly sexy best friend? How will I ever decide?"

I slide my hands around her back, holding her in place. "I have a way for you to decide." Her fingers comb through my hair. I love her hands on me. It doesn't matter where. Her touch sparks hope inside me.

"What's that?"

"One orgasm for no and two orgasms for yes."

She throws her head back in laughter. "How can I argue with that decision-making?"

"Exactly." I slide my hand up to the back of her head. I lift my chin and press my lips to hers.

I woke up at 6 a.m. and sneaked out of Eve's room. I hated leaving her and her warm, naked body pressed against mine. But Jake would have surely caught us if I didn't leave. Of course, I couldn't fall back asleep, so I sat in bed and sketched. The pencil gliding across the paper always soothes me and drowns out all the other noise in my head. I could always escape to drawing. I can spend hours sketching anything and everything, finding inspiration in whatever's in front of me. Currently, I'm sketching a sunflower breaking through concrete. As of late, most of my sketches have been of sunflowers.

Next to me, on the bed, my phone buzzes with an incoming message. I pick it up, and Eve's name flashes on the screen.

EVE

I'm so sad you had to leave this morning.

LACH

Same. Did I wake you up?

EVE

Yeah. It got cold real quick once you left. I
didn't want to say anything because I knew
you'd stay, and climbing out my bedroom
window might have been the only way to
escape.

LACH

I would have done it for you.

EVE

I know, but you were in your boxer briefs,
and there's snow.

LACH

Since someone kept me up late last night,
I'm going to take a nap before my shift
later.

EVE

Okay. I'm going to try not to make awkward
eye contact with my brother. Wish me luck.

LACH

Good luck, Sunflower.

I'm standing behind the bar at Porter's when the front
door opens. A familiar face emerges, a dusting of snow
covering his shoulders. He finds an empty stool at the bar a
few feet away from me. He shrugs out of his coat and

neatly hangs it over the back of the stool. I wait a few minutes, expecting the rest of the Single Bros. Life crew to follow, but no one comes. I mosey to where he's seated.

"Hey, Miles. What can I get you?" I grab a cardboard coaster and slide it toward him.

"Actually, I was wondering if Rylee was working?" He adjusts his black-rimmed glasses.

"No. She's not here."

His shoulders drop, a frown falling on his face. "I know she's good with advice, and I could really use some right now."

He looks like someone just stole his puppy. Rylee always gives straight-to-the-point advice. It can't be that hard, right? I rest my palms on the bar and lock my elbows. "Lay it on me. Maybe I can help."

"There's a girl I like."

Oh fuck. If he's looking for dating advice, I'm the last person he wants to listen to, seeing as how I'm in my own dating predicament myself. I nod along anyway.

"And I've gone out with her twice. But somehow, the second date went worse than the first. I don't know what to do. I have a feeling I only have one more shot with her. If I don't do it right, she'll never want to go out with me again."

"How do you know that's the case?"

He rests his elbows on the bar. "Because if I screw it up, I wouldn't want to go out with me. So I really need to wow her."

Color me curious. I wonder what he considers a bad date. Did he spill a drink on his shirt? Food stuck in his teeth? Maybe he had a streamer of toilet paper stuck on his shoe after using the restroom? The perk of not dating: you don't have bad dates. "How bad could the dates have been?"

"Our first date turned into a double date with my parents. Not by choice. They happened to be at the same restaurant I took her to. That was awkward, especially when my mom pulled out baby pictures she had in her purse. After the date, I convinced myself I wouldn't get a second date, but she said yes. For the second date, I made sure my parents had plans, so I could stay as far away from them as possible. I was so nervous about making it the best date that I rambled about anything and everything. Did you know sea cucumbers can expel their internal organs to ward off predators?"

I shake my head.

"Neither did she. But she does now."

I blow out a deep breath. We now know the downfall of knowing random facts. This is going to require a beer. Pushing myself to my full height, I grab a pint glass and fill it with beer from the tap. Since he's been in here several times, I know what he drinks. I place the full glass on the coaster. "It's on me."

He eyes the beer before reaching for it and taking a sip. "Thank you."

What do I tell him? It's obvious he needs help, but I'm not the one who should give it to him. Where's Rylee when you need her? I can't stall much longer. By then, he'll have finished his beer. Dates. Dates. Dates. OneDate. I perk up. "I think I know what your problem is. You need to build up some confidence for when you go out on your dates."

"And how do I do that?"

"Nora's creating a dating app—"

"I have the date. I just need to not have her hate me by the end."

"No. This isn't a traditional dating app." I pull out my phone and unlock the screen. I click on the app, and my profile pops up. "This app is for when someone needs a date to a function but doesn't have one. It's no strings attached. No expectations. You just show up as someone's date. You could use it to go on some practice dates. Get comfortable dating without all the pressure."

He checks out my profile and some of the menu options while nodding. "How do I join?"

He passes back my phone, and I shove it in my pocket. "You'll have to talk to Nora. It's still in beta testing, but it should be live soon. I'm sure she'll hook you up."

"Thanks. OneDate seems like it could be the cure to my problem."

I'm a fucking genius. Move over, Rylee. There's a new advice giver in town. Just kidding. Rylee can keep the position. This shit's stressful. On the note of providing amazing advice, I really wish someone could give me some in return. It's getting harder and harder the longer we wait to tell Jake.

Chapter 32

CALLING MR. SHART

Eve

Have you ever been forced to do something you don't want to do, but it's the responsible thing to do? This is me. I'm going on record to say that adulting sucks. All I want to do is stomp my feet, cross my arms, pout, and say no. It worked when I was five. Why can't it work now? Over the past two weeks, my anxiety skyrocketed every time I thought about picking up the phone. Life would be so much better if I didn't have to make this phone call. Ugh. Fine. He deserves to know. But I already know what his reaction will be. How could I do this? I'm trying to trap him. It's my fault. Blah. Blah. Fucking blah. Shit Bag doesn't believe in consequences for his actions. Let me point to Exhibit A. Cheating on his wife with me as his girlfriend. Why is this so much harder than when I told Lach I was pregnant? Maybe because I'm dreading having to tell Fuck Nugget he's going to be a daddy. I'd much rather have it be Lach's. Surprise, surprise, life has to punch me in the tit and give me the worst possible human as the baby daddy. I cross my arms over my chest and pout. I need to rip this off like a leg wax strip.

Grabbing my phone from my pocket, I scroll through my contacts until I find his number and unblock him. Calling Mr. Shart flashes on the screen. It rings a few times. I throw up a silent prayer that his voicemail picks up, and I can just leave him a courtesy message. Unfortunately, everything is against me, and he picks up on the fourth ring.

"Eve, I'm so glad you called. I knew we could work this out."

My jaw clenches. "Oh, there's nothing to work out," I seethe. "And I don't think this phone call is one you're expecting."

"Of course I was expecting your call. It's okay to still be in love with me. I feel the same."

He loves me but can't even say it. Ugh! Why the fuck do I care? I don't. This is just one of the many reasons he's a piece of shit. I jump to my feet. If only there was a way I could punch through the phone and wring his neck. "Oh, fuck no! Sorry to burst your overinflated ego. But I'm calling to tell you I'm pregnant." Goodbye, hairy wax strip. "And it's yours." It's silent for a few seconds, which is out of the ordinary for the used douche. I check my phone to make sure he hasn't hung up on me, but the timer continues to tick away.

"What do you mean, pregnant?" His words are a low whisper.

"I'm pregnant, as in with child. A small fetus is growing inside my uterus. It will make its grand appearance in about six months. I'm that kind of pregnant. And unfortunately, it's yours."

"How do you know I'm the father when you were

sleeping around as soon as you left the hotel room in Florida? Or the guy claiming to be your boyfriend?"

I pinch my eyes shut, needing to channel my inner zen. "Based on time of conception, you were the only one I was sleeping with."

"What the fuck, Eve? How could you do this?"

I rear my head back. I shouldn't be surprised this is his take because I called it, but I am. "Excuse me? It takes two people to have a fucking baby, asshole."

"I have a wife," he whispers. "I can't be having a kid with someone else."

I pinch the bridge of my nose as I pace from one side of the living room to the other. "Perhaps you should have thought of that before sticking your dick in me while having a wife."

"What do you want? Money? Five thousand? Ten thousand? My wife can't know about this."

"You're a real dick." I shake my head. While the cash would be nice, the payoff makes me feel cheap. Maybe it's pride, but I would rather do this without his hush money than be paid off. "You want to buy me off now?"

"I may have to pay you in payments to keep it a secret. But I can move some money around in a few accounts—"

"It's called child support. Unless you want to sign your rights over, then you don't have to pay anything." I drop my head to my hand. "Look, I really wish you weren't the father. But you are, unfortunately. Just so you know, I'm more than happy to do this without you. I'd much prefer it that way. But I also can't deny you the right." Even though I wish I could. "I just wanted to tell you because it's the right thing to do." I throw up another silent prayer that Satan's Butthole actually does sign over his rights. That would make things a hell of a lot easier. Bonus. I would never have to deal with him again. You didn't give me my first prayer, you could do me a solid and give me this one.

"Are you moving back?" he asks.

"No. I'm staying in Harbor Highlands. Alright, so there—I told you. Goodbye."

There's nothing but silence on the other end. He says nothing. Since I'm done talking, I press end. Flopping onto the couch, I cover my eyes with my forearm. I'm relieved that's over. I'm stressed as fuck, but relieved, nonetheless. If he wants to be in the baby's life, we'll make it work, but I certainly don't want him in mine.

I still have ninety-nine problems, but telling Fuck Face isn't one of them. Now it's telling Jake, which might be the scariest one of them all since it'll be like a gut punch and a right hook simultaneously. I pick up my phone again and send a message to Lach.

EVE

I told Pax about the pregnancy. Now we wait and see what he wants to do.

LACH

I'm right by your side. Every step of the way.

A flutter fills my chest. Like millions of butterflies taking flight. Why couldn't I have met Lach like five years ago instead of two and a half months ago? Maybe my life would look a lot different from how it looks now. I could still have my studio. This baby could have been Lach's. We could be planning our future together instead of planning how we're going to tell my brother. Hell, I would even take four months—then this baby could be his instead of the dickhead's.

EVE

> Now that we have slain one dragon, how are we going to tell the other one?

LACH

> Abandoning our lives and running away to Europe together isn't an option?

EVE

> As tempting as that sounds, probably not. I hated the cross-country move, and one across the pond sounds less appealing.

LACH

> Worth a shot. We'll talk later and come up with a plan.

EVE

> Then afterward, we get to reward ourselves for creating such an amazing plan.

LACH

> That's kind of what got us here in the first place.

EVE

> Then we've come full circle.

I just hope the circle doesn't explode into a fiery ball of we-fucked-this-up.

Chapter 33

ARE YOU READING MY BOOK?

Lach

I quietly toe open the door to Eve's room, her sweet coconut scent wafting around me. Once inside, I push it closed but don't let it click shut. Jake's working the closing shift for Rylee tonight, and Eve should be home any minute now. Which means we get a few hours alone. This week has been busy. We haven't had more than a few minutes to see each other, let alone talk about our Jake plan. Any spare time I've had has been filled with looking at apartments.

Recently, I started a few freelance drawing projects. I found a freelance marketplace online for creators to open a landing page and upload a portfolio. Within an hour, I had a customer commission a drawing from me. I figured any extra money I can get now will help later. I throw myself onto her bed and kick my feet up. Leaning against the headboard, I link my hands behind my head. On her nightstand, something familiar catches my eye. Reaching over, I grab the paperback. It's the same one she was reading while we were driving back from Tennessee. A bookmark sticks out of the top. I slide my finger over the edge until I reach the spot she left off and start reading. Books have never been my thing, but after a few paragraphs, I'm fully immersed in the story.

"What are you doing?"

The suddenness of Eve's voice startles me, sending the book flying from my grasp to hit the floor with a resounding thud. "Nothing," I spit out. Heat creeps up my neck. Shit. How long have I been reading? I never heard her come into the house, let alone push open the door.

A teasing smile flirts on her lips. "Are you reading my book?"

"No." I shake my head, adjusting myself to sit up on the bed. "Not anymore," I mutter. "How long have you been standing there?"

"About a minute." She saunters into the room and to the side of the bed before bending over and collecting the book off the floor. "Did you pick up where I left off, or did you start from the beginning?" Her thumb flips through the pages like a Rolodex, a smirk on her plump pink lips.

"Wherever you had your bookmark."

Her gaze meets mine. A glint of lust shimmers in her irises. "So the scene where the assistant sneaks under her boss's desk without him knowing." She shoves the bookmark between the pages and sets it on the nightstand. Her fingers grip my knees and move me to the edge of the bed, and I willingly follow her lead. Slowly, she pushes my knees apart while she stares at me through her lashes. As she drops to her knees, her hands glide up my thighs. Her hooded gaze lifts to mine, and her teeth sink into her bottom lip. Her pupils fully dilate as an inferno of heat burns behind them. I don't know where this is going, but I'm fully invested in finding out.

"Well, since you read ahead, you'll have to tell me everything that happens."

Fuck. I bite my lips together. The scene I read was hot as hell. While I was reading it, I imagined Eve doing the same exact thing. I won't lie, my dick got a little hard. And now she wants me to describe the scene. I clear my throat. "Like you said, the assistant sneaks into her boss's office and under his desk. She waits for him to come in, and when he does, he takes a seat in his chair."

Still kneeling on the floor, hands at her sides, she peers up at me. Her voice is soft and seductive, like dripping honey. "And then what happens?"

I swallow. Hard. "He still doesn't know she's there, so he picks up the phone and makes a phone call. That's when he feels her hands slide up his thighs."

Her hands softly glide up and down my thighs, over my jeans.

Oh shit. Is she going to act out the scene? My dick twitches, knowing how the scene ends.

"Then what happens?"

"He quickly glances down," I drop my gaze to Eve, "and notices it's his assistant under his desk. She licks her lips, and her hands continue to slide up to the waistband of his slacks." My heart rate spikes as her hands do the same.

"Grab the book and read it to me." She nods toward the nightstand, a salacious smile gracing her lips.

I reach over and pick up the book. I open it up at the bookmarked spot and start reading at the top of the page. "I lean back in my chair as her dainty fingers work to pop the button of my slacks. The other line picks up. 'Mr. Olsen. I've been expecting your phone call.'" Eve quickly undoes the button on my jeans and slides the zipper down.

My dick is now at full attention. Hard. Thick. Throbbing. She peels the fabric away, giving herself just enough room for her fingers. I continue reading. "I clear my throat, trying to redirect my concentration, but it's hard when my assistant is between my legs rubbing my dick." Eve's fingers caress my dick through my boxer briefs. I pinch my eyes shut, loving her touch.

"Keep reading."

My eyes pop open at Eve's words. Right. The book. "Uh." I stumble to find where I left off. "'Good afternoon, Mr. Parker. I'm glad we can finally connect to talk about the merger.' She hooks her fingers under the waistband and tugs on my slacks, urging me to lift my hips, and I do." Eve mimics every word I'm reading. Her fingers pull on my jeans until they hit the floor. My dick strains against the thin cotton of my boxer briefs. Eve licks her lips as if she's waiting for the first taste of a lollipop. I lift my hand, wanting to run my thumb over her plump pink bottom lip, but when I'm inches away, she pulls back.

"Nuh-uh. There's no touching in the story."

"How do you know?"

"I may have read this book a few times. Keep reading."

I shake my head but pick up where I left off. "Her hand cups me over my boxers. Caressing. Massaging. My head falls back and hits the chair. I mouth, 'Oh fuck,' and this spurs her on even more. Mr. Parker continues to talk, but I don't know what he's saying. All my thoughts are on the woman between my legs jacking me off over my boxers." The words come out shaky and uneven as Eve's hand slides up and down my shaft, her grip alternating between hard and soft. A dark spot forms over the head of my dick as a bead of pre-cum soaks the fabric. "She sits up and runs her tongue over the fabric covering my dick. Her hot breath on me causes me to squirm in my seat. 'Uh. Yes. Mr. Parker.

That sounds great.' I don't know what he said, so I hope it's good." Eve does the same. I groan as her warm breath ignites a spark that shoots a lightning bolt directly to my balls.

"Keep going. We're not even to the good stuff yet," she whispers as she continues to slide her lips over the bulge tenting my boxer briefs.

I refocus my eyes and continue reading. "She pulls at the elastic waistband until my rock-hard dick springs free. For a brief second, she fixes her gaze on the head; then, her eyes slowly rise to meet mine. Her fire-engine red lips curve into a smile. I wonder if her lipstick is going to stain my dick. That's exactly what she wants. For her to leave me with a souvenir that she was in here choking on my dick. Her tongue slides up the underside of my shaft, and I bite back a moan."

The cool air hits my hard dick as it releases from the confines of my boxer briefs, but it's quickly replaced with Eve's warm mouth. Following the words from the book, her tongue slides up my shaft. At the tip, she swirls around the head, lapping at the pre-cum that pools on the top. "Ah fuck. I love your mouth on me."

She releases me from her mouth. "He doesn't say that."

As quickly as she was gone, she's back to bobbing up and down on my dick. My gaze dances over the words as I try to find where I left off. "While she sucks on my dick, her other hand massages my balls. My teeth grit together, fighting a groan. Mr. Parker continues to talk, but I have to pull the phone away so he doesn't hear my heavy breathing."

Eve's hand slides up and down my dick in tandem with her mouth. Using her other hand, she pulls my boxer briefs down to my thighs. While her mouth and hand work together, her other hand cups my balls, gently rolling them in her hand.

"Fuck. Eve."

"We're not even at the good part yet. Keep reading."

Seeing as I read this chapter minutes earlier, I know exactly what happens. I'm on pins and needles, wanting to know how she's going to act it out. I continue reading. "She licks the underside of my shaft as if I'm a lollipop as she gently squeezes my balls. Mr. Parker mentions a three o'clock meeting on Friday, but I don't catch where. I hope my assistant knows. Wait, she's currently between my legs, on her knees, feasting on my dick. Her other hand disappears for a moment and reappears with a small egg-shaped item."

With my dick in her mouth, Eve blindly reaches to her nightstand. She pats around as if she knows exactly what she's looking for. A second later, she pulls out a pink egg-shaped vibrator. My lips part. My pulse quickens. With Eve slurping on my dick, it's hard as fuck to keep the words in focus.

"She pushes my desk chair back, and it rolls easily. My dick hits the back of her throat, and I nearly come. 'Yes. Yes. Mr. Parker. That. Sounds. Perfect.' With my dick still in her mouth, like a magician, she leans forward, lifts my balls, and—"

A small buzzing sound fills the room before Eve lifts my balls and shoves the egg underneath. "Ah! Fuck!" The vibration shoots in every direction. The book falls from my grasp and hits the bed. My eyes pinch shut. I fist the blanket. Eve's tongue slides up and down my dick. A tingle starts at the base of my spine. I release another deep moan. "Your mouth feels fucking fantastic. As much as I want to come down your throat, I'd much rather be inside your tight pussy. Then I can watch as you come undone on my dick." I push to my feet. She releases me with a pop and falls back onto her hands. I hook my arms under hers and pull her off the floor.

"We were just getting to the good part." She licks her glistening lips.

"I'm rewriting the story. My ending is better." I shove my boxer briefs all the way off. Frantically, I claw at her shirt until I peel it over her head. My gaze drops to the swell of her tits confined under the pink lace bra. "This has to go." Reaching behind her, I flick the clasp undone and the straps loosen, falling down her arms. I tug it off, and it hits the floor near my boxer briefs. Her nipples pebble in the cool air.

"My turn." Her hands grab my shirt, and I help her as she pulls it over my head. She flings it behind her.

"Something's wrong with this situation."

"What's that?" She frowns.

My gaze drops from her face and down her body, admiring every inch of her. "You're still wearing entirely too many clothes."

I spin us around and lift her enough to toss her on the bed. She giggles. The bed dips as I rest a knee on the mattress and crawl over her body. I undo the button of her jeans. She wiggles, helping me as I peel them and her underwear down her legs. I nudge her legs with my knee and nestle myself between them. With my dick in hand, I slide the head over her pussy. "You're already drenched for me. Did sucking my dick turn you on?"

Her hand cups her tit, her fingers pinching her nipple. "Yes."

"But would you rather have my dick in your pussy?"

"Yes," she moans. Her back arches off the bed when I rub my head over her clit.

"Tell me how much you want it, Sunflower."

"Lach. Don't fucking tease me." She lifts her hips, rubbing herself on my dick.

I chuckle. "I wouldn't dare." Stretching my arm toward the nightstand, I grab a condom from the drawer, but her fingers on my wrist stop me.

"We can go without."

I freeze. My eyes meet hers. "Are you sure?"

She drops her hand to the mattress. "I mean, I'm already pregnant. I've been tested, and I'm negative for everything."

"Me too. Well, not pregnant, but I'm negative."

She laughs. Reaching up, she cups my cheek, and I lean into her warmth. "Then I suggest you fuck me."

I bend down, my lips inches from hers. "Anything for you, Sunflower." With one hard thrust, I'm fully inside her.

Chapter 34

FUCK

Eve

I suck in a sharp breath as I relish in his cock stretching me. Savoring it. My back arches off the bed. There's nothing better than his warm body over mine, cocooning me. Even more so when he's fully inside me.

Lach groans against my lips. "You feel so fucking perfect. Everything about you is perfect." His mouth skates over my cheek until his head is buried against my neck. He rocks his hips, sliding in and out of me. Every push and pull driving me higher and higher. It won't take long until I'm catapulted into the stratosphere.

Sex has never been this good. With Lach, it's an out-of-body experience. It's like capturing the most beautiful sunrise. Splashes of pinks and purples streak across the sky, much like the tingles soaring through my body like a shooting star. Lach's hand slides up the back of my leg until he reaches my knee. He pushes my leg to my chest. It's a little easier now since I started doing more yoga. His pace increases, pounding into me as his groans grow louder. I never. *Thrust.* Want. *Thrust.* It. *Thrust.* To. *Thrust.* Stop. *Thrust.* My nails claw at the sheets to keep me grounded.

"Hold this." Lach sits up and moves my hand to my bent knee. He pats around until he finds the discarded egg vibrator tangled in the blanket. He presses the button, and it vibrates to life. Leisurely, he rocks his hips into me. With the egg in his hand, he lowers it until it rests against my clit.

The vibrations shoot from between my legs to every toe and fingertip. Then it's like a firecracker exploding. "Ah! Fuuuck." There is no slow buildup. No crawl to pleasure. It just detonates. Lach has the button, and he's pressing it. Over and over again. On my clit. "Oh my god. Lach!" My entire body convulses with pleasure. Pure orgasmic pleasure.

His movements slow, but he never stops. "I'll never tire of watching you come undone. Do you have another one in you, but this time riding my dick?"

I'm still collecting my breath from the last. One orgasm from Lach is amazing. Two is a fucking dream. "Are you threatening me with a good time?" My words come out breathy.

Lach pulls out of me, and I whimper from the loss. He lays down on the bed, and I hike a leg over his hips. Reaching between us, I brush the tip of his cock over my pussy before aligning myself with him. Slowly, I sink down, savoring the stretch. No matter how many times we have sex, each time feels more amazing than the last. His calloused hands slide up my thighs until he reaches my waist. I slide up and down his cock, taking all the pleasure I possibly can. My head falls back on a moan. His fingers dimple my soft skin, guiding my movements. I lean down, my long hair cascading around us like a curtain. My nails dig into his chest, leaving crescent-shaped marks as I increase my pace. With each stroke, the anticipation builds and builds, bringing me closer to the edge of another intense orgasm.

"Fuck. Sunflower. Ride my cock like you own it."

His grunts mix with my moans in perfect harmony—each stroke driving me closer and closer to bliss. He bucks his hips up, slamming into me from below. Each one gets harder and harder as he chases his own orgasm. A white-hot fireball shoots through my entire body and hits me right in my core. Waves of bliss pour through me. A second later, Lach groans out his orgasm, filling me.

I collapse on top of him, my cheek resting on his chest. The rhythmic thumping of his heartbeat almost lulls me to sleep. His fingertips glide up and down my spine. "That was… amazing. Well, every time is."

His shoulders bounce with laughter. "I'm happy to serve." He presses a kiss on the top of my head.

"As much as I want to lie in bed with you just like this, I need to use the bathroom." I reluctantly push myself up out of Lach's grasp. The blanket falls as a rush of cold air hits me. Jogging to the other side of the room, I grab my robe hanging from the closet door. While squeezing my legs together, I throw it over my shoulders, shoving my arms through the sleeves. I find a bath towel on the floor and use that to clean myself up temporarily.

"I'll be right back. Then we can do that again." I wave my finger over the bed where he's still lying down, the blanket resting low over his hips. I can't help but drool over his bare chest filled with colorful ink. My nipples perk up under my plush robe, more than ready for round two. *Concentrate, Eve,* I scold myself. *You have all night.*

"I'm going to get a bottle of water. You want one?"

Lach slides his legs over the edge of the bed, reaching for his boxer briefs with his toe.

"Yeah. Sure. It's best to stay hydrated for all our extracurricular activities." I pull open the door, take a step through the doorway, and immediately come to a halt. A boulder sinks from my throat to the pit of my stomach. "Oh. Shit," I murmur.

"What's wrong?" Lach's heavy footfalls rush up behind me. With a hand on my waist, he comes to a stop. "Fuck," he whispers.

Chapter 35

I HATE THIS

Eve

"What the fuck is going on here?" Jake glares murderous daggers at me and then Lach. I've seen Jake mad before, but the look on his face puts mad to shame.

"Nothing" is on the tip of my tongue, but based on Lach's current state of dress, or undress, "nothing" is not the word I'm looking for here. "Oh. Um. Uh." All the words are failing me right now. Lach and I still haven't discussed what we were going to tell Jake. Hence why I'm tongue tied at this moment.

Lach steps around me and guides me to stand behind him. "I hate you had to find out this way, but—"

"But what?" Jake grits between his teeth. He takes a step toward Lach, causing him to push against me. I rest my hands on his hips to keep him steady. Or me steady.

"Eve and I are… together."

My heart leaps in my chest. We've told each other we

want to be together, but this is the first time we've told anyone else. Unfortunately, it's my brother, and after we had sex, which has now kind of killed my orgasm high.

"Together? Fucking? Is that all this is? She's my little sister. I asked you to look after her, and what the fuck do you do? You fucking sleep with her!"

Lach holds his hands up in defense. "Look, I didn't know she was your sister when it happened."

"When the fuck did it happen!?" He glares at Lach, then me.

"In Florida. We met at the resort where Dessa and Garrett got married." Lach's voice is slow and deliberate as if he's trying to calm a fierce tiger ready to pounce.

Jake's nostrils flare. His eyes narrow to tiny slits and bounce between me and Lach. "So you didn't know each other when it happened? What did you do when you found out?"

Lach tenses under my grasp. I tag myself in and step out from behind Lach. "This isn't how we wanted to tell you."

Jake directs his wrath toward me. "And how the fuck exactly were you going to tell me? By letting me catch you actually fucking?"

I flinch at his words. That almost happened once. His arm sweeps me away.

Lach steps forward, putting himself between me and Jake. "Don't push her." His voice is strained like he's holding back his anger.

Jake ignores me and gets in Lach's face again. "I confided in you to watch over her. Keep her safe. Instead, you sleep with her. And behind my back! You're my best friend! And this is how you repay me!" Jake's fingers clench into a fist.

"I know." Lach's face falls. "This isn't how I wanted you to find out."

"But you still did it anyway!" Jake seethes, his face flushing molten. The muscles in his forearms flex with every clench and unclench of his fingers.

Oh shit. He's going to punch Lach. I don't even think. I just spit out the next words, hoping to take some of the heat off Lach. "I'm pregnant!"

Both Lach and Jake freeze. Lach pinches his eyes shut. I hold my breath.

"Excuse me? You're pregnant?" Jake turns his head so fast toward Lach I'm surprised he doesn't get whiplash. "You got my sister pregnant?" He glares at him so hard the vein protruding from his neck is seconds away from exploding.

"No." Lach shakes his head. "It's not mine."

Jake jerks to face me. "You cheated on my best friend?"

"No!" I sigh. "It's not like that at all."

"Then someone tell me what the fuck it's like then!" Jake roars.

"It's my ex-boyfriend's, but I only found out recently that I'm pregnant." I do my best to remain calm with hopes to keep Jake from hulking out.

"What the fuck is going on?" He pushes his hand through his hair. Jake jerks to Lach, his jaw clenching. "Are you having your fun now, and you'll leave after the baby is born since it's not your responsibility?"

Without missing a beat, Lach answers, "No. I'm not leaving her."

My heart soars as much as it can soar, given the circumstances.

Lach clears his throat. "I apologize for not telling you, but I will not apologize for doing it. Because that would mean I regret it happening, and I don't regret a single thing when it comes to—"

Time slows to almost a standstill. Before Lach can finish, Jake rears his arm back, and it shoots forward like a bullet from a shotgun. His fist connects with Lach's cheek with a sharp thwack. Lach stumbles backward, and I jump out of the way to avoid getting toppled to the floor.

When I collect my balance, I turn to Jake. "What's wrong with you!?" I race to Lach's side. Blood seeps from a cut on his lip. "Are you alright?"

"I'm fine." His words are soft. He brushes his thumb across his lip, smearing the blood.

I've only seen Jake lash out a handful of times, and that's when someone threatens the things he cares about, like his bar and me. But Lach is his best friend. He should know he's not the bad guy. I jerk to face Jake.

"What the hell is wrong with you?" I jump to my feet and stomp the two steps toward Jake. "If you're going to be mad at him, you have to be mad at me. This is just as much my fault." My heart pounds a million miles a minute. I stab my finger at his chest, and he doesn't flinch. "Actually, I'm going to go out on a limb and say this is all my fault. I pursued him. He didn't want to start anything between us, but I couldn't help myself—"

"Eve," Lach interrupts, his hand on mine.

I turn to him. His eyes are soft, pleading that I don't take the blame for this. "No. He doesn't get to be mad at only you." I return my attention to Jake. "No! If you're going to be mad at anyone, be mad at me."

"He knew exactly what he was doing!" Jake jabs his finger at Lach. "I trusted him! And he does this?" He directs his anger at Lach, taking a step closer to him. I'm afraid he's going to punch him again. "Get out. Get the fuck out of my house," Jake spits, the vein in his neck throbbing.

With a hand on his forearm, I attempt to spin him around, but he doesn't move because he's a brick. "Where is he supposed to go? He has nowhere else to go."

Jake scoffs. "I don't give a shit, but he's not fucking staying here. He betrayed me. Lied to me. He can't do that shit and expect me to also give him a place to live. He can leave now and get his shit tomorrow when I'm not here."

Panic pounds in my chest. This can't be happening right now. None of this. "Jake, you can't be serious. You're being irrational."

"Irrational would be strangling him with both hands. I think I'm being perfectly rational," Jake deadpans before he stomps away.

Lach rests a hand on my arm. "It's okay."

I spin around to face him. Fear. Panic. Hopelessness. And everything in between races through me. "No. It's not. He's being irrational," I choke out.

"He's not. I did all those things he said."

"But he punched you." My voice softens. "You're bleeding." Tears prick the corners of my eyes, and I reach up to brush my thumb over his cut. He flinches at the contact.

"I deserved it." Stepping out of my reach, he picks his shirt up off the floor and shoves it over his head. Next, he finds his jeans and tugs them on. His hand rubs his jaw where Jake punched him.

"Where are you going to go? Let me come with you. Give me a minute to get a bag together." My gaze flits around the room, figuring out everything I need to pack.

He clasps his hands on my biceps. "You stay here."

The tears grow bigger until they're too big to hold back any longer. One slides down my cheek and then the other.

Lach lifts his hands and brushes them away with his thumbs.

My heart thunders in my ears. "Where are you going to go?" My words are barely a whisper. I don't want him to go. I don't want to be without him.

"I'm going to make a couple of phone calls. If I have to, I'll get a hotel room."

My heart plummets to my stomach, a cold dread washing over me. "I hate this."

His face falls, and he nods. "I know. I do too."

"What do I do?" I've never felt so helpless in my entire life. Even when I was a teenager with shitty parents, who were basically non-existent, at least I had Jake, but now I don't even have him.

He cups my cheeks, his warmth the only thing that's comforting. "It's best I'm not here right now. Jake needs some space, and me being in his house won't make anything better. We'll figure this out. I promise."

My eyelids droop. I wait for Lach to kiss me, even if it's on the forehead. To offer me comfort that everything will be okay like he says, but it doesn't happen. His warm touch disappears, and his hands fall to his sides. My heart breaks for a completely different reason. Glancing up, I meet Lach's eyes. His once bright blue irises dull to almost gray. The same heartbreak I feel is etched on his face. He pivots on his heels. I watch his retreating frame until he disappears from the doorway. I hold my breath, hoping he comes back to tell me he changed his mind, but the sound of the back door closing echoes through the house and smacks into my chest. The last of my tears roll down my cheeks. I wipe them away. All the fear and hopelessness dissolves into hurt and anger. My blood boils, and Jake is sitting in the bullseye of my wrath. The pounding of my feet throughout the house rattles the walls and everything on them. I find Jake in his bedroom, pacing back and forth.

"What the hell is wrong with you?!" His head jerks up to meet mine. "I can't believe you just kicked out your own best friend."

He freezes a few feet away from me. "A best friend wouldn't sleep with his best friend's sister and keep it a secret for months."

"We didn't want to hurt you. Why can't you see that?" Jake has always been the last person I wanted to hurt. He's always been there when I've needed him. I don't want to lose him over this, but I also can't lose Lach.

He scoffs. "Well, congratulations. You did exactly that."

"I didn't tell you either. This is just as much my fault." I point to my chest. It's not fair for Lach to take all the heat for this. There's only one person being unreasonable here, and it's Jake.

"You're my sister."

"And he's your best. Fucking. Friend." I blow out a deep breath and stare up at the ceiling. Yelling at each other won't get us anywhere. "Look," I lower my tone, "we both know that sometimes our friends are worth more than the blood family we have. So congratulations for once again pushing people out of your life who care about you. Just like you always do. You can be sad and miserable for the rest of your entire life. But I'm going to live mine. Just so we're clear, I'm not going to stop seeing him. I don't care what you say. He's the one man who has made me feel good about myself. Even though this baby isn't his," I rest a hand on my belly, "he wants to be in my life. *Our* lives. And I want him, no, I *need* him in mine. So, if you want to kick me out too, go right ahead. Otherwise, I can't stand to look at you, because I can't believe you're doing this."

He says nothing. We have a stare-off, the intensity of

the moment thick in the air. He's acting like a stubborn, overprotective older brother, but he doesn't need to shield me from Lach. His best friend. His lips part a fraction as if he's about to say something, but he slams them shut. With a sharp jerk, he rips his gaze away and forces his way past me, his body brushing against mine. I spin around as he stomps down the hallway. I follow him, hot on his heels toward the back door. With a yank, he throws the door open, letting out a loud bang as it slams shut behind him.

An entire gauntlet of emotions race through me. More tears fall and fall and fall. I wipe them away, but they won't stop. I jog to my bedroom, the floorboards creaking beneath my feet, and slam the door shut. Climbing onto the bed, I curl myself into a ball. I knew it was going to be difficult, but I didn't expect it to play out like this. Jake's always been the protective older brother. He's always watched out for me. Always been there for me. But he doesn't understand he's trying to take away the best thing that's ever happened to me. What if Lach decides this is too much for him? That I'm not worth all this trouble and leaves? What if he goes to Rachel's? More tears fill my eyes and fall, staining my pillowcase.

My phone chimes with a message. Stretching my arm over to the nightstand, I glance at a blurriness of jumbled words on the screen. I lift the corner of the blanket and dry my tears.

LACH

It'll be okay. I promise. We'll figure it out.
I'm staying at Rylee's tonight. And we'll
figure everything out later.

We. He said we. He still wants *us* to be a *we*. I type back a reply.

EVE

I miss you. I wish you were still here.

LACH

Same, Sunflower.

I'm going to grip the tiny thread of hope with all my might because that's all I have right now. He's all I have right now.

Chapter 36

ISN'T LIFE GRAND?

Lach

I crack an eye open to find little, bright hazel eyes staring at me from inches away.

She squints. "You snore."

"Abby! Leave Lach alone. He's trying to sleep," Rylee yells down the stairs that lead to the basement where I'm currently lying on the couch.

Abby twists to face the stairs. "But he's awake!"

"Probably because you woke him up!" Rylee volleys back.

I stretch my legs on the leather couch and rub the sleep from my eyes. "It's okay. I'm awake."

"See?" Abby turns to face Rylee as she comes down the stairs, her other daughter in her arms.

"I'm sorry, Lach. I hope she didn't wake you."

Abby scrunches her nose, pointing to my cheek. "What's wrong with your face?"

"Abby!" Rylee scolds.

"What?" Abby whines.

"Go upstairs and finish your breakfast." Rylee points to the stairs.

Abby huffs before climbing to her feet. "Fine." She runs off, stomping up the stairs. If anyone else in the house was sleeping, they're awake now.

"Sorry about that. She's more and more like Trey every day. You'd think she was his biological daughter." Kaelyn wiggles in her arms, but Rylee keeps her wrangled like a champion cowgirl.

"It's fine. She's kind of charming."

"She's going to be the death of me or especially Trey when she gets older." Rylee laughs and shakes her head. "Can I get you anything? Ibuprofen? Ice pack?"

"Nah. I'm okay." I scrub my hands down my face, being gentle with the mangled side. I make a running tally of everything I need to do today. Mostly, get my shit from Jake's.

"You're welcome to stay here as long as you need. I know it's not the most luxurious accommodations, and you'll probably have a seven-year-old waking you up every morning, but don't feel obligated to leave right away."

I stifle a yawn as I rise to the sitting position. "Thanks. I do have to get my stuff from Jake's. That's my first priority."

"I know he'll be at the bar most of the afternoon. I'll tell Trey to make room in the garage if you need it."

"Lucky for you, the fire destroyed most of my belongings, so I only have a couple of suitcases and a few of boxes." And that's another thing to add to my ever-growing to-do list. I need my own place. Then I need to furnish it while also tiptoeing on eggshells to see if I'll still have a job once the dust settles.

"You know Jake will come around. He's just... He's hurt." She shrugs.

"Yeah. I'd like to think so, anyway." A part of me is relieved that Jake knows. We don't have to keep our relationship a secret anymore. It would have been better if he didn't find out the way he did. Truth be told, I have no one to blame but myself. I had weeks to come clean and tell him. Instead, I chickened out. Mostly because how do you tell your best friend you're falling for his sister? There's no how-to guide for that. Instead, I took a fist to the face, and now I'm couch surfing. Fuck. Isn't life grand?

"So you and Eve..." Rylee's voice pulls me from my thoughts. "Is it official now?" A wide grin covers her face.

"We're just going to tiptoe around this for a little while longer. Let Jake's anger come to a simmer before we flaunt our relationship." How long will it last? I don't know. But I have time. Eve's worth every ticking second of time.

"That's understandable. Just so you know, I'm Team Lach." She holds up her fist in solidarity.

I chuckle. "Thanks. Some days, I don't feel like I have too many people in my corner."

"I'm pretty sure everyone is in your corner." She flashes me a warm smile. "You're welcome to invite Eve over. But no hanky-panky." She shakes her finger at me. "There's a good chance you'll have a seven-year-old chaperone. Also, if you want a shower, I put a towel on the sink for you. There's shampoo and a spare toothbrush in there as well."

I shake my head and laugh. "You're such a mom."

"Well, just wait. Your time is coming." She hoists Kaelyn higher on her hip. A loud crash sounds through the floor. Rylee sighs. "I need to see what's getting destroyed in my house." She spins around and climbs the stairs. "Abby, get off the counter!" Rylee's voice carries through the entire house.

Shit. Does she know? Did Eve already tell her? It's most likely Rylee's voodoo fall-in-love shit. This could be my life one day. Maybe sooner rather than later. My lips tug into a half smile. Honestly, it doesn't seem half bad.

After a shower, I text Eve. She tells me she and Jake are at the bar, so I use that opportunity to run over there and get the rest of my stuff. Since I don't have much, it only takes an hour to pack and be out. I tell her to come over to Rylee's later, and Abby will be chaperoning. I also tell her to bring the book we were reading before Jake caught us. When Eve is done with work, she comes over, and we watch a cartoon movie about Minions, but it didn't matter what we watched. All that mattered was my arm was around Eve, her warm body pressed against mine while Abby sat next to Eve, kicking her feet and munching on popcorn. It wasn't the most ideal circumstances, but I'll take what I can get. Lucky for us, Abby fell asleep snuggled against Eve halfway through the movie. Rylee collected her and brought her upstairs, leaving us alone.

"Did you bring the book?" I slide my fingers over her shoulder, hoping she did.

She bends over and digs in her purse, pulling it out. "Are we doing this? Here?" She lifts a brow.

"I enjoy reading with you." A smile flirts on my lips. I sit up, taking the book from her grasp. "Plus, we left off at a very crucial point in the story. I need to know what happens next. Does she get caught? Did Mr. Parker hear anything and out them?"

"Oh! You're really into the story. So you're aware there's no explosives and bloodshed at the end." She shrugs. "Just a happily ever after."

"I'm all for a happily ever after." Over the next several

hours, we pass the book back and forth, each of us reading a chapter, until Eve drifts off to sleep against my chest. I ease her into the lying position on the couch and cover her with a blanket. I find a small stuffed animal of Abby's, along with a princess blanket that's entirely too short for me and stretch out on the floor.

The next morning, every inch of my body is sore, as if I slept on the floor. Oh wait, I did.

From above me, Eve stirs awake. "Sorry, I fell asleep and stole your bed."

"Don't be sorry. I'd sleep on the floor a million times for you."

She giggles. "Hopefully, soon, that won't be the case anymore."

I rise to my feet and wince as my muscles stretch. Eve rises too. I tug her to me and press a kiss to the top of her head. We quickly say our goodbyes, and I walk her to the front door.

Since Jake hasn't fired me yet, I check out a couple of apartments before my shift. Luckily, the swelling on my face has gone down, but there's still slight bruising, and the scab on my lip is very attractive. If anyone asks, I'll tell them I ran into a wall. They don't need to know the wall was Jake's fist.

The first two places were way too small, even for two bedrooms. There was zero outdoor space, which wouldn't work with my plans. The park a block away was sufficient though. The third place had a wide-open floor plan with two bedrooms. It would have been perfect, but again, no outdoor space. The fourth place is in Dessa's old neighborhood. Rows of townhomes fill both sides of the street. The rent is more than what I was paying before, but so far, it's the best option out of all of them. Two bedrooms. Check. Lots of space. Check. And a small backyard. Check. A sandbox can fit next to the house and maybe a small swing set. I take as many photos as possible so I can show Eve later to make sure she approves. I'm doing this for her. For us.

Porter's
ALE HOUSE

"Holy shit!" Nora says. "Did you do some street fighting over the weekend?"

"Not exactly. On the plus side, Jake now knows about me and Eve." I pull a beer from the cooler and pass it to a customer.

Nora props herself against the bar next to me, crossing her arms over her chest. "Did you finally tell him?"

I huff out a laugh. "If by tell him you mean he caught us in her bedroom after sex, then yes. I told him."

She gasps. "Oh, shit." She points to my face. "Jake did that?"

I nod. "I can't blame him. I'd punch me too."

A light bulb flickers to life above her head. "That's why he was in here earlier, rearranging the schedule. He asked if I could work some closing shifts with you this week. Which actually works better with my schedule, anyway."

"Yeah, I'm guessing he won't want to see me for a while." I rap my knuckles on the bar top. "It might be best if I find another place to work."

Her forehead wrinkles. "Do you think he'll fire you?"

"I'd fire me."

"You're dating his sister. It's not like you killed a man."

"I broke his trust, so that's pretty damn close." I rub the back of my neck.

"Okay, all that aside. You and Eve?" Her eyes light up with an eagerness to hear my answer.

"I'm going to let the dust settle before we pick up

where we left off." I can't keep the smile off my face. "She's it for me. I don't want anyone else, but—"

"You don't want to get between her and her brother," Nora finishes. Her lips press together as silence fills the space between us. "Jake would never keep his sister from happiness. I'll call him an asshole if he does. But I can't blame him if he needs some time to let everything settle." She rests her hand on my forearm. "Don't give up on your happiness. You deserve it too."

Happiness has always been out of my grasp. A brush of my fingertips away. All I needed to do was step forward, and I could clutch it with both hands. All I needed was Eve to encourage me to take that step.

Chapter 37

OR IT'S GAS

Lach

Later in the week, Eve assured me Jake wouldn't be home all night. I hate what I did to him. It eats me up inside that he's mad at me. For the last decade, he's been my one constant in life. Now I'm the asshole. I can accept that he hates me as long as there isn't a rift between him and Eve. She needs him more than I do.

Pushing open the back door into Jake's house unleashes a cacophony of emotions. Some are good, like the ones surrounding Eve. The cruel ones mix well with the bitter taste of betrayal. It's only been a week since I was last here, but it feels like a lifetime. Eve jogs into the kitchen from the living room, the widest, most beautiful grin on her face. Her growing belly, round and firm, bumps against mine as her arms wrap around my neck. It seems like overnight, the baby decided to grow. Pregnancy is strange.

"I've been waiting all day to see you."

"I'm here now." I press my lips against hers. We've

been working opposite shifts, so it's been hard to see each other. All we get are the late-night phone calls and text messages. "Are you sure Jake won't be doing any surprise pop-ins?"

"I bought a wireless motion detector alarm, so it will alert me of any movement in the back."

I laugh. "We could have used that earlier."

Her hand clasps around mine and leads me toward the living room. "Tell me about the townhome." She lowers herself to the couch, and I take the cushion next to her. "Did you like it?"

"I did. It has two bedrooms on the second floor. They're pretty close to each other, so the baby won't be far. There's a full bath upstairs and a half bath on the first floor. Both the living room and kitchen have plenty of space."

"And cupboard space?"

"I think so." I pull my phone from my pocket and unlock the screen. Opening the photos app, I scroll through all the pictures I took. "There's even a small yard. I think we'll be able to put a little sandbox over here and maybe a small swing set on this side of the yard." I swipe my finger across the screen to show her the next photo.

She tenses, and her face drifts up to meet mine. Her lips press together.

Shit. She hates it. This isn't what she wanted. "What's wrong? You don't like it?"

A smile takes over her face. "It's perfect."

"Really?"

"Yeah. I mean, I'd live in a cardboard box with you if I had to. Not saying I want to, but you get the gist." She giggles. "Most importantly, you thought about the baby." She freezes. With a flicker of uncertainty, her eyes shift back and forth, searching for something.

"What's wrong?" I scan her body for an injury, but she's been sitting next to me the entire time.

"I think the baby moved, or it's gas," she whispers. Her gaze drifts up to mine, a smile curving her lips. She grabs my hand and rests it on the soft cotton shirt covering her stomach. "I don't know if you can feel it."

I hold my breath, afraid to move and miss it, but after several seconds pass, nothing happens. "I might feel the baby or your gas?" A giggle escapes her lips, her belly shaking with mirth. I drop my hand.

"It's still early. Maybe no one else can feel it yet." Her fingers grip my chin, forcing me to meet her gaze. "I'm taking that as a sign the baby also agrees."

"Or we're deciding based on your gas." I raise an eyebrow.

She playfully backhands my chest. "I'm making the executive decision, and it was the baby."

I laugh. Fuck. I never expected my life to do a complete one-eighty in the span of two months. Single-handedly, one woman changed the course of my entire life for the better. I don't want to imagine what my life would be without her. She's my sunflower. Pointing me toward the sun. Filling me with warmth.

"I'll call the landlord tomorrow." I brush my thumb over her cheek. "We'll move in together."

"Sounds perfect." Her soft smile warms me.

"Only one small problem. We can't move in for two months."

"It wouldn't be a Lach-and-Eve relationship without a few bumps." She places a hand on her stomach and wiggles her eyebrows. "We've waited this long. What's sixty more days?"

Every day, I fall deeper and harder for this woman. Leaning in, I press my lips to hers in a chaste kiss. I pull back, but close enough that our lips still touch. "Can we read your book?"

Eve's hazel eyes glint in the lamplight. She jumps off the couch and strolls to her bedroom. She emerges with the book in hand. The cushion dips as she takes a seat next to me. I wrap my arm around her shoulder, tucking her against my side. Her finger slides over the pages until she finds the bookmark.

"Do you think she's going to take the new job?"

Her gaze lifts to mine. "That's a spoiler. I can't tell you that."

"I think if she does, the relationship is over. I want to believe she'll stay, but he did her dirty by ignoring her at the party. So she has every right to leave."

Eve chuckles. "You're really into the story, aren't you?"

"You told me romance stories have to end in a happily ever after, but I don't see how this one can. There are too many forces pulling them apart. I need to find out."

She giggles and snuggles deep against me. "I assure you there's a happily ever after." She opens the book, pulls out the bookmark, and passes it to me. "It's your chapter."

I grab the book from her and clear my throat. She rests her head on my chest, right over my heart. "Chapter eighteen."

Chapter 38

GRUNTS AND FLYING FISTS

Eve

Over the past month, I've given Jake the silent treatment, which is much easier for him since his style of communication mostly consists of grunts and flying fists. Needless to say, I'm the talker out of the two of us, and I'm ready to spew all the words at him. I'm on the opposite side of the kitchen, leaning my butt against the counter, shooting eye bullets at Jake over the rim of my mug. His large frame makes the small round table look like it belongs in a dollhouse. The rustle of a newspaper fills the kitchen as he turns the page. I've always looked up to my brother. He was the only person who was a constant in my life for so many years. Then he wasn't, and then I bailed. I held nothing against him. He did what he needed to do to survive, and I did the same. No more running. I'm exactly where I want to be. I place my mug on the counter and cross my arms over my chest.

"I'm sorry we didn't tell you sooner." The top of the

newspaper rustles as it falls to the table. He peers up at me with his typical blank expression. While I tend to serve my emotions on a silver platter, Jake keeps his locked up tighter than a casino vault. "But I meant what I said—I'm to blame for this too, not just Lach. When we first met in Florida, we didn't know each other. Then, when we did, the attraction was already there. We couldn't fight it."

"That's not the point."

I fling my arms into the air. "Then tell me what the point is."

"He lied."

"So did I! It wasn't right, but we did it to protect you."

The newspaper crinkles in Jake's grip like a tin can. "Protect me from what? I don't need protecting."

"Protect you from getting hurt."

He scoffs.

I dramatically wave my hands in front of me. "That's right. I forgot. The big bad Jake doesn't have feelings. Guess what? You proved that one wrong. You wouldn't have punched your best friend if you didn't care. But it was still no reason to punch him. You're welcome to tone down the big brother act. We're adults now."

"I'll always be your big brother, and I will always protect you."

"Except when you bailed for over a year." I cross my arms over my chest and glare at him. Was it a low blow? Yes. I know he was dealing with his own shit, but he did abandon me when he said he wouldn't.

"That's not fair."

"You're right. It's not. But neither is punching your best friend." I raise a brow. All he does is continue to glower. He's never been good with his feelings, especially since the accident. When I turned eighteen, I shouldn't have left, but he seemed to be doing better. I needed to rise on my own two feet instead of standing behind Jake. He had the bar to run, or maybe the bar was only there to mask what was happening deep inside. I blow out a heavy breath. I need the two people I care most about to stop fighting not only for me but for each other. "Look, I get it. Lach's your best friend, and he hurt you. I'm not innocent in all this either. But why all the hostility? Wouldn't you want me to be with someone you trust? Who you know won't hurt me?" Jake says nothing, so I continue. "That's what I don't get. And you know Lach is exactly that type of man."

"He has his own issues to deal with."

I roll my eyes. "Everyone has issues. Much like my older brother."

My romance with Lach has been a whirlwind. Sure, we don't know every single facet of each other's lives, and we're still getting to know each other. But he's right. At the beginning, Lach was very hot and cold, apprehensive about us. While Jake was a big part of that, I know deep down there was more. There's a reason their friendship runs as deep as a trench. When he's ready, he'll open up. He's very guarded, much like my brother. Maybe that's why they're so close. But I know Lach wouldn't go all in if he didn't have feelings for me as well. That's all the reassurance I need right now.

"He wants to be there for me. And I want to be there for him." I rest my elbows on the counter and scrub my hands down my face. Sometimes it's like talking to a brick wall. "I won't stop seeing Lach. If you want to be in my life and your niece or nephew's life, then you need to talk to him. Without the flying fists. Or I'll get you some giant inflatable boxing gloves. I don't want to choose between my brother and my boyfriend, but if I have to, I'll pick him because he's not making me choose. So this bullshit needs to stop. You need to realize how much better he's made my life. And I know you miss your best friend. You're extra grumpy, and it's annoying."

Jake sits in the chair in complete silence. Maybe he's letting my words sink in. Maybe he tuned out everything I just said. I rest my hands on the counter, throwing everything out there because I give zero fucks anymore. Someone else now commands my attention. I rest a hand on my stomach. "Also, I'll be moving out next month." His gaze jumps to mine. "Lach found us a great townhouse, and I'll be moving in with him."

He nods before picking up the paper again, shoving his face between the pages. All I can do is shake my head. I will go on living my life, and he can stew in his. I have more important things to do, like packing my belongings. Again.

Chapter 39

SIX-PACK APOLOGY

Lach

The past two months has been much of the same. Jake avoiding me. Eve avoiding Jake. Even the vibe at Porter's has been off. Everyone is tiptoeing around each other, or maybe it's me. Sure, I have the most amazing woman by my side now, but at the expense of my best friend. It fucking sucks. When I picked up the keys from the property manager, I was shocked when she mentioned my employer had given her one of the best references she ever received. I was tempted to ask her if she had called the right number, but I only provided one number, and it would be odd if a stranger gave me such a positive reference. Eve mentioned she had a friendly chat with Jake, but I wonder how friendly it was. She stood up to Goliath, and she did it for me. I'm keeping her.

To say I was excited about leaving Rylee's couch is an understatement. Don't get me wrong, Abby's adorable, but I won't miss waking up to her inches from my face. It was really sweet the one time she brought me a glass of orange juice though.

Moving my belongings in was a breeze. All I had were my clothes, a computer, a few boxes, a TV, and a stack of artwork. Eve was a different story. She has a bed, two dressers, a loveseat, recliner, and a small pub table at Jake's. All the other miscellaneous items we need have been ordered, and we're waiting for them to arrive. All the baby furniture was delivered in record time, even though the baby hasn't arrived yet. Eve brought over a suitcase full of clothes that will tide her over until we can get everything else.

I slide the scissors through the tape on the top of the box, breaking the seal. With a flick of my wrist, I open the flaps and pull out all the wood pieces along with two plastic baggies. One holds a variety of nuts and bolts. The other includes an Allen wrench and several metal brackets. In the palm of my hand, I hold everything that will keep this crib together. I'm somewhat skeptical all this will hold anything over five pounds. Among the foam padding, I find the instructions. The thick paper feels sturdier than the crib. I scan the diagram of pictures and then all the parts. Seems easy enough. I toss the paper to the side, it floats to the floor, and I unwrap all the wood pieces.

A knock on the door echoes through the townhouse and to the second floor. I climb to my feet and jog down the stairs to the front door. Since we don't have curtains yet, I peek out the wide-open window. My chest tightens, and my brows pinch together. He's the last person I'd expect to see standing on my doorstep, especially after avoiding me for the past month. Unless he's back to finish what he started. At the door, I twist the knob and pull it open.

"What are you doing here?"

Jake's gaze lifts to mine. "Eve yelled at me."

I rest a hand on the doorjamb. "So you came here to tell me Eve yelled at you?"

He squares his shoulders, but his scowl diminishes a fraction. "Not entirely. But she made me realize I really shouldn't be mad. In fact, I should be happy. Not only is she with a guy who makes her happy, but also someone I know is a good guy who won't treat her like her ex."

A part of me questions if Eve wrote a script for him to recite. But I know coming here saying what he said, even if it's scripted, was genuine. He wouldn't have done it otherwise. "Thanks. I appreciate it. I know sneaking around behind your back wasn't the right decision. I'm sorry for that."

Jake nods. "Also, I brought this." He holds out a gift bag with cartoon giraffes, elephants, and tigers printed on it with white tissue paper spilling out the top.

I lift an eyebrow. It's too pretty to be something Jake put together himself. "What's this?"

"A gift for the nursery. Nora helped me wrap it."

I nod. "That explains the presentation. Thanks."

"And this is for you." He passes me a six-pack of my favorite beer that can only be bought in Wisconsin.

The fact he drove across state lines to bring me a peace offering is telling. Granted, it's only a twenty-minute drive, but it's the thought that counts. "Thanks. Do you want to come in?" I fully open the door and step out of the way. Jake passes through, and I close the door behind him. He toes off his shoes on the mat next to the door.

"This is a nice place you got here." He glances around the bare walls and stacks of boxes.

"Thanks. It's still a work in progress, but it's an upgrade from my previous apartment. Plus, I wanted Eve and the baby to have a nice place to call home."

Jake crosses his arms over his chest, his gaze settling on me. "You know you don't have to do this, right? You don't have to take care of her."

I freeze. My blood is on the brink of boiling. I thought he came here to make amends. Not this. I square my shoulders, preparing for another fight. "Look, if you've come to hassle me about my relationship with Eve, you can leave now." I point to the door. "But know this, I'm doing this just as much for me as I am for her and the baby. I want to be with her. I need to be with her. I love her."

The words have always been on the tip of my tongue, but I was hoping she'd hear them before her brother. Fuck it. Here are my cards. "I love your sister. She makes me want to be a better man for her, but also for myself. She's my every breath. I want to take care of her. I want to give her the entire fucking world. If you can't see that, then go."

He holds his hands up in defense. "I just wanted to see where your head was at."

"I don't need any of your big-brother tests."

He nods. "So you love her?"

"More than anything."

"Got it." A few seconds of silence pass between us before he says, "I always wished Eve would grow up and have a strong head on her shoulders, but I didn't anticipate her being as fierce as she is. Good luck, and you have my blessing."

I laugh. "After you punched me in the face, you do realize I was going to do it whether or not I had your blessing."

"I'd expect nothing less."

I pull one bottle from the cardboard carrier and set the rest on the counter. Twisting off the cap, I take a long pull. "You want a water or something?"

Jake shakes his head. "No. I'm good." He inspects a box with parts for the crib. "Working on something?"

I take a drink, enjoying the slightly fruity ale. "You ever put a baby crib together?"

"Can't say I have."

"Great! Then you can help me." I grab the other five beers and stroll through the living room to the stairs that lead to the second floor. Jake follows close behind.

Two and a half hours and two extra screws later, the crib is assembled. Both of us stand in front of the crib and admire our handiwork.

"Do you think we're supposed to have leftovers?" I hold out my palm with the two screws resting in the middle.

He shrugs. "Don't they usually provide extras, just in case?"

"Sure. Seems reasonable." I grip the railing of the crib and give it a firm shake. It feels fairly sturdy. I walk around to the other side and do the same. This could hold a baby. "Climb in and see if it holds you." I nod at the crib.

Jake bends down and picks up the directions. "I read somewhere that the max capacity is like fifty pounds. I'm just a few pounds over that."

I rub my chin. "That's not going to work."

The plush carpet rubs against my arm. The tiny light from the drill is the only thing helping me see under the crib as I screw in the last two-by-four to the legs.

"Oh, don't you two look cute assembling a crib together?"

I jerk and smack my head on the wood. A loud thud echoes through the small room and wince. Twisting to my side, Eve stands in the doorway with a wide grin on her face. I roll out from under the crib and rise to my feet. "What do you think?" I motion to the crib.

"Looks good. You two assembled this by yourselves?"

"We're more than just good looks. We're carpenters now." I wrap my arm around her shoulder and press a kiss to the top of her head without a second thought. When I pull away, I glance at Jake. The corner of his mouth twitches. It's the closest thing to a smile anyone will see from him.

Eve wraps her arms around my waist. "Whatever helps you sleep at night."

"You need to be our tester, though," I say.

Eve freezes. "Your tester?"

"Yeah. Get in the crib." I lift my chin, nodding at the crib.

She giggles. "Why?"

"If it'll hold your weight, it'll surely hold the weight of a ten-pound baby."

"Ten pounds?" Eve screeches.

"Could be twelve pounds," Jake adds.

"Wait! Why is the number going up?" Her wide-eyed gaze flits between me and Jake.

"When you were born, you were a pretty big baby," Jake says.

She presses a hand to her chest. "But that doesn't mean I'll have a big baby."

"Genetics play a role in it," I add. "So we need you to get in the crib." I drop my arm and hold out my hand for Eve.

"Are cribs meant to hold the weight of adults?"

"No. But we've made a few…" I glance at Jake and shrug, "modifications."

Eve's lips press into a thin line. "If this collapses to the floor… I don't know what I'll do, but you'll owe me. Owe me big. Both of you." She points a finger between me and Jake. "I'm thinking a full spa day." She turns to me. "And dinner. Like the best dinner anyone has ever eaten."

I laugh. "Anything you want."

Jake removes the side railing and rests it against the wall. With Eve's hand resting in mine, she steps up into the crib and sits down in the middle, cross-legged.

A few seconds pass, and she blows out a breath. "I think we're good."

"Maybe we should leave you there all night just in case," I tease.

"Oh, hell no! I'm not sleeping in the crib." She uncrosses her legs, and I help her to her feet.

"Alright. I think my job here is done," Jake says.

Eve wraps her arms around him in a hug. Jake reluctantly hooks his arm around her waist. "Thank you." I don't know if it's for helping with the crib or coming here to mend our friendship. Maybe both.

After they release each other, he clasps my shoulder. "Take care of her. If you don't, I know where you live."

I smile at him. "Got it."

Eve walks Jake to the front door. After it clicks shut, her feet pad up the stairs and meet me in the nursery. She wraps her arms around my waist. "So everything is back to normal?"

I brush a strand of hair off her forehead. "Is it the way it was? No. But it's a new normal. It might take time."

"Good, because I really didn't want to have to make a choice between my brother and my boyfriend."

"We're a title now?"

"Boyfriend seems easier than 'guy I slept with, who didn't get me pregnant, but now I'm currently sharing a townhouse with.' 'Boyfriend' has a better ring to it."

"And I finally get to sleep next to my girlfriend with no interruptions or sneaking out early in the morning." I spin her in my arms so she's facing me. My thumbs brush over her cheeks, and I drop my forehead against hers. She lifts her chin, pressing her soft lips to mine.

She pulls away slightly. "I have a twenty-five-week ultrasound next week. It was pushed back a few times due to scheduling conflicts, but since I've been feeling fine, Sofia said it was okay. Anyway, it's routine. To make sure the baby is healthy. If you want to—"

"Yes."

She laughs. "I didn't even finish."

"If you're asking me if I'll go with you, the answer is yes. I would want nothing more than to be there with you."

This baby may not biologically be mine, but it feels like it is. I'll be there for both of them as if it is.

Later that night while Eve's asleep, I slide down the bed until my head is next to her belly. "Hey, you. I guess I don't know if you're a boy or a girl yet. Doesn't matter." I shake my head. "I know I'm not your biological father. But I will love you as if I am. See, I grew up without parents, and I never want you to go through what I did. I will do everything to take care of you and your mom because I love you both more than anything. I can't wait to meet you." I lightly rest my hand on her belly above the blanket. This is exactly where I'm meant to be.

Chapter 40

ARE YOU THE FATHER?

Eve

My eyes tick along with the second hand as it moves clockwise. Where is Lach? He said he didn't want to miss this. The paper on the table crinkles beneath me. The stark white walls reflecting the harsh fluorescent lights amplify my anxiety tenfold. What if he forgot? I should have sent him a reminder. Maybe he changed his mind, and this is all too much for him, and he no longer wants to be with me because I'm having someone else's baby. What if he got into an accident on his way here? He could be lying in the ditch dead somewhere, and no one knows where he is. My chest tightens as a giant lump forms in my throat, choking me. I wish I hadn't forgotten my phone in the car.

The door swings open, and a woman with strawberry blonde hair and a white lab coat strolls in. "Hi, Miss Porter. My name is Cindy. I'll be performing your ultrasound. Sofia couldn't be here today. How are you?"

She gives me a warm smile, but it does nothing to calm my anxiety. "G-good," I choke out. Except that my boyfriend may be gasping for his last breath. "A little nervous."

"Is this your first pregnancy?"

I nod.

"Nerves can be expected, but I'm sure everything will be fine." She flips through a few papers on the clipboard before returning her attention to me. "We'll just run through some standard procedures to make sure the baby is healthy. If we're lucky and the baby is in the right position, perhaps we'll be able to see the sex as well."

She continues talking, but my mind drifts back to Lach. Where is he? I pick at my cuticles, needing something to do. I know this isn't his responsibility, but I could really use his support right now.

"I'll have you lie down, and we'll get started," Cindy says.

I nod and lie back. She presses a few buttons on the ultrasound machine. My gaze darts between what she's doing and the door. I drum my fingers against my thigh, trying to rid myself of any nervous energy, but it's not helping. Beeping from the machine fills the room as it springs to life. A second later, a knock on the door cuts through the beeping. I roll my head toward the door. A woman with short, black hair peeks her head in through the crack.

"I have a Lachlan Murray here."

"Yes! He can come in." My heart beats again. He's here. He made it. There's no accident. No ditch. He's here. A wide grin spreads across my face when he comes into view.

Immediately, he races to my side. "I'm so sorry I'm late. A road crew was working on an underground pipe that burst. Traffic was backed up for miles. I got here as fast as I could."

"Worst-case scenarios were flashing in my mind," I whisper.

"I'm here now." He brushes his thumb over the top of my hand.

"You're just in time. I'm Cindy, the sonographer."

"Lachlan. But you can call me Lach," Lach replies.

"We haven't started anything yet. Are you the father?" Cindy's face drifts up from her paperwork.

My gaze shoots to his. This isn't something we discussed beforehand. Who would discuss this? It's not like it would come up in everyday conversation, mostly because all our friends know he isn't the father. His eyes meet mine. They're soft and full of love.

"Yes. Yes, I am." He drops his gaze to mine.

A tear pricks the corner of my eye. We both know this baby isn't his, but he's claiming them as his own. More and more every day, I find myself falling harder and deeper for him. How did I survive without him? Lach not being in my life seems like a lifetime ago. He squeezes my hand before linking his pinky with mine.

"Great. Let us get started."

I slide the hem of my shirt over my belly. The cold jelly contacts my skin, and I flinch. She slides a wand around, smearing the jelly. A few seconds later, a whooshing sound fills the room. I roll my head away from Lach as he looks up. A grainy black-and-white picture fills the small monitor next to us. I gasp. There's a head. A chest. Arms. Tiny hands. Legs. My breath hitches, and my entire body trembles with elation.

Lach squeezes my pinky and leans down. His warm breath rolls over the shell of my ear. "I got you, Sunflower. I got you."

From Lach's words, all the tension escapes my body. Him here, by my side, is exactly what I need. The fetus wiggles back and forth while Cindy slides the wand from one side of my belly to the other.

"It appears everything is progressing as normal. That little dot is the heart." She points to the screen. "Would you like to know the sex?"

I glance at Lach, and he squeezes my pinky. I'm unable to fight the smile forming on my lips. Turning my attention back to Cindy, I nod. "Yes."

"Alright. Let's see if we can get them to cooperate." She moves the wand to the side of my belly. "Right there." She freezes. "It looks like you're having a boy."

Lach points at the screen. "Right there. That's his…"

"No. That's his arm. Right there." She points to a smaller gray spot on the screen.

For the next ten minutes, we continue to watch him wiggle and squirm on the screen. I'm growing a little human inside me. A little boy. Cindy takes a couple of sonogram pictures for us to take home. When we're finished, she cleans the gel off my stomach and informs me everything will be sent to my doctor, and she'll get in touch with me if there are any issues.

Back at our now-furnished townhouse, I sit on the couch, thumbing through the pictures. This ultrasound hits differently than the first. This time I can see all the limbs, fingers, and toes. He's no longer a kidney bean. My finger slides over the glossy black-and-white photo. It's real. The cushion dips beside me as Lach takes a seat.

"Is everything okay?" Lach's voice is soft.

I nod. "Yes. Everything is almost perfect."

"Almost perfect?"

I peer up at Lach. "I wish this baby was yours." A tear rolls down my cheek.

Gently, he brushes it away with his thumb. "To me, it doesn't matter. I'm there for you and him, no matter what."

"What did I do to deserve you?"

"You kissed me at a resort bar. I've been lost in you ever since." A smile flirts on his lips.

I melt into him, resting my head on his shoulder. "Imagine if none of that happened?" I blow out a heavy sigh.

He wraps an arm around my back, holding me tight. "I'd rather not. Life without you is unthinkable for me. I've lived it for the past twenty-nine years, and I don't want to go another day without you."

I relish his warmth, taking comfort in his words. I don't know what I would do without him in my life.

Chapter 41

PINEAPPLE PIZZA

Lach

It only took a month for both of us to not only have free time but also a day off together. I've been taking as many freelance gigs as I can. Babies aren't cheap, and I want to help Eve as much as possible. We use our time together to collect the last of Eve's things from Jake's house.

"When's the pizza going to get here? I'm starving." Eve flops down on the bed, resting a hand on her belly.

"I think you're the only person I know who's excited for pineapple pizza," I take a seat next to her.

"It's just so good."

"Said no one ever," I counter.

"I'm not eating it for me. I'm eating it for the baby. The baby gets what the baby wants."

"We could've at least gone half-and-half or something."

"Speak to the man in charge." She points to her belly.

"Not only does he like fresh pineapple pizza, but cold, left-over pineapple pizza is his jam."

I scoot away and lean down so my face is inches from Eve's belly. "Hey, buddy. It's time we have a chat, man to man. I need you to develop better food tastes. The pineapple pizza just isn't cutting it."

Eve's belly bounces as she laughs. There's a knock on the front door, and I jump to my feet. In the entryway, I twist the knob and yank it open. It's not pizza.

"What are you doing here?" Eve's ex, Pax, stands on the doorstep, just as shocked to see me as I am to see him.

"Can I talk to Eve?"

"No." I deadpan. "She doesn't want to talk to you."

"And you know this how?"

"Lach! Hurry! I need pizza." Eve whines from the bedroom.

Pax shifts to see around me. "Eve! Are you in there?"

I slam the door, hoping like hell he gets the hint. Eve strolls out of the bedroom and comes to a stop. She stares at my empty hands. "Where's the pizza?"

"It's not here." I scowl.

Her brows knit together. "Then who's at the door?"

"No one."

Another knock comes from the door, followed by a muffled, "Eve!"

Her eyes drift from me to the door, then back to me before weaving past me and pulling it open. Her back stiffens like an iron beam.

"Eve," Pax says. His gaze drops to her belly. "Oh shit. You are pregnant."

Eve sighs. "I told you that when I called you. Did you think I was lying? Never mind, it's not important. Why are you here, Pax?" The annoyance is dripping from her voice. I don't blame her because I'm right there too.

I move to stand behind Eve. I'm here if she needs me for anything. She peers over her shoulder and gives me a small smile before her attention drifts back to Pax.

Pax rubs the back of his neck. "I needed to see you. I miss you." He looks up to me and then back to Eve. "Can we talk alone?"

"No." She crosses her arms over her chest. "There is nothing we need to discuss unless you want to sign over paternity rights. Otherwise, we can discuss child support when the baby is born." She glares at him.

His eyes dart everywhere and anywhere besides Eve—the one person his attention should be on. I'm sure he's stalling to conjure up some stupid excuse. This confirms how much of a piece of shit he is.

"My wife can't know about this. Any of this," he grits through his teeth.

"Sorry to burst your I-want-my-cake-and-eat-it-too bubble, but it doesn't work that way. She will find out. You can't keep your child from her for eighteen years. Since you're in town, your best option is to come with me tomorrow, and we'll get a paternity test. When it proves you're the father, you can relinquish your parental rights." She blows out a breath. "Then you can continue on with your life as if nothing happened."

Holy shit. Is he going to go with this plan? It would make Eve's life a whole lot easier. She wants nothing to do with Pax. She's more than capable of being a great mom to her baby boy, and I will be right there by her side. The baby won't be without a father. I'll be a father to him.

A car door on the street interrupts us. A young man steps out in jeans and a hoodie with a Harbor Highlands Pizzeria logo printed on the front. He jogs up to the door. "I have a pizza for Lach."

I sidestep Eve and Pax, passing the delivery guy some

cash for the pizza. Eve's nose follows the lingering aroma of the savory tomato sauce and the sweet and tangy smell of the pineapple.

"I'll call you tomorrow, Pax, and we'll go to the clinic for the test." Before he can say anything else, she closes the door on him.

I laugh. "Clearly we know which is more important to you between pizza or Pax." I set the pizza box on the coffee table in front of the couch.

"Pizza would win one hundred percent every time." Eve takes a seat and flips open the box, grabbing a slice. "Also, don't come between a hungry pregnant woman and food."

"Noted." I grab a slice for myself. "Do you think he'll go through with it tomorrow?"

Eve finishes chewing and then swallows. "He'll do anything to avoid threats to his lifestyle. He's selfish like that. I don't know how I didn't see it before. He doesn't want a kid. I would rather be a single mom than have a piece of shit like him around. It would be more of a headache than being helpful."

I nod. "I have your back, no matter what happens."

A radiant smile spreads across her face as she beams up at me, her eyes sparkling with happiness. "I know."

We finish eating in comfortable silence. That's one thing I love about being with Eve. We can be content just being in each other's presence. No need to fill the silence with meaningless words. Our words are invisible, but we both feel them. Eve leans over, resting her head on my shoulder. She pops the last bite of pizza crust into her mouth and moans in satisfaction.

Dessa and Riley always talk about when you find the one, you just know it. I never believed it. I always thought it was horseshit. Until now. I can't explain it. It's a tightness in my chest. A flutter in my stomach. I don't want to be with anyone else. I think back to the woman at the bookstore. She told me it wouldn't be worth it if it wasn't hard. Eve is worth it. She's worth every punch in the face. Every surprise ex visit. Because I also get every smile. Every laugh. Every kiss. We will emerge stronger because we faced those challenges together.

We finish packing the last of Eve's stuff, haul everything to my truck, and head home. *Our* home. After we move the last of the boxes into the townhouse, we're both exhausted. Eve sits up in bed, leaning against the headboard as she reads the book we've been reading together out loud. I'm only half listening, though. Something else is on my mind.

I reach over and grab the pen sitting on top of my short stack sketchbook on the nightstand. Grabbing Eve's hand, I lay it flat on the bed, palm up.

She stops reading and peers down at me. "What are you doing?"

"I got an idea for a sketch."

"So you're using me as the canvas?"

"Seems like the perfect spot. Just keep reading."

I twist my body to shield her eyes from what I'm drawing. She laughs but continues reading the book. I slide the ink pen over her skin, starting with the outside lines. The black ink is a stark contrast against her light skin. I draw small flourishes around the outside and lightly shade on the inside. Every now and then she twitches as the pen tickles her skin. When I'm satisfied, I pull the pen away, dropping it to the comforter.

"Are you finished?" she asks.

"Yeah, I think I am." I sit up so she can get a full view.

Her gaze drops to her wrist, and she gasps. The book falls from her grasp and lands on the comforter. Tears prick the corner of her eyes. She lifts her wrist to get a closer look at the cursive lines of "I love you" surrounded by sunflowers. Her gaze drifts to meet mine, and her lips part.

"Do you mean it?"

I hate that she even has to ask the question. "With my whole fucking heart. I love you, Sunflower."

A tear rolls down her cheek, and she wipes it away, making sure not to use her hand with the drawing so it doesn't smear.

Rising up, I move to sit next to her. "I've been gasping for breath my entire life. And you're the breath I didn't know I was missing. I love your laughter, your quirkiness, your fierceness, and spontaneity."

She rests a hand on my cheek. "I love you, Lach. I love your thoughtfulness, your protectiveness, and how sweet you are."

Leaning in a few inches, I press my lips to hers. It's soft and gentle and perfect for this moment. She gasps and pulls away. Her fingers splay over her growing baby bump. She freezes, and her eyes widen.

"Is everything okay?" I scan her face and down her body to her belly.

Her head bobs up and down. She grabs my hand and places it on her stomach.

"What are you—"

"Do you feel that?" she whispers. "It's not gas this time."

My gaze drops to my hand. Against my palm, her skin twitches. My mouth drops open. I move down the bed to get closer to her stomach. Holy shit. As fast as it happened, it disappears. "That's crazy." I peer up at Eve.

"It is." She smiles at me and leans against the headboard. "Tell me something real."

I rub my chin, thinking of the perfect answer. Then it hits me. "Something real…I hate peas."

"Really?" she whines. "Who hates—" she begins before abruptly stopping and widening her eyes. "Wait! Is that—"

I roll my head back in laughter. "*10 Things I Hate About You*. Yes. You gave me Patrick's name. I had to see for myself who I needed to live up to."

"I promise there is no comparison between you and Patrick Verona. I'd say I got the better deal."

I look down at the comforter and pick at an invisible thread. Eve knows me. The real me, but she doesn't know all of me. I'm terrified if I tell her she'll not want to be with me. My past is my past, and I prefer it stays there. I peer up at her. "You're my first actual girlfriend."

She sits forward, dropping her hands to the bed. "You've never had a girlfriend? I figured you had a trail of broken hearts following you around."

I bark out a laugh. "If I broke their hearts, that was on them. I never got that involved. I never wanted to." My gaze drifts to hers. Blue eyes meeting hazel. "Until you." While it's something real, I don't know if it's the real she was looking for. Right now, it's all I got. It's always hard handing over one hundred percent of yourself. I've never done it. I don't know if I can. "So what about me? I know I'm not your only, but what about number two or three?"

She laughs and buries her head in her hands. "Is it sad to say, I don't even know. I dated. A lot. I hated the idea of being alone. Some were more serious than others. But I do know you're the one who means the most to me." She leans back, resting against the headboard. "Looking back, I don't even know if I liked Pax. He was there. It was convenient. I always like the comfort of knowing someone was there. Which always got me in trouble." She waves a hand over her belly. "This being the most recent. But I wouldn't change it for anything." A laugh bursts out of her. "Look at us. You don't do relationships, and I can't seem to stay out of them."

"Maybe that's how we make it work so well." I shrug.

"How can you be such an amazingly sweet and caring guy? I'm such a hot mess. I don't deserve someone like you."

I grab her hand, the one with the drawing on her wrist, and flip it over. My fingers trace over her palm. "I love that you're a hot mess."

Her jaw drops, and she giggles. "Thanks for that." She tugs her hand away, but I refuse to let her go.

"You didn't let me finish. I love that you're a hot mess because I want to see all of you. The good, the bad, and the hot mess. I want to be your rock during all those times. To help you. Comfort you. Cheer you on. Anything you need me to do. I'll be a hot mess with you. I love you."

"Good save." Her hand wraps around my wrist, and she pulls me to where she's sitting. I drop my hands on either side of her hips. My lips are inches from hers. "Did you ever play hockey? Because you'd make a good goalie."

"No, but we can play a little stick-in-the-net action if you'd like."

"Now you're speaking my language." She wiggles her eyebrows before leaning in, pressing her lips to mine.

Chapter 42

HOLD MY HAND

Lach

A month later, things between Jake and me still aren't back to how they used to be, but at least I don't flinch every time I'm in his general vicinity. The beer he brought over was a good peace offering but not the fix. I know it will take time, at least longer than working a few shifts together, and I can wait. If the tables were turned, I would have reacted the same way. Both of us want the best for Eve, and a rift between us isn't that.

I exit the walk-in cooler with a case of beer in my hands. My phone vibrates in my back pocket. I rest the box on the edge of the cooler and pull it out. Eve's name flashes on the screen. With my hip, I slide the box so it fully rests on top. I stroll to the opposite end of the bar, where it's a little quieter. I press talk.

"Hey, what's up?"

"Lach." Her voice is shaky.

Panic sets in. "What's wrong?"

"S-something doesn't feel right. I don't know what it is, but it doesn't feel right."

Fuck. A rope tightens around my chest. She's scared. I need to be strong for both of us. "Alright. Call the doctor. Tell her we're going to the hospital. Can you do that, Sunflower?"

"Y-yes."

"I'm on my way to pick you up."

"O-okay."

I end the call and whip around. Jake's at the other end of the bar with Nora. When he spots me, he nudges Nora to finish making the drink and advances toward me. "I've never seen all the color drain from your face. What's wrong?"

"I need to leave. Something's wrong with Eve. I don't know what it is, but I have to take her to the hospital," I spit out. I yank my keys from my pocket, not even waiting for an answer.

Nora leans around Jake. "Go. We got it here." She glares at Jake, almost willing him to say no.

His eyes meet mine. "Eve needs you."

I take off in a full sprint across the bar and out the door to my truck. The engine roars to life. The tires squeal and kick up rocks as I peel out of the parking lot. All the buildings and houses flash past me in a blur. My only focus is to get to the townhouse and to Eve. As soon as I pull into the short driveway, I slam my truck into park. Leaving it running, I shoot off like a cannon to the front door. Eve's in the living room, sitting on the couch, holding her right side. Within seconds, I'm kneeling in front of her.

"Are you okay?"

"I have a sharp pain on my right side and a pounding headache."

"Did you call the doctor?"

She nods. "Yes. She'll meet us at the hospital."

"Okay. Let's go." I rise to my feet and help Eve to hers.

At the hospital, I pace the waiting room while I wait for them to finish a few tests. Nervous energy flows through my veins like a raging river. There's no way I'd be able to sit and relax. It's not even a word in my vocabulary right now. I need to know she's okay. That the baby is okay.

A woman in a white lab coat pushes through a set of double doors. My gaze bores into her, waiting for her to say something. Call my name. Call Eve's name. Anything.

"Lachlan Murray?" She glances up from the clipboard in her hands.

"Yes." I race to where she's standing. "I'm Lachlan. Is Eve okay?"

"Eve is okay. I'm Sofia, Eve's doctor. Follow me, and we'll go see her."

I nod. She turns on her heel, and I follow close behind. We stroll down a hallway, passing door after door until we turn down another hallway. She stops outside a room and waves her hand for me to enter. Instantly, my eyes connect with Eve's as she lays in a bed. I'm gutted. If someone were to rip my heart out and stomp on it, that would feel better than seeing her like this. I rush to her side. She gives me a warm smile. She's in the hospital bed, and she's trying to provide *me* comfort. My girl is strong. She's fierce. She's a fucking warrior. I grab her hand and intertwine our fingers. It's probably frowned upon if I crawl into the bed with her, so holding her hand in mine will have to do. Eve squeezes her fingers around mine.

"Hi, Eve and Lachlan." Sofia enters the room. "We've done a few tests, and Eve has developed preeclampsia. It's a blood pressure condition that can occur during pregnancy."

"Okay." Everything around me fades away. "What can we do? How do we fix this?"

"The only cure is delivery, but with Eve at thirty-three weeks, we would like her to remain pregnant as close to full term as possible. I recommend Eve monitor her blood pressure at home, avoid high-stress situations, and do her best to manage her stress. Here are some pamphlets for more information." She passes me a small stack of papers.

It's easy for her to say to stay stress-free when she's not the one who's diagnosed with preeclampsia. "Okay." I nod before twisting to face Eve. "We got this."

Sofia discharges Eve and exits the room, giving us a few minutes alone.

Eve sits up in the bed, swinging her legs off the side. "I don't know what to do. Working at Porter's won't be viable for much longer. But I have bills to pay."

Lifting her hand, I press my lips to her knuckles. "I'll take care of you. I want to take care of you. And the baby. I have some money saved up from all my freelance gigs."

"Lach." Her eyes soften. "I can't. That's yours."

"I wouldn't offer if I didn't want to. If you and the baby weren't in my life, I'd be nothing. Just let me do this. Please," I plead. I feel helpless. There's nothing I can do to help her besides this.

Her thumb brushes over my finger. She lifts her hand, pressing a kiss to my knuckles. "You're holding my hand."

Fuck. I am. It never even crossed my mind when I did it. It just happened. But I don't hate it. In fact, it's another one of those things that feels perfect. "I don't want to hold anyone else's hand but yours."

I often think, what if? What if my parents didn't abandon me and put me into foster care? What if George and Sue were still here? What if I never took the bartending job at Porter's? Where would my life be? But there's no more what-ifs. I'm right here with Eve by my side because of all those things, and I wouldn't change it for the fucking world.

Chapter 43

SPARK OF HOPE

Eve

The doctor told me to be as stress-free as possible. You know what doesn't help to be stress-free? Thinking about how to be stress-free. It's stressing me out. Not only do I have my health to worry about but also the health of my baby boy.

I place the pint glass under the spout and pull the tap. The beer flows into the glass until it kisses the rim. I grab a cardboard coaster and slide it to the customer across from me. At the register, I ring in the total and glance up at a sign that reads Number of Days Without an Eve Accident: Ninety-three. A smile tugs at my mouth. I've come a long way. Not only with not breaking bottles but with my life. In elementary school, I remember we would draw pictures of what we wanted to be when we grew up. My drawings comprised of a ballerina, a singer, and a teacher. None of them were of me working at my brother's bar and pregnant with my married ex-boyfriend's child while dating my brother's best friend. I doubt any six-year-olds have drawings like that. Life has a way of throwing wrenches at your plan, but what defines you is how you come out on the other end. I've come out being the happiest I've ever been, and I think that's pretty damn good.

I close the register and return to the customer with their change. With a lull in customers, Rylee stops next to me. "How are you feeling?"

"I'm doing good. Luckily, I haven't had too much discomfort like I've heard others have. But I don't know what I'm going to do."

Rylee turns to me, giving me her full attention. "About what?"

I rest a hand on my growing belly. "Being pregnant and working in a bar isn't the most ideal situation. Then, with my preeclampsia and working random shifts, it gets even harder."

Rylee nods along. "Oh yeah, I've been there."

"What did you do?"

"When I was pregnant with Kaelyn, Jake was really accommodating. Essentially, he made me a bar manager and put me on paperwork duty. He always made sure someone was working with me who could do the heavy lifting and always put me on day shifts. If I had an appointment, he ensured my shift was always covered, even if he had to do it himself. He'll do the same for you."

I blow out a deep breath. "Working in my brother's bar was certainly never the dream."

"Yeah, it wasn't mine either, but honestly, I wouldn't trade it for anything else. I get to work with my best friends. We're more like a family than anything."

"Lach says the same thing." A slow smile stretches

across my lips. "While I love the atmosphere, I don't know if it's what I see myself doing for the rest of my life."

"You're a photographer, right?"

"Was." I give her the short version of my lackluster photography career from having my own studio, then losing it, to my most recent failure as an assistant.

"What if you did that again? Build your own photography studio."

A laugh bubbles out of me. "I'm thirty-four weeks pregnant with zero energy. I do not have two brain cells to rub together in order to open a business again."

Rylee's eyes light up like the flip of the switch on a neon bar sign. "Here me out. You have all the photography equipment, right? Camera. Lights. That kind of stuff."

My brows pinch together. I'm not entirely sure where she's going with this. "Um. Yeah."

"I've had an idea for a present for Trey. But didn't know how to exactly go about it because it's Trey, and he's sort of protective." She leans in so only I can hear. "How would you like to do a boudoir photo shoot?"

"I've never actually done one. I don't have a studio or anything." I'm familiar with the style of photos, but I've only ever done weddings, family portraits, and graduations. Boudoir photos are intimate, sensual, and romantic. They're empowering—why have I never done these before?

Rylee rests a hand on my forearm, excitement radiating from her pores. "We can do it at my house. We can set up in the basement. Or I have this antique chaise longue in the living room. Or the bedroom. I'll make sure Trey and the kids are gone. I'll provide the space if you can provide the skills. And of course, I'll pay. Plus, I know Trey would be more comfortable if it was another woman versus a man taking the photos. I don't need him roaming the city wanting to rip some guy's head off." Rylee chuckles and shrugs a shoulder.

Rylee's eagerness is infectious. I'd love to get back into photography. I can easily do this. Even while pregnant. I'll just need help to haul some of the heavier equipment. A spark of hope ignites inside my chest.

"Let's do it." This is my leap of faith. My fear of failure has always prevented me from resuming professional photography. But opportunities are fleeting, and I don't want to miss out on any more.

Nora strolls into Porter's for her shift and stops at the bar. "What are we doing?"

"Eve's going to do a boudoir photoshoot for me." Rylee beams.

"Yes! I call dibs for next!" Nora raises her hand in the air. "I've always wanted to do one of those for myself. Then I can hang the photo over my bed."

Rylee claps her hands together. "I bet Dessa, Olivia, Charlie, Parisa, Hollyn, and Tatum would all book sessions with you. We could fill your calendar for the next three months."

My head spins with this idea, but the warmth that fills my body tells me this is exactly what I should be doing. I'm buzzing with anticipation of getting started. Tears prick my eyes. I'm doing this. I wipe them away. Both Rylee and Nora's gazes shoot to mine. Concern etches on their faces.

"Sorry," I sniffle. "Happy tears. I blame it on the pregnancy. I think I've cried more in the past three months than I have in my entire life."

Rylee laughs. "Oh, the uncontrollable hormones. I don't miss those." She wraps her arms around me in a hug.

Before my shift is over, Rylee and I figure out a date that will work best for the photoshoot.

When I arrive home, Lach is sitting on the couch drawing on his iPad. As I close the door behind me, he looks up and sets the iPad on the coffee table. He rises to his feet and greets me at the door with a chaste kiss.

I bite my lips together, eager to share my news with him. "So you'll never guess what happened today."

"What's that?"

He grabs my purse from me and follows me into the kitchen. He sets it on the kitchen island, and I drop a stack of mail in my hand next to it. "I'm going to do a boudoir photoshoot for Rylee." I flash him a wide grin.

"I don't know what that is."

"It's a photography style that's more sexy and romantic with lingerie. She wants to give the photos to Trey as a gift."

He frowns, holding up his palm. "I don't need to hear any more about my friends in lingerie." He drops his hand and wraps it around my waist. "More importantly, you're going to get back into photography?"

"Yeah. I'm going to start small and see where it goes first. But I'm ready to start again."

He grips my chin, forcing me to look up at him. "Whatever you do, I support you all the way."

I melt against him. "I love you."

"Love you too, Sunflower."

Lach releases me and moves to sit on a stool. While sorting through the mail, a letter from the clinic catches my attention. Everyday since my trip to the clinic with Pax, I've been anxiously waiting for the results to arrive. Even though I know he's the father, this will provide legal documentation. I flip it over and run my finger under the flap, breaking the seal. I pull out the piece of paper and unfold it. Quickly, I scan all the words.

"What's that?" Lach nods at the paper in my hand.

"It confirms what I already knew. Pax is the dad." I tuck the letter back in the envelope and push it to the side. I stare at the next letter, and my brows furrow. Holding it up, I ask, "Who's Archibald Murray?" I peer up at Lach. He's silent. "Wait. Is that you? Is your first name Archibald?"

His cheeks flush. "Yeah. Clearly, I never use it."

"I could call you Archie!"

"Or not." He laughs.

Lach's real name is Archibald. I never knew this. Why didn't I know this? What do I actually know about Lach or Archibald? A tear rolls down my cheek. My shoulders shake, and I slap a hand over my mouth.

In an instant, Lach jumps from the stool and is at my side. "What's wrong?"

"I don't know anything about you besides your penis size, which I like, but I know nothing else." My sobs grow louder.

He laughs. "I'm glad it's to your satisfaction, but you know more than that. Plus, we're still getting to know each other. Our relationship is a little different from most, but it's ours."

I sniffle. "Rylee said the hormones would get to me. But it's getting to be a lot." I dry my damp cheeks. "Yesterday, I cried over a cat video because the cat tried to jump from the bed to the windowsill, and he didn't make it. And I just felt so sad for the cat because he couldn't jump. Then there was a video of a dog trying to get a bone from the bottom of his water bowl but couldn't because it wasn't a real bone. It was printed. All the dog wanted was his bone." My eyes open like faucets, and the tears flood down my face.

Lach wraps his arms around me and tugs me to his chest. "It's okay."

"And I didn't even know your first name." Another sob racks through me.

His hand slides over my head and down my hair. "It's not something I announce to the world."

"But these are things I should know. It's like we don't even know each other."

"Hey, look at me." I peer up at him through wet lashes. "You know a lot about me. You know my favorite breakfast food is pancakes. You're the only one who knows I enjoy reading romance books, mostly because I do it with you, and you know I love you more than anything. We have a lifetime to get to know each other."

I nod. I know he's right.

His lips press into a thin line, his Adam's apple bobbing as he swallows. "You asked me about the significance of my tattoos, and I told you I drew them, which is still true, but it's deeper than that. The most significant one is the gears that run along my spine."

Chapter 44

TWO BROKEN SOULS

Lach

This is the part of my life I've always kept buried deep underground. Never to be dug up. But it's still part of who I am, regardless. Eve deserves to know. I want to tell her. I grab her hand and lead her into the living room. I take a seat on the couch, and she sits next to me. The gears tattoo is the one most people ask about because it seems so random, but for me, it's the one that makes the most sense. I always give them some bullshit reason. They don't need to know that part of my life. But I trust Eve.

"It was after a rough time in my life. I spent my childhood in foster care. For whatever reason, my parents didn't want to be parents anymore." Eve gasps but says nothing as she lets me continue. "For many years, I bounced around from house to house. I don't know if they didn't want me or couldn't handle me. As I got older, it got tougher because I understood it wasn't permanent." She inches closer to me and rests a hand on mine. I give her a half smile. "All that changed when I turned fifteen. A couple, George and Sue, took me in. I believed it would be like all the others. Within two years, I'd be in another home. But one year passed and then another. I certainly wasn't the perfect kid. I was shit at school, mostly because I didn't go. There was even a time or two I found myself in the back of a police car." A humorless laugh escapes me. "Sue was an artist, and she convinced me to go to an art class with her. That's when I discovered my outlet for all my rage, hurt, anger, and loneliness." Eve squeezes my hand before flipping my palm over and linking our fingers together. I lift our intertwined hands and press a kiss to her knuckles. "At the two-year mark, I was preparing to get shipped off, but it never happened. Sue and George were the only people to show me love and acceptance when no one else had. When I turned eighteen and graduated from high school, I was no longer in the system, so I was on my own."

"Did you stay in contact with them?"

I nod. "I did. It wasn't a lot, but I would send pictures of my artwork to Sue and tell them how my life was going. But eight months later, they were both gone. A car accident on an icy road."

"Oh my gosh. I'm so sorry, Lach."

My lips press into a thin line. "The only stability I had in my life was gone. Ripped away from me. For the longest time, I wasn't living. Only going through the motions. That's when I got the gears. They were helping me go through the motions of everyday life. Every turn kept me moving." My gaze drops to the carpet, and I blow out a deep breath. Fuck. I've kept the full story secret, but surprisingly, after telling Eve, I feel a thousand pounds lighter. "Then I met your brother. I was working random odd jobs, and he told me to come work for him. I'd make triple in tips alone than what my current paycheck was providing. Once again, I finally found the family I never had."

"That's why it was so hard to tell my brother about us," she whispers.

I press my lips together and nod. "Yeah. I didn't want to lose what family I had again."

She leans into me, resting her head on my shoulder. "Thanks for sharing that with me."

I release our linked hands and wrap my arms around her. "Thanks for letting me get it out."

"We have similar pasts. Maybe that's why we're drawn together. While I technically had parents, they certainly weren't winning any parents of the year awards. But I had Jake. He did his best to not only be the big brother but also the parent. After the accident, there were a few years where Jake couldn't look after me anymore because he needed someone to look after him."

I nod along as she talks. I'm familiar with Jake's story. While I was going through my hard time, he helped me by telling me his. Trauma bonding. It helped us to know we weren't alone.

Eve continues, "But when he acquired the bar, things seemed to have turned around for him. I graduated and was determined to leave Harbor Highlands and make something of my life. It went well for a while. Photography has always been a passion of mine, so I started working with local photographers. Eventually, I met this other girl who also loved photography. We both saved up all our money and started our own business. Right before we were going to open the doors, she cleared out what little we had in our bank account and disappeared. The police did nothing because her name was on the account as well. My only option was a lawyer, but she took all my money. I was stuck cleaning up the mess with zero money to my name."

"Shit. That's rough," I murmur.

She nods. "I worked random jobs like taking Santa and Easter Bunny photos at the mall. Eventually, I started working for Pax as his assistant. The pay was great. My plan was to do that for a while, save as much as possible, and then maybe start my own business again, but everything blew up in Florida. Met you. Then this," she rests a hand on her belly, "happened. That brings us to the present."

"I think we can both admit we've gone through hell and back but came out better on the other side."

Her hazel eyes meet mine. "I couldn't have done it without you."

"Same, Sunflower. Same." We were two broken souls who found each other to become whole.

Chapter 45

BIRTH OR ANAL

Eve

Our conversation left me feeling closer to Lach than ever before. Opening up to me took a lot of courage. It's hard to be vulnerable, to bare your soul to someone. It's a raw and unsettling experience to let someone else see our cracks. I'm not here to make them bigger. Instead, I want to heal them. Much like he's doing with me. Love is deeper than someone's warm bed, even though a bed with Lach is glorious. It's deeper than that with him. It makes me appreciate what we have even more. I took Rylee's advice and talked to Jake about lightening my workload while I'm pregnant and even going part-time to give me more availability for photography. Word has spread quickly between all the women who work at Porter's and even their friends and friends of friends. I promised them after the baby is born, I'll get them scheduled.

I'm currently in the stockroom with Rylee, helping her take inventory, which seems easy enough except when people move things and don't put them back where they belong.

"Do you have plans for a baby shower?" Rylee slides a box of straws across the shelf.

"Um. It's not something I even thought about with everything going on." With moving again—thankfully not halfway across the country—Pax showing up, and my preeclampsia diagnosis, a baby shower has been on the bottom of my to-do list.

Rylee turns to face me, leaning a shoulder against the shelf. "If it's okay, I'd love to throw one for you."

My heart swells, and tears prick my eyes. I know baby showers are for family and friends to show support and comfort for the mother and baby. With Lach and Jake as my only support system, I often feel alone. But Rylee, who I've only known a few months, wants to throw me a baby shower. It's now nearly impossible to keep the tears from spilling down my cheeks.

"I didn't mean to make you cry!" Rylee drops her clipboard on the shelf and wraps her arms around my shoulders.

"I just… I don't… know why… I'm crying." I choke out between tears.

"Hormones. They're a real bitch." Rylee giggles and squeezes me tighter. "What do you say? Can I throw you a baby shower?"

"I don't even know who would show up."

"Trust me. There isn't a shortage of people who would love to support you and Lach."

"But it's not even his baby." Rylee passes me a tissue, and I dry my cheeks.

She rests a hand on mine. It's comforting. Something a friend would do. "I've known Lach for as long as I've been working at Porter's. He's never been involved with someone like he is with you. He's not going anywhere. That baby might as well be his. When Trey and I got together, I saw the same thing when he would play with Abby. He adores her and loves her as if he was her biological father. It doesn't take blood to be a family."

I nod along. The tears well up again, and I fight to keep them at bay.

"You're part of our family now. Just so you know, we can be a little dysfunctional at times, but the love is there, and that's all that matters." She gives me a warm smile. "So what do you say? Baby shower?"

"I would love that. Thank you."

She wraps her arms around me in another tight hug. "This is great! We can do it at my house. I have a ton of space. Plus, there's a baby balloon arch that needs to make a second appearance."

Rylee's house is gorgeous. It's a large two-story modern farmhouse-style home. If a house could give me an orgasm, it would be this one. Orgasm aside, I don't know how she did it. In a week, Rylee pulled off organizing a baby shower. Never underestimate a woman on a mission. I expected no one to show up, but the house is full. Rylee, Nora, and Dessa are here, along with Charlie, Olivia, Parisa, Hollyn, and Tatum, who all know Lach from the bar. They welcomed me with open arms. We've spent the last hour chatting, eating, and laughing, and it's been the best day a pregnant woman could ask for.

Rylee organized a variety of games for us, which included *The Price is Right* for baby items. My eyes bugged out at the price of what all the baby items cost. I will need to save a few more pennies in my piggy bank. For another game, everyone brought a baby photo of themselves, and we have to guess who the baby was. Rylee won with only having two incorrect. Pin the sperm on the egg was hilarious, and somehow, Dessa got it every time.

Nora rises to her feet with a stack of papers in her hand. "We have one more game to play. If you ask me, we saved the best for last. Don't flip your paper over yet." She walks around and passes us each a piece of paper and a pen. Once everyone has their paper, she says, "Okay. Turn them over!"

I stare, wide-eyed, at the sixteen different squares with pictures of women with various facial expressions.

"You have to guess if the picture is birth or anal!"

The entire room bursts into laughter. Leave it to Nora to pick this game.

Rylee points to one picture. "Olivia, this woman looks familiar. What are you letting Ledger do to you?"

Olivia laughs. "I'm going on record to say Ledger has never put his cock in my ass." She shrugs. "Now, my vibrator is a different story."

The room falls into another fit of laughter. Time ticks by as we make our guesses. Based on all these pictures there's a fine line between pain and pleasure. Honestly, I'm hoping all of them are anal because I don't want to imagine the agony of what birth may look like. Unfortunately, I was wrong. All wrong. All the images I thought were anal were birth and vice versa. Olivia got them all right.

After most of the guests leave, I lower myself to the couch, not wanting to move for the next twenty-four hours. There was so much food, and laughter, and so many gifts. I don't know where I'm going to put everything. But I'm so grateful. Rylee, Dessa, and Nora join me in the living room.

"Ugh, I'm going to kill Lach." Rylee, Dessa, and I turn to Nora. She peers up at us from her phone. "Sorry. I hope you haven't gotten too attached because he's a dead man."

"Technically, he's not the baby daddy, but he gives me massages and food, so I'd like to keep him around for a little longer. What did he do?" I ask.

She slams her phone down on the couch cushion. "He told Miles about OneDate, and now he wants to join to get dating practice. The app is not a tool for education."

"What's the harm in him joining?" I shrug. "He's a really nice guy."

"Sure, he's a nice guy. But he also has the 'I want a girlfriend' flashing billboard above his head. The purpose of OneDate isn't to find a partner but to help ease the pressure from others about not having a partner. Miles will be five seconds away from asking out anyone he goes on a date with."

"I think you're being a little harsh," Rylee interjects, crossing her leg over her knee.

"Nope," Nora says with a firm shake of her head. "I'm trying to run a legitimate business. Not a daycare service."

"If you don't want him on the app, you could show him the ropes on dating yourself." Rylee lifts a brow.

"Ugh, I'd rather let him join the app."

Rylee smiles triumphantly, "There you go. You have your answer."

Nora glares at Rylee. "You're supposed to be on my side."

"We are on your side," I add. "But Miles is a nice guy. He deserves a fair chance, just like everyone else."

"Fine," Nora sighs. "But if he asks out every girl he goes on a date with, you all owe me a new handbag." She points her finger at each of us. We all laugh but agree.

When I arrive home, I'm exhausted, but it was still one of the best days I've ever had. Lach helps me haul everything inside and into the nursery. I'll work on putting it all away later. Until then, I'm ready to relax, take my socks off, and put my feet up. I ease down on the couch and rest my feet on the coffee table. I wiggle my little sausage toes. My naked sausage toes. Damn. I don't remember the last time I had a pedicure, let alone painted my nails, and I'm in need of pretty nails. I lean forward and stretch my hand out, but my belly stops me. That's not going to work either.

I rise from the couch and waddle up the stairs. In the bathroom, I grab a bottle of pink sparkly nail polish from a drawer in the vanity and head back downstairs. I pass Lach while he brings the last of the shower gifts inside. He eyes me warily but says nothing. The silverware drawer rattles as I yank it open. Next, I find the duct tape and pull a strip from the roll.

"What are you doing?" Lach's voice sounds from the living room.

"Improvising."

"For what?"

I emerge from the kitchen, wielding a wand of three butter knives secured together with duct tape. At the end of the wand is the nail polish brush, again securely fastened with duct tape. "I want to paint my nails, but this baby is preventing me from accomplishing that. This would be a great invention, by the way. Pregnant women all around the world would rejoice. They can paint their nails again."

"Or they could ask their husbands to help them." We both freeze at the word "husband." That's a road not traveled for either of us. He quickly recovers. "Or boyfriend. Partner. Pretend baby daddy. Come here." He moves to the end of the couch to give me room to sit and stretch out. He grabs a pillow from behind him and sets it on his lap. "Sit on the other end and rest your foot here."

"You're going to paint my nails?" A warm sensation explodes through my chest, much like when he tells me to ride his cock.

"An attempt will be made, but I'm sure it will be better than whatever you plan on doing with this." He takes the wand from me, rips off the tape on the brush end, and tosses the rest onto the coffee table.

I take a seat on the couch and lean against the armrest. Lach lifts my leg and sets my foot on the pillow. He dips the brush into the bottle and slides it over my toenail, leaving a streak of pink sparkle in its wake. If it's possible to fall even more in love with this man, I just did.

"Where do you see yourself in five years?" I ask.

Without missing a beat, he continues to run the brush over the next nail and says, "In five years, I see myself doing exactly this. Sitting on the couch with you, painting your toenails while terrible reality TV plays on the television because that's what you like to watch."

"Wait." My heart stammers. I would sit up if I could, but I can't. "You're only painting my nails because I'm pregnant and can't. So what are you saying? In five years, you want to—"

"Yep. Toys will be strewn across the living room. We'll have at least one more. Maybe two. But we'll definitely need a bigger house by then."

"Dammit, Lach."

He freezes and lifts his gaze to meet mine. "What?"

"You're saying all the sweet things to me."

"I only say them because I mean them, Sunflower." His

warm breath blows across my toes. "All done." He screws the brush cap back into the nail polish bottle.

"Give me ten minutes for my nails to dry. Then I'm going to show you exactly how much I love you. In the meantime, I have a game for you. Will you grab my purse?" I point to the opposite side of the coffee table. Lach grabs it and passes it to me. I dig inside, pull out a folded piece of paper, and pass it to him.

"What's this?" He peels back the edge of the paper.

"It's a game. You have to guess if it's birth or anal."

"What the fuck?" he screeches and tosses the paper to the coffee table.

I fall into a fit of giggles. Dammit. I peed myself, but it was worth it.

Chapter 46

TWO WEEKS

Eve

When I arrive at Rylee's house, I step out of my car and hoist my camera bag over my shoulder. I've read a lot of horror stories about pregnancy, but I think I fared well. I somehow escaped full-blown morning sickness. Heartburn is a bitch. The preeclampsia is the worst of it. I did limit my coffee intake, which wasn't a terrible sacrifice since I found a caffeine-free herbal ginger tea I enjoy. Fatigue tends to hit me by midafternoon, and then I'm like a toddler who didn't get a nap. Not to mention the July heat suuucks. Sometimes I find sweat in places I didn't even know could sweat. I've learned air conditioning is my friend, and I will happily pay that electric bill.

Before I'm halfway up the sidewalk to the front door, Rylee greets me.

"What can I help with?"

"If you could grab the two bags in the back seat with the lighting, that would be great."

"Of course." Rylee collects the bags, and I follow her into the foyer.

"So we can start in the living room with the antique chaise lounge or the bedroom."

"Let's start in the living room and work our way to the bedroom." I pause, rehashing my words. "That sounds like a bad date, doesn't it?" We both laugh. This is like learning to ride a bicycle again. It's been years since I've done it by myself, but I should be able to hop on and start riding. I scan the room to determine the best angles and perfect lighting. "With the sun shining in through this window, we could get some dramatic lighting that could look really great." I point to the large floor-to-ceiling window on the south wall.

"You're the professional. Also, thank you so much for doing this. I know Trey's going to love these. Even more because it was you seeing me half naked and not some stranger." She turns to face me. "Your due date is coming up, isn't it?"

"Two weeks."

"It's getting close. And you're sure you are up to this?"

"Yes. I need to get out of the house. I've done all the nesting I can possibly do. Plus, this is relaxing." Photography is my happy place. I forgot how much I missed it until now.

"Great! I'll change, and we can get started." Rylee disappears down a hallway.

I pull the lights from the bag and set up what I can. I push the chaise to the perfect angle close to the window.

Rylee struts into the living room wearing a black lace corset and garter under a sheer black robe.

She looks sexy and fierce. I have to pick my jaw up off the floor. "You look amazing."

"Thanks." Pink tints her cheeks. "I bought it for myself

after Kaelyn was born to make myself feel good. My ex-husband was not the nicest. Actually, that's too generous. He's an asshole." She laughs. "Months after Abby's birth, I still carried some baby weight, and he made sure to point it out."

"What's with asshole exes?" We share a laugh.

"Yeah. So, I was determined never to feel like that again. Trey is a much different story. After I bought this set and showed him, he went out and bought me a pink, red, and white one to go with it."

"That's amazing." Lach and I are still exploring our relationship, but I can't imagine him being like Rylee's ex. He's been amazing this entire time. I couldn't ask for a better not-baby-daddy baby daddy.

"Where do you want me?" Rylee plays with the edge of her sheer robe.

"Let's start on the chaise. You can lie down and raise your hand over your head." I demonstrate the pose.

Rylee gets into position, and I snap a few photos. I offer a few more pose suggestions and snap more photos. "Why don't you part your lips a fraction?" *Click.* I stroll to the chaise and gently slide a lock of hair over her chest. "Oh, that's hot. Trey is going to love these." *Click.* I move around as best as I can to get different angles. Some close-ups and some wide-view. Hello, bicycle! I'm ready for the Tour de France. A buzz of energy courses through my body. This is exactly what I need to be doing with my life.

"Alright, move back just a little bit." Rylee rolls her shoulder, leaning away from me. "Lift your arm a little higher. And scoot back a little more."

Rylee inches back. Suddenly, her arms are flailing in the air, and she hits the floor with a heavy thud.

I lower my camera. "Oh my god. Are you okay?" I slap my hand over my mouth to contain my laughter.

"I'm good." Rylee giggles while on the floor. "Did you get that? Because that was graceful as fuck." I double over in laughter, squeezing my thighs together. A wetness pools between my legs. "Oh my god, I think I just peed myself," I say between giggles.

Rylee sits up and rests her hands on the chase. Her laughter dies. "Are you sure that's pee?"

Now that I think about it, I'm not entirely sure. My chest tingles. I might vomit or faint. Maybe both. Is this happening? I peer up at Rylee. "I think my water broke."

She jumps up from the floor and leaps over the chaise. "Okay. We have to get you to the hospital." She grabs my camera from me and sets it on the couch. With her arm linked with mine, she ushers me toward the door and helps me with my shoes. "We'll take your car since mine's in the garage, and you're parked in front of it."

I nod along because I don't know what else to do. Clueless first-time pregnant woman here. I'm happy I'm with Rylee, who's been through this two times.

She shoves her feet into a pair of slip-ons. "Do you have a bag packed?"

"I do. But it's at home."

"Okay. We'll call Lach on the way to the hospital and have him grab it." She yanks open the front door.

"Um, Rylee?"

"Yeah?"

"Do you want to change first?"

She glances down at her black corset and garter. "Shit. That would've been embarrassing. Yes." She races across the house and emerges a few seconds later in capri leggings and a T-shirt. The outline of the garter is visible under the black leggings. She holds up a bath towel. "Your seats will thank you later."

"Are you still wearing the corset underneath that?"

"Yes."

"I think I like you even more."

Rylee closes the door behind us and helps me into the passenger seat. I'm having a baby. I'm going to be a mom. Once I'm settled, she jumps in the driver's seat. Since my phone is connected to the car's Bluetooth, we use it to call Lach. It rings a few times before he picks up.

Chapter 47

TAKE CARE OF HER

Lach

I stroll through the front door of Porter's early for my shift. Since Eve's at Rylee's doing her photoshoot, I got tired of sitting by myself. Jake's talking to someone seated at the bar. Their back is to me, so I'm not entirely sure who it is. Jake waves me over.

"Lach, I want to introduce you to an old friend, Beckett."

Recognition hits me. "Beckett Holloway. You're kind of the local hockey hero." In high school, he went to three state championships and played for Boston College before making his NHL debut for the Minnesota Mavericks.

He holds out his hand, and I give it a shake. "You can call me Beck."

"Sorry to hear about the injury a few years back. That's a tough break."

"Or it was a sign for me to retire." He laughs. "Plus, I heard this guy," he hikes his thumb at Jake, "keeps losing all his bartenders. I got some free time on my hands, so why not come back home?"

"With Eve on maternity leave and Dessa part-time, I could use the extra hands," Jake says.

"That's great. I'm looking forward to working with you." I lift my backpack higher on my shoulder and head toward the employee room.

"Hey, Lach!" Jake catches me at the end of the bar, and I stop. "This came to the house for Eve. Could you give it to her?"

"Yeah. Sure." I glance down at the manila envelope. The return address is a law office in Knoxville, Tennessee. I slide my bag to the side and unzip the top, shoving it in my backpack. As I continue down the hallway, my phone buzzes in my back pocket. Eve's name flashes on the screen.

"Hey, Sunflower, what's up?"

"Lach. It's Rylee."

My heart leaps to my throat, and I come to a screeching halt. Why is Rylee using Eve's phone?

"What's going on? Where's Eve?"

"She's right next to me. Her water broke, and we're going to the hospital right now."

"Hi, Lach," Eve says.

"Sunflower, how are you doing?"

"I'm okay. Slight cramping, but I'm okay. Can you grab the hospital bag from the house and meet me there?"

Shit. She's having the baby. "Yeah. But isn't it early?"

"Yes. But I think he's ready to join us."

"I'll meet you there." I disconnect the call. A rush of adrenaline propels me back out to the bar. I come to a stop where Jake and Beck are still talking. "Eve's water broke. I have to meet her at the hospital."

Jake's eyes widen. "Go. We got it."

I nod and spin on my heel, ready to sprint out the door, but Jake's voice stops me.

"Take care of her. I'll see the three of you soon."

The corner of my mouth curves into a smile. When Eve and I started our relationship, I never wanted Jake to be caught in the middle. He only wants what's best for his sister. I'm glad to know he now trusts me to be the one to look after her and not just keep her out of trouble. It took some time, but those wounds are healed, including the ones on my face. Now it's time for us to take our relationship to the next level: raising a baby together. Without another word, I'm pushing through the door and racing to my truck. I jump inside and turn it over. My tires spin on the pavement as I step on the gas. I get to our townhouse in record time and grab the hospital bag Eve packed.

Eve's having the baby. I know he's not biologically mine, but fuck, he feels like mine. I'm going to be there for him as if he's mine. It doesn't matter if we're blood or not. He'll always be my son. The entire drive across town is a blur. At the hospital, I park in the first available parking spot. I shove the envelope Jake gave to me in the front pocket of Eve's bag and torpedo across the parking lot and inside. After I find what floor Eve is on, I forgo waiting for the elevator and hoof it up the two flights of stairs. I come to another waiting area when I spot Rylee standing near the large window that faces Lake Superior.

"Rylee!" She spins around, and I jog to her. "Where's Eve?" My chest heaves as I collect my breath.

"They took her through the doors." She points to a set of double doors behind me. "I'm sure it's to check to make sure everything is okay."

Spinning around, I spot the reception desk and close

the distance. "Excuse me. I'm Lach Murray, I'm looking for Eve Porter. She just came in here. Her water broke."

"Yes. They took her to a delivery room. If you want to have a seat, we'll keep you updated." She points to the waiting room chairs.

"Really?" I slam my hands on the desk. "That's all you can give me? She needs me. I should be there with her."

"Lach." Rylee's hand rests on my arm. "Come. It will be okay. She's in good hands. She'll let the doctors know you're here."

I nod and follow Rylee to a row of chairs in front of the window. Rylee takes a seat, but I can't sit. I want answers, but no one can give me any. My feet carry me from one end of the row of chairs to the other. I repeat the path over and over again; I'm surprised I don't wear a hole in the carpet. Seconds turn to minutes. The minutes add up to half an hour. Then three-quarters of an hour.

"Lachlan Murray." My name draws my attention to a doctor, Eve's doctor, standing in front of the double doors. I race over to her.

"Yes. Is Eve okay? The baby?"

"Both Eve and the baby are doing great. We had to perform an emergency C-section. Everything went as planned. Would you like to see them?"

Dumb fucking question. "Yes." I follow Sofia through the double doors and down a short hallway. She comes to a stop in front of an open door. Eve's lying in bed, holding her baby boy. My heart swells to twice the size. Once for Eve and the second for the little boy in her arms. I rush to her side. "I'm so sorry I couldn't be here for you."

She peers up at me, pure elation and happiness adorning her eyes. "It's okay. You're here now."

I press my lips to her forehead. I glance down at the

baby in her arms, swaddled in a blanket. His tiny fingers wiggling in the cool air. "Does he have a name?"

"He does. Lach, I'd like you to meet Asher Lachlan Porter." She smiles up at me.

"Lachlan, huh?"

"I kind of like the name and guy I got it from. Archibald was also in the running." She flashes me a teasing smirk.

"I like Lachlan better."

"Would you like to hold him?"

"Yeah." I take a seat in the chair next to her, and she passes me Asher. I stare down at his little nose and little mouth as his lips move. I'm going to love him as much as I love his mom. "Oh. Jake gave me this. I thought it might be important." Carefully, I bend over to pluck the envelope from the hospital bag and pass it to Eve.

"What's this?"

"I don't know. You'll have to open it."

Her eyebrows pinch together as she breaks the seal and slides out a piece of paper. Her eyes follow the words, reading line for line. She drops the letter to her lap. A vacant, emotionless look fills her eyes and spreads across her face.

"What does it say?"

Her lips pull into a smile. "Pax signed over his rights."

With Asher in my arms, I lean over to Eve. "I love you, Sunflower."

Her hand rests against my cheek, and I lean into her warmth. "I love you too."

Epilogue

TWO MONTHS LATER

Lach

Kids are no joke. Eve and I haven't had a night alone for two months. In fact, it's been hard for us to even spend time with each other. While I'm working the close shift at Porter's, Eve watches Asher. During the day, while Eve is killing it with her photography, I'm chilling with my buddy. She's been killing it with her photos. She has bookings through December. While she still doesn't have a studio, she's been able to manage to do everything on location. To say it's exhausting is an understatement, but I know it won't last forever.

Two bright, big, blue eyes, sparkling with mischief, stare up at me, then shift to the ceiling, taking in the world or the townhouse. He continues to chug down the bottle like a college senior at a keg party. He wiggles his legs as he continues drinking.

I stare down at him, and his eyes connect with mine. "I want you to know your mom is the most amazing, fierce, determined, beautiful-inside-and-out woman I've ever known. You're not biologically mine, but you'll always be my son. We're family. I'll always be there for you and your mom."

"Dammit, Lach."

I jerk my head up to see Eve standing in the doorway. She swipes a tear off her cheek. She strolls into the nursery and takes a seat on the rocking ottoman in front of me.

"You can't say things like that."

"I meant every single word."

"I love you."

"I love you too, Sunflower."

She leans in toward Asher. "Whoa!" She rears back, her body recoiling like a spring. "We have a DEFCON One explosion."

I lean down for a whiff. "Damn. I don't know how someone so little could create a big stink like that."

"Here," Eve holds her arms out. "I'll change him."

I pass her the empty bottle. "I got it. Why don't you pick out a movie for us to watch?" Leaning in, I press my lips to hers.

She pulls away a fraction of an inch. "I think I know the perfect one." Eve rises to her feet. I smack her ass as she turns. Her head spins around, and she flashes me a sexy smirk as she saunters out of the nursery.

"Alright, little man. Time for damage control." I keep my head away from ground zero. Rising to my feet, I shuffle to the changing table and set him down. I peel away the blanket wrapped around him and pull the snaps from his onesie. "Oh, you really did a number here. You had some force behind that one. Also, I didn't know poop could be that shocking shade of green." I wrinkle my nose. After I clean him up and snap on a new onesie, I lay him down in his crib. His blue eyes blink up at me and slowly grow heavy.

"Good night, buddy." I tap the button on the mobile above his crib, and a sweet, tinkling melody fills the room. With the baby monitor in hand, I shut off the light and climb down the stairs. When I reach the living room, Eve is sitting on the couch with a bowl of popcorn in her lap. "So, what are we watching?" I take the cushion next to her, leaning my shoulder against hers.

"This." She flashes me a bright smile before pressing a button on the remote. A scribbled sketch of the Seattle skyline shines bright on the screen while "Bad Reputation" by Joan Jett and the Blackhearts plays through the speakers.

My lips pull into a smile. "Perfect." Life couldn't get any better. But tomorrow might prove me wrong.

The following morning, I stroll into the nursery. "Hey buddy, are you ready for your first outing?" Lifting him out of the crib, I press a kiss to his forehead and carry him to the changing table.

Asher wiggles and coos while I pull the snaps from his onesie. My head rears back, and I frown. "Well, I'm glad you dropped this bomb before we left and instead of in the car. You would have gassed us all out." I hold my breath while I work on putting him in a fresh diaper.

Two months ago, I found a farm online and knew I needed to take Eve. Since Asher was born, we've been too busy to get out of the house, but time is running out. After clearing both our schedules, I told Eve this weekend was ours, and we're taking a little family road trip. After I'm finished changing Asher, I hold him to my chest and head down the stairs to where Eve is packing half the kitchen.

"Are you moving out?"

Eve peers up at me from stuffing diapers into a bag. "We need all these things. Sometimes Asher gets fussy, and he doesn't want breast milk, so I have to bring formula." She holds up the container of formula before dropping it in the bag. Then I have to bring the warmer because no one wants cold formula. Then I have to pack my breast pump just in case and extra pads so we don't have another nipple leakage incident. I got snacks. She lifts an economy size bag of sour gummy worms.

"Only the best road snack."

She smiles. "Duh. And I packed an extra stash of diapers and two changes of clothes for Asher."

I bend down, pressing my lips to her forehead. "Alright, you seem to have it handled."

She blows out a deep breath. "I think so."

"But you know we are only going to be gone for like half a day."

Leaning toward Asher, she tickles his belly. "You underestimate what this little man can do in six hours. You're a little terror, aren't you? You're our little terror, though."

"He gets that from you, by the way."

She glances up at me, rolls her eyes, and spins on her heel. Before she can walk away, I wrap my hand around the back of her neck, pulling her close. The softness of her skin is a contrast to the firmness of my grip as my lips find hers.

Asher coos in my arms.

I pull away from Eve and chuckle. "Yeah. Yeah. I know you don't like the PDA. But I can't help it. Your mom's hot.

All I want to do is kiss her. You'll understand when you get older."

"How about we don't encourage him to grow up faster than he already is?"

"Fine. How about I pack the car, and we'll get on the road?" I pass Asher to Eve.

Two trips to the car later, everything is packed, and we hit the road.

Porter's ALE HOUSE

"So where are you taking us, anyway? Because we're kind of out in the middle of nowhere." Eve turns to face me.

For two hours, the only things passing by were endless rolling fields, a blur of green and brown under a pale blue sky. "It's a surprise." I glance at her from the corner of my eye.

A soft laugh bubbles out of her. "I kind of figured since you've been hounding me for the past month to take a weekend off."

"Time's running out. So it was important." After a few minutes, I turn right. We drive under a ranch-style sign that says Sunshine Haven Farms.

A sharp gasp escapes Eve as she spins to face me. "Is this what I think it is?" She glues herself to the window, and we pass a massive field of towering sunflowers reaching toward the sun. "This was totally worth all the secrecy." A wide grin, stretching from ear to ear, illuminates her face, crinkling the corners of her eyes.

After I park, I strap Asher to my chest with a newborn sling. We pay for our tickets and set forth to the expansive sunflower field. The crisp and mild September air floats around us. Eve stares in wonder at the velvet golden petals. I can't keep the smile off my face while I watch her admire the towering sunflowers. We stroll along the path, hand in hand, admiring the sea of tiny suns as the blue sky and sun shines down on us. We approach a small alcove, and I nod for Eve to stop.

"There's something I have for you." Eve gasps. Her fingers cover her mouth as her lashes flutter uncontrollably. Oh shit. Does she—? I reach into my back pocket, her eyes laser-focused on my every move. With a folded letter in my hand, I hold it out to Eve. "Your brother gave this to me about a week ago."

Her hand drops to her side, and her shoulders fall. As inconspicuous as possible, she blows out a breath. "What is it?" She takes the letter from my grip.

"It's a down payment. For a house. For us to grow our family." My gaze meets hers.

Her mouth drops open with a gasp, then snaps shut in surprise. All the color leaves her cheeks. "Is this for real?"

The corner of my mouth curves up. "It's real. I crunched the numbers, and pretty much what we are paying now for rent is close to what a mortgage payment would be. We can start looking for a home. For our family."

Tears pool in the corners of her eyes. "This is amazing." She glances at me, the paper, and then back at me. Her hand reaches up and brushes my cheek. The sunflowers shine down on us. Our lives were once gloomy, dark skies, but now there's nothing but sunshine.

"Did you think I was…?" My brows raise.

"No!" Her words come out in a rush. "I mean," she lifts a shoulder, "if you were, I'd do it, but Sandy at the Book Bar might be disappointed we didn't use her engagement sign at the store. Also, we'd miss out on the discount."

I laugh. "We can't miss out on the discount." I wrap my arm around her shoulder and haul her to me.

On our way back to Harbor Highlands, Eve tells me she wants to stop at Porter's to thank Jake in person. As we walk into the bar, it's fairly quiet, but it's still early for a late Saturday afternoon. Jake greets us with a head nod from behind the bar. When he's finished serving the customer in front of him, he meets us at the open end of the bar. Eve wraps her arms around her brother and thanks him. He half pats her back. It's the biggest hug from Jake anyone will ever receive. After they break apart, she passes Asher to him to hold. I can't help but laugh at how tiny he looks in Jake's arms, much like a linebacker carrying a football. This is my family, and it's the best fucking family.

Nora

Eve's and Lach's voices get my attention. Then I hear Asher's name. I slam the locker door, and it clanks against the metal latch. From the back room, I race to the bar. "I want baby snuggles!" My shoes squeak on the floor as I stop next to Jake. I pluck Asher from Jake's grasp, but he gave him up pretty willingly. With Asher in my arms, I bend down and rub my nose against his teeny, tiny button nose.

"You know," Lach says, "you could have one of your own, then you'd get twenty-four-hour baby snuggles."

"Why do that when I have yours?" I coo at Asher. "Auntie Nora is here, and I'll spoil you with all the love and toys imaginable."

"How's OneDate going? Get Jake to join yet?" Lach playfully elbows Jake.

"Nope." Jake spins around and storms off, ending his participation in further conversation.

"Since Jake's out, what about Miles? Has he been behaving himself?" Lach takes a seat on a bar stool.

It's been almost a year since I began developing OneDate. So far, the soft launch has been successful. Miles has been behaving himself, except for a few minor hiccups. "It's been good. He's been good." Asher scrunches his face and fusses in my arms.

"Oh! He's dropping bombs." Eve collects Asher from me. "I'm going to take care of the damage." Eve walks down the hallway with Asher and the diaper bag in hand.

I was apprehensive about Miles joining OneDate in the first place, but I underestimated a guy who is desperate to find love. When he threw out statistics and percentages about the number of people who are looking for their soul mate, I kind of blacked out and agreed to let him join as long as he stopped talking. Was it the smartest move? No. But it got him to shut up, and that's what was important in the moment. I won't admit it to anyone, especially Miles, but he's not a bad guy. He teeters closer to shy and socially awkward, but deep down, a good guy.

My phone alerts me with a message. I pull it from my back pocket. It's not the message on my screen that draws my attention but instead an alert from OneDate. When I open the app, it's on the screen I was last on. Miles has an event today, and his date just canceled. An hour before it starts. Dammit. There's no way someone else could arrange a new date with him on such short notice. I swallow. The lump of dryness in my throat not going away. There's a good chance I'm going to hate myself later for this, but I shove my phone in my pocket.

"I have to go," I say to Lach and race out the door before he can say anything.

Thank you for reading I Wanna Be Your Lager! Want more Lach and Eve? Claim your copy of their fun bonus scene when you join my newsletter!
https://authorgiastevens.com/bonus-iwbyl/

Get read for Nora's fake dating story in Stout Of My League!

He has something I want. I have something he needs. The tradeoff... fake dating.

Bartending pays the bills while I develop OneDate, an app for finding a plus-one. But Miles Kayson, hopeless romantic and walking first-date disaster in black-rimmed glasses, is determined to use my app to charm his dream girl.

Until one small rescue turns into a huge mistake.
Now his entire family thinks I'm his soulmate.

To keep up the lie, we strike a deal. I'll be his fake girlfriend for his help in return. Strictly business. Zero feelings.

Except our fake relationship includes practice dates.
The practice dates turn into spicy lessons.

And suddenly we're standing too close, touching too long, and kissing like we forgot it's only for show.

Miles is sweet, earnest, and dangerously good at proving nice guys do it better. He listens. He learns. And he's very eager to please. But he's not my type and definitely out of my league.

If I'm not careful, I'll forget this was only supposed to be fake.

https://authorgiastevens.com/stout-of-my-league/

I WANNA BE YOUR LAGER COCKTAIL

Hush Hush

Ingredients:

- 1 1/2 oz Tequila - 1800 coconut
- 1/2 oz RumChata
- 1/2 oz Blue curaçao
- 1/2 oz Lime Juice
- 2 oz Pineapple juice

Directions:

Pour over ice and stir.

Drink Created By: Cindy C. -Cocktail Concoctionist

Acknowledgments

First and foremost, I want to thank everyone who picked up this book. I think I will forever be in awe that you want to read my stories.

I have to thank my husband. I don't know if I would have ever started writing without his words of encouragement. Thank you so my entire extended family. They're so supportive and read my books, and we avoid discussing the spicy scenes at family gatherings.

A big shout out to Brandi Zelenka. You were there for me every step of the way and I don't think I could have done this without you.

To my creative team, you pushed me to put out the best book possible and I am so thankful to have you on my side. Thank you to my editor, Brandi at My Notes in the Margin. I tend to give you a hot mess and you make it brilliant. And thank you to Maddie at Davenports Edits for all your extra helps on polishing this book.

Thank you to Katy Cuthbertson for all your work and support, especially your eye for commas. You've been a huge help.

Thank you to my beta readers Rachel Story, and Randi Gauthreaux. You gave me invaluable feedback to help make my manuscript sparkle. Thank you to my proofreaders Jessie Bailey and Tonya Fender. You've helped me out so much.

Thank you Jane at Torch Lit Ink. You made everything run smoothly.

Thank you to my wonderful Sassy ARC Readers! I appreciate you so much.

Most of all thank you to all the bloggers, bookstagrammers, and booktokers for reading and sharing your excitement for this book. It means the world to me and I can't thank you enough. And of course, thank you to all the readers for reading my words. I hope I've been able to give you a fun escape for a few hours.

See you at the next book! Stay sassy!

About The Author

GIA STEVENS

Gia Stevens resides in Northern Minnesota with her husband and cat, Smokey. She lives for the warm, sunny days of summer and dreads the bitter cold of winter. A romantic comedy junkie at heart, she knew she wanted her own stories to encompass those same warm and fuzzy feelings.

When she's not busy writing your next book boyfriend, Gia can be found binge watching TV shows that aired five years ago, taking pictures of her cat, or curled up with a steamy romance book.

Visit my website for more information.
https://www.authorgiastevens.com

Also By

GIA STEVENS

Want to read more sassy heroines, swoony heroes, and fun and flirty romance books?

Visit Gia's website to find a complete list of all her books.

www.authorgiastevens.com

www.ingramcontent.com/pod-product-compliance
Lightning Source LLC
Chambersburg PA
CBHW060855210726
48293CB00006B/1806